Echo of a Distant Planet

Powell River Books
Powell River BC, Canada

Book sales online at:
www.powellriverbooks.com
phone: 604-483-1704
email: wlutz@mtsac.edu

10 9 8 7 6 5 4 3 2 1

Echo

of a

Distant Planet

Wayne J. Lutz

2009

Powell River Books

Science Fiction by Wayne J. Lutz

Inbound to Earth
Echo of a Distant Planet

Other Books by Wayne J. Lutz
in the series *Coastal British Columbia Stories*

Up the Lake
Up the Main
Up the Winter Trail
Up the Strait
Up the Airway
Farther Up the Lake
Cabin Number 5

Front Cover Photos:
Top – C-130s landing at Clarke Air Base, Philippines;
photo by Staff Sgt. Daniel C. Perez
Bottom – M81 Galaxy in Ursa Major; image from
Hubble Space Telescope

Contents

Our Year 1981: Distant Planet

I am conscious of being only an individual struggling weakly against the stream of time.

Ludwig Boltzmann (1896)

Chapter 1

Signals

The goal was to send a signal across the expanse of space. Not just data, but a message that could be received and interpreted by an intelligent mind. The first experiment involved the medium for transmission. Content would come later.

The signal held the promise of timeless travel – designed to exceed the speed of light by exploiting space-time. Rather than a violation of the laws of physics, it was dependent upon a process that harnessed those laws. The target was a planet with an abundance of water, where intelligent life should be prevalent.

The first step was the signal itself. Communication would follow naturally, with physical contact an eventual outcome.

A concentrated signal transmitted across the span of interstellar space risked missing all potential recipients. So far, no intelligent beings had been confirmed, even considering the high probability of higher-order life on such a watery planet. Life there might not yet be fully evolved.

The quantity of living beings in the universe was totally unknown. But if the signal was properly transmitted and remained targeted on the first receptor found, it should eventually pay dividends. The temptation, of course, was to jump from one target to another, until feedback was received. But if the anticipated life wasn't mentally powerful, time could be wasted by such lack of patience. The receptor might require considerable time to recognize the signal; even longer for it to be properly interpreted.

Such were the odds facing the Minds, and they had to convince their superiors this approach was the wisest choice. When it came to decisions regarding the direction of this project, no one wanted to discuss critical engineering decisions with anyone else. The constituents who supported the Minds failed to adequately explain their logic to the Force and the Guides. And the Minds thought it was their right to avoid the politics surrounding the project. As a result, no one really understood what was going on. Lack of proper dialogue plagued the biggest communication project in the planet's history.

1981: Earth

The great thing about time is that it goes on.

Arthur Eddington (1928)

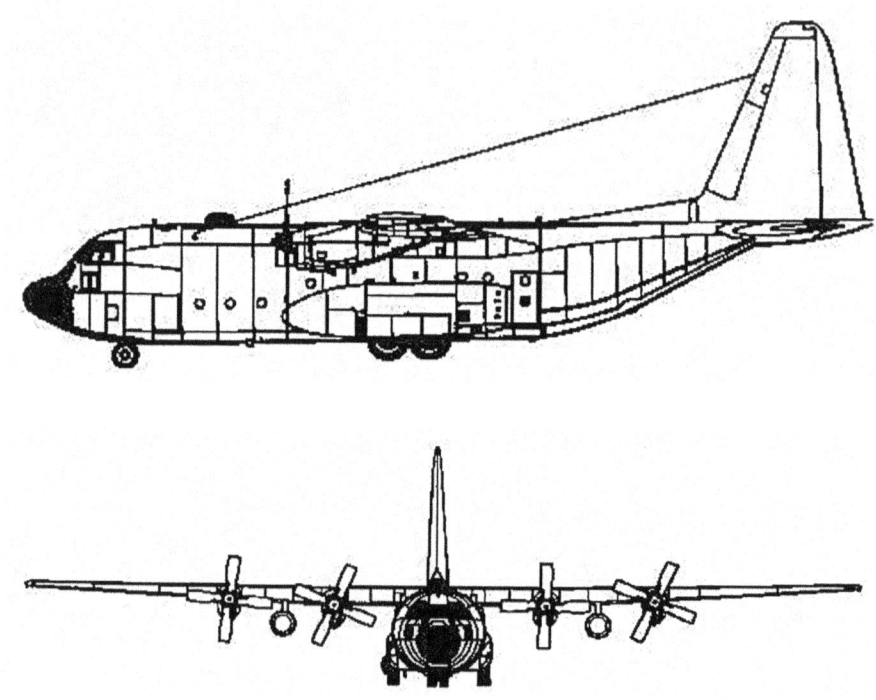

C-130 Hercules

Chapter 2

Awakening

Lieutenant Shawna Whitney never awoke easily, even on the best of mornings. This was the second day in a row that she opened her eyes remembering the tragedy. She was shivering – trembling and sweating silently in the damp room. More the reason to try to drop back into sleep, and attempt to forget.

It wasn't the kind of nightmare that cleared with the light of day and was promptly forgotten. Instead, Shawna vividly remembered an accident that hadn't yet happened – next month's tragic mishap in Hangar Two. In her mind, the future shattering of metal on concrete was far clearer than last week's embarrassing chewing out by Colonel Penland. The accident in Hangar Two formed a stark reality that didn't yet exist. In contrast, she didn't dwell on Colonel Penland's tirade at the standup briefing. Hangar Two and the future were not as easily pushed aside.

This wasn't Shawna's first such memory of a time that doesn't yet exist, but still she sweat, and still she shivered. And, as always, it would pass. Familiarity had a way of promoting acceptance.

The morning boded frustration the moment it began. Shawna eventually would be able to push Hangar Two from her mind – she was an expert at concentration. But those C-130s were already inbound, and that meant a day of confusion. Rotation day brought new aircraft, and worst of all, new people. These large turboprop airplanes seldom flew all the way across the Gulf of Mexico without major mechanical problems, and today wouldn't likely be an exception.

For a moment longer, she brooded about the upcoming day, and then swung her small frame out of bed. It was half-dark. The noisy window air conditioner had thrummed all night, blasting its musty odor. Another day in paradise – hot, humid, and unchanging. The Panama dawn seldom varied.

She pulled back the curtains and stole a peek. Towering cumulus clouds, thunderstorms in-waiting, straddled the orange glow on the eastern horizon. In the distance, ground-hugging evaporation fog partly obscured the lush, dark-green jungle canopy. Her hair would be in for another curly day.

Shawna Whitney, age 24, U.S. Air Force aircraft maintenance officer – now there was a joke. Her mechanical expertise was nil. When her old Ford sputtered, Shawna would pull over to the side of the road and raise the hood, but only in the interest of personal safety rather than mechanical expertise. Then call the Auto Club. If only there was an Auto Club here.

But she was a competent maintenance officer. Being an MO involved basic communications skills, both technical and personal. Her job never put grease under her fingernails. That was fortunate, since Shawna self-described herself as a member of the school for the mechanically declined. But she was also from the school of systems management. In front of the colonels, she could keep up with the best of the maintenance officers. But it seemed best to kid along with her colleagues when they picked on their "girl MO." That didn't mean it didn't bother her.

The best way to fight this dichotomy was to do a good job. And Shawna knew she contributed to the mission. She preferred to work low-key, but always with ingrained leadership traits that came from somewhere. But from where? It seemed to be neither from her family background nor her selected course of education. Yet, she was somehow a natural leader. A wise sense of command often showed through her guise of gruffness.

No makeup today. It was a waste of time in the Panama drip. The bike ride to work was about two miles, and that's all it would take to get her sweating in the pre-dawn sauna. Add to that, this time of year, a one-in-two chance of getting rained on.

Lieutenant Shawna Whitney, dressed in her fatigues, was ready to go. Maintenance Control was pretty informal at Howard Air Force Base, at least in terms of dress. If she had to leave the comfort of the air-conditioned control room for a trip to the flightline, her sweat would be a lot less obvious in fatigues. Today, she hoped to stay secluded in her little office, a raised stage-like platform separated from the dispatch area of Maintenance Control by height rather than a physical partition. Most days, except for lunch, she was able to remain relatively isolated. But the scheduled C-130 rotation was today, so all bets were off.

* * * * * *

Biking out of the bachelor officers quarters, Shawna generated her own breeze, her fatigue hat wasn't yet moist at the headband. Her nearly-black hair was approaching regulation limits, but that wasn't watched as closely here as elsewhere in the Air Force. She usually kept her hair short anyway. It was a lot cooler that way. But now her hair was almost shoulder length and more wind-blown than curly. She wore it pulled back into a bun with a red cloth tie. The tie wasn't exactly regulation either. But the Air Force of the early 1980s was working hard to avoid scaring off its few women. Shawna took full advantage of that fact.

At the first downhill grade, she let her bicycle coast. As the bike picked up speed down the winding street, the air felt cooler. She glided through the married officers housing area, mansions by Air Force standards – old, solid tropical homes with sprawling lawns and huge front gardens filled with towering plants – white Angel's Trumpet and orange Birds of Paradise.

The low-pitched whine of the headlight generator buzzed against her rear tire, increasing in pitch as she picked up speed. She nudged the handbrake. The squeal of the brakepad against the metal rim momentarily blocked the background chirping of the crickets. Not too fast now – the main intersection was approaching.

From the stop sign at the bottom of the long hill, Shawna could see the base spread out on the flat plain. Seemingly endless rows of stark rectangular buildings and round-arched hangars stood in front of the dominating runways and huge paved aircraft aprons, all the way to the jungle horizon.

A puffy cumulus cloud blocked the sun, bright rays poking out in all directions. Within a foreground of formidable military force, tropical beauty was easily taken for granted.

Shawna's bike had coasted all the way down the hill, but after the stop sign, it was time to start pedaling again. She could already feel her hat's moist band sticking to her forehead. Today, even in the air-conditioned sanctity of Maintenance Control, the sweat might not end.

Chapter 3

Low-Level

Soon after dawn, they broke away from the Panamanian jungle on the northern coast. They crossed the shoreline with all four turboprop engines reverberating against the cliffs of a small bay. Even from inside the noisy C-130 Hercules, the flight crew could hear the change in pitch from their own echo. No longer was the sound moderated by the lush green growth of the jungle. The placid bay beneath them reflected the roar of the engines and thrust it out toward the open ocean and back upward towards the cockpit. It was the reassuring roar of airpower.

In the early morning light, the shadows on the shoreline below were distinct. In the middle of the bay, a small sailboat dipped its sail delicately towards the water, capturing the light breeze from the Caribbean Sea. Few pleasure craft were awake this early.

Second Lieutenant Dana Munson, Minnesota Air National Guard, sat contentedly in the Herk's co-pilot seat, looking through his lower cockpit window, just to the right of his rudder pedals. He watched the sailboat pass below the aircraft. The C-130 was skimming low enough over the bay for Dana to see two dark men dressed in swimsuits aboard the boat, waving outstretched arms over their heads. Dana smiled to himself and then returned his attention to the instrument panel, where he was supposed to be backing up the aircraft commander.

In the left seat, a graying, posture-perfect lieutenant colonel eased the control wheel to the right in a shallow turn. The colonel scanned the coastline, glancing occasionally at the instrument panel, flying mostly by feel. His movements on the controls were precise, yet smooth, and the aircraft reacted accordingly. He glanced down at his turn coordinator and smiled to himself when he saw the ball perfectly centered. When you fly precise, you fly coordinated.

The aircraft was in air-drop configuration for this mission, but its cargo compartment was empty. The pallets bearing supplies for U.S. Army ground forces had already been dropped into their jungle destination. This low-level air-drop mission, cutting across the jungle 500 feet over the canopy of green, was all but over. At the Army drop site, small Container Delivery System pallets had been tugged from the cargo compartment by parachutes cascading from the C-130's gaping rear cargo door, scoring an almost direct three-ship hit on the ground site. This had been a morning twilight jaunt to maintain mission flight proficiency in a time of restless peace.

The station-keeping radar panel capped the top of the instrument glare shield, a reminder of the morning's formation of three C-130s, now well separated, each on their own tour of the Panama coast. Today's resupply mission supported the Army's simulation of an aggressive Cuban attempt to disrupt the operation of the Panama Canal. A Cuban threat didn't seem very likely, but it was a nice diversion from a routine cargo hauling mission.

"Let's go up," said the colonel, with a glance at Dana.

The colonel eased the four throttles forward with his right hand, as he simultaneously pulled back smoothly on the control wheel. The nose of the C-130 rose distinctly above the horizon in a steep climb. Dana felt himself pushed back comfortably in the right seat as the g-force peaked and then returned to normal. Not exactly a fighter aircraft, but this baby could sure perform at its near-empty weight.

Leaving three thousand feet, the colonel turned his gaze towards Dana and gave a satisfied nod that indicated it was time for the boss to relinquish control of the aircraft.

"You've got it," said the colonel.

Dana sat up straight in the seat, as if imitation of the colonel's posture would lead to the same smoothness on the controls. He felt taller now, both in height and attitude. His attitude was never lacking, but his stature was. Dana had barely made the Air Force's minimum pilot height requirements of 5-foot, 4-inches, just one of his many worries along the way. Among other Air Force pilots, it made him look even more like a kid, which, in reality, he was.

"I have the aircraft," said Dana, confirming his status on the flight controls. "How high?"

"Five-point-five, northbound for now. We'll need to get ready for arrival into Howard in a few minutes. But first let's just enjoy the ride."

"My wife's a taxpayer," said the flight engineer, nestled behind the pilots in the center seat, and even younger than Dana.

"So am I," said the colonel. "After protecting our country today, we deserve a few first-class air miles."

"You call that protecting?" said the flight engineer. "It seems more like harassing the jungle monkeys. I bet we made a real *Whoosh!* when we crossed Checkpoint Bravo five hundred feet above the deck."

The colonel laughed carefully. He knew his by-the-book attitude was well known, and he wanted to keep it that way.

As Dana leveled the aircraft at 5500 feet, he focused his attention on the altimeter, then pulled back gently on the throttles. He glanced below the throttle quadrant to the laminated card covered with greasepencil – reminders of the aircraft's critical speeds at takeoff and final approach. Dana was now miles ahead of the aircraft, preparing for landing. He relaxed his grip on the yoke. It was always better to fly with fingertips for a better feel of the controls.

Dana had been in awe the entire week. It was his first real mission as a pilot with the Air National Guard. He had no more than returned to Minnesota from flight training in Arkansas when he was on an aircraft bound for Panama. It had all happened fast.

This morning Dana felt in-tune with this airplane – the resonance of the propellers, even the smell of the cockpit. It was the odor of old metal mixed with oil and hydraulic fluid, a musty smell enhanced by the cool air pushed from the overhead vents. The air conditioner was trying to keep up with the Panamanian heat and humidity, and was barely the winner.

Dana Munson had spent five years with the Air National Guard as an enlisted crew chief, mothering a C-130 in and out of its parking spot, refueling, and performing general maintenance on his assigned airplane. He had enjoyed the work in Minneapolis, but a pilot slot had been his constant dream. That was what had brought him to the military in the first place. So he finished his bachelor's degree at the University of Minnesota and was ready for the next pilot selection board. Every night he did stretching exercises to try to increase his height that extra half-inch. But it was his commendable record as a crew chief and his nearly two hundred hours of civilian flying that put those gold bars on his uniform and won him a pilot slot. He earned it, and he cherished it.

Dana's two-week rotation in Panama was now half finished. Only Minnesota aircraft were flying these air-drop missions today. Their rotational partners, the North Carolina Air Guard, had worked all night, preparing their C-130s for departure for the States later this morning. Four more C-130s, inbound from California, would replace them. On any given day, there were eight Herks at Howard Air Force Base to perpetually guard the skies of Central and South America. It was a continuous rotational mission called Volant Oak, shared by the various units of the Air National Guard.

"Where to?" asked Dana.

He glanced to his left, and the colonel gave a shrug which meant the lieutenant could point the nose where he wanted.

"Clear left?" asked Dana.

"She's clear," said the colonel.

Dana rolled the aircraft into a 30-degree bank to the left, provided some back-pressure on the control wheel, and advanced the throttles a bit to hold the altitude. The C-130 stabilized in a left turn, the altimeter pegged level at fifty-five hundred feet.

Dana continued in a complete 360-degree turn, practicing his control of the aircraft. He rolled the C-130 out of the bank, and then flew parallel to the shoreline again. After a few minutes of straight-and-level, he banked back to the right to join the course towards the air base.

The sun was now blazing through the windshield, angled directly at Dana. The flight engineer stretched to the left side window and removed a dark green sun-visor from its clipped storage location. He handed the visor to Dana, who attached it to the narrow clip-on tubing above his windshield.

"Thanks," said Dana.

"You're welcome. You butter-bars need all the help you can get," said the flight engineer.

Dana smiled, shrugging off the teasing insult about his newly acquired second lieutenant's gold bars. Inwardly, he swelled with pride. It seemed impossible he was really handling the controls of a C-130. For the time being, he could maneuver this aircraft anywhere he wanted to go. A 120,000-pound military cargo airplane was in his hands, and he was living his dream.

Chapter 4

Maintenance Control

First Lieutenant Shawna Whitney tapped in the entry code. She held her breath as she rotated the doorknob, setting a determined mood. This was going to be a day that required her to maintain her cool.

The duty officer this morning was Todd Chandler, and Shawna detested him. She also felt terrible about what she knew lurked in his immediate future. But he was going off duty in a few minutes, and it was best to play the game. It was easier that way.

"Morning, sir." Shawna was determined to get things off to a good start. Todd would be gone from this dark room in a few minutes.

"Hi, Shawna. None too soon."

"That doesn't sound good."

"Just kiddin'. All's well in the world of darkness."

Todd was dressed in his informal blues, no tie and no ribbons. No surprise. For Captain Todd Chandler, this was as informal as it got. He did try hard as a maintenance officer, but he certainly could put his foot in his mouth on a regular basis. He worked the graveyard shift by choice so his days were free for his precious bass fishing and sailing adventures.

Todd successfully avoided most of the results of his middle-of-the-night ineptitude. Often it was Shawna who paid for the after-effects when the colonel arrived for duty in the morning.

Shawna stood just inside the doorway, waiting for her eyes to adjust to the subdued light. The room resembled an air traffic control radar facility, with wall-to-wall display panels above three worktables at the front of the room. Banks of telephones and radios complemented the display boards. The small room also included her desk on its raised platform near the rear, next to the entry door. It wasn't a working area for the claustrophobic.

Todd was seated at the rear desk. Two other controllers were in position at their panel displays at the front of the dark room – minimum manning for the night shift.

"Morning, Lieutenant," said the tech sergeant at the weapons control display board.

"Hi, Ted," replied Shawna. Ted was an outstanding controller. Too bad he wasn't on Shawna's shift.

Shawna reluctantly turned her attention toward the specialist controller next to Ted. She could do without this fellow.

"Good morning, Jim," said Shawna.

"Morning, ma'am," replied Jim.

He probably used that term just to piss her off.

"How did the engine change go?" asked Shawna.

She still stood motionless at the entry door, allowing her eyes to adjust to the darkness.

"Done," said Todd. "They still have engine trim runs this morning, but the A-7 squadron has two spare aircraft for today's missions. Looks like the fighter jocks will be no problem for you today."

Shawna was now adjusted to the dim light. She walked to the *No Exit* door at the far end of the thirty-foot control room and entered the area behind the display boards. The wall separating this small storage area from the main control room was little more than a few pieces of plywood and a line of electrical panels.

She flipped the switch for the single overhead florescent light. The small bulb flickered and then flooded the storage room with light. There wasn't much to see except their personnel lockers, a purring refrigerator, and a tall government-gray supply cabinet. A straight-back armless chair and two pairs of combat boots adjacent to the lockers completed the room's meager contents.

Shawna took a few steps into the room and opened the refrigerator door. On the top shelf was a large plastic container of orange juice. She poured some of it into a paper cup for her traditional morning dose, and returned the jug to its shelf, leaving the door of the fridge open for a few moments in case she wanted more.

As she raised the cup to her lips, she heard the radio call of an inbound aircraft. The sound came directly through the electrical panels that divided her from the control room's work area.

"Howard Command Post, Titan One-Three is fifteen minutes out, alpha two for nose wheel shimmy."

The weapons controller on the other side of the false wall waited for the answer from the Command Post. When none resulted, he transmitted his reply on the UHF radio.

"Titan One-Three, Maintenance Control copies. We'll relay to the Command Post. You'll be parking in Charlie-Four."

Without warning, a stabbing memory of Shawna's nightmare pierced her brain. It was a painful thrust, quick and concentrated, and almost immediately it was gone again. The intense spike of memory simply disappeared. Her cup of orange juice was trembling in her hand.

Why would she so intensely remember her horrible dream at this moment? But it had happened before in this exact same location behind the electrical panels.

Damn this place! I won't be coming in here again.

The small storage area was a tough place to avoid because it served as the control room's only private space. But she could live without it. She rapidly regained her composure. She'd been through this before.

"The arrival time of the California Air Guard C-130s keeps slipping," announced Todd, his raised voice projected towards her through the thin plywood partition.

Shawna didn't reply immediately. Instead, she squeezed her eyes shut. And when she reopened them, she tried to relax her entire body. The orange juice was no longer quivering in the cup.

"Okay, sir," she replied. "We'll get you out of here in a few minutes."

She took a final gulp of juice and placed the paper cup on the wooden shelf next to the refrigerator. She slammed the refrigerator door with a determined push, and started back towards the control room, preparing herself to face the routine of the morning.

"So what's the problem with the inbound C-130s?"

"An air traffic delay," said Todd. "They supposedly had overflight permission from Mexico, but it sounds like they still got routed the long way around."

"How late?" asked Shawna.

"The estimate is five after eleven, and that ain't good. The outgoing North Carolina troops are getting restless. They're at Base Ops with their Customs checks complete. So they can't leave the area. I bet they're getting grumpy."

"Not good," said Shawna, pausing at the control room's grease-board flying schedule display. "It'll mean a quick turnaround to make the Bogota run."

"It gets worse," said Todd.

"How worse?"

"Well, the outgoing mission commander has reminded us that his flight crews can launch when the first replacement bird is an hour out," said Todd. "But the arrivals are in trail of each other by at least a half-hour between aircraft. We won't have the last one down until about one o'clock, and the North Carolina aircraft will be long gone by then."

"So, let's have Colonel Penland tell them to wait until the last bird is down," said Shawna.

"Fat chance. Did you ever try to tell those Air Guard boys anything?"

"Never had to."

"Be glad. And, if that's not bad enough, guess who's bringing a B-model?"

"A B-model C-130?" Shawna was hoping she misunderstood.

"That's the one, Miss Shawna."

Todd seemed to be having fun laying the day's bad news on his replacement duty officer. He paused for effect and then continued.

"Their fourth airplane broke at home just before departure. The spare aircraft also crapped out, so they switched to a B-model."

"No way!" barked Shawna. "What are we going to do with a B-model? Without external fuel tanks, they've got worthless range. Penland won't buy it."

"What's to buy? The B-model is already on its way, stumbling in from somewhere over the Gulf of Mexico. But it's not that bad. Most of the parts are common to the E-model, even the engines."

"Most. Not all," said Shawna. "The B's range is the big problem. I doubt we can send a B-model down-country at all."

"It will be a rather useless airplane," said Todd. "Maybe we can make her the cannibalization bird."

"Just what we need – another hangar queen. Penland hasn't intervened at all?" asked Shawna.

"It's too late," said Todd. "They launched before they notified us."

"But they can't do that."

"Like I said, try to tell the Air National Guard."

Shawna stared at the flying schedule board, pretending to study the plan for the day. She was still recovering from the episode in the back room, but she wasn't about to show it. There was no further shaking, no hesitation in her voice, but she was still recovering. Shawna took a deep breath, turned from the board, and headed towards her desk on the raised platform in the rear of the control room.

The government-gray desk was a shared work area for duty officers, and Todd had already cleared his papers from the desktop in preparation for his exit. All that remained was a government-issue desk calendar, the multi-line telephone console, and an in-box. Looking down, Shawna noticed the in-box contained only two items – on top was a single-page summary of the week's flying schedule with a few red marks where changes had occurred. Peaking out below the flying schedule was a copy of the base newspaper, folded to fit the box.

Shawna ignored the flying schedule and pulled the newspaper from underneath. The headlines of the paper read: "Torrijos Issues Ultimatum." She would read it later, but she doubted she would understand it. Local politics were complicated.

Todd was standing next to the desk now, ready to turn over his shift to Shawna. None of her replacement controllers had arrived yet, but Todd wouldn't wait for them. Shawna wheeled the desk chair out from under the desk and sat down, then rolled herself forward to take her position of command. Of course, she knew, as did everyone else, that it wasn't really a command position. Instead, she was here to keep everybody in harmony, as much as possible. It was a totally impossible task, but she did it the best she could. Better than most maintenance officers – even the guys.

"Have a good one," said Todd, waving to Shawna as he departed.

Not much of a turnover briefing. Not much of a maintenance officer.

"Thanks," said Shawna. "Sweet dreams."

Chapter 5

Canal Zone

Second Lieutenant Dana Munson removed his right hand from the control yoke to assure the aircraft was properly trimmed. The C-130 stayed perfectly steady. Dana flexed his fingers inside his flight glove and then gingerly gripped the control wheel again.

"This is what those taxpayers should see," said Dana. "What's wrong with this picture? Do you think they would understand I need their money to learn how to fly this airplane?"

"That's the way the game is played," said the colonel. "Don't be so sure you're not earning your pay. Somebody's got to drive this thing."

"Thing?" said the flight engineer. "Watch out 'cause she's listening. If you don't treat her with respect, she'll burp on you at the wrong moment."

Dana eased his grip on the control wheel again. He had to keep reminding himself to fly with a gentle touch. The altimeter had drifted upward over a hundred feet since he rolled out of the bank. *Release that back-pressure.*

"What do you know about the new guys from California?" asked Dana. He was trying to act unconcerned as the huge four-engine turboprop droned along at 250 miles per hour. In reality, his attention was riveted on the Herk.

"What about them?" asked the colonel. "They probably think Minnesota only knows how to fly in the snow."

"Well it's hard to imagine what they're like," said Dana. "Tough to visualize them without thinking about all of that Hollywood crap."

"The Hollywood Guard," said the flight engineer. "That's what they call themselves. I doubt they have an ounce of common sense."

Dana laughed, but the colonel responded quickly: "Don't be so sure. I've worked with them before. No better, no worse than anybody else. They'll pull their share."

"Better than those hillbillies?" asked the flight engineer. California was replacing the Air Guard unit from Charlotte, North Carolina, on the standard two-week rotation. Usually, no one in the Air Force had a lot of good things to say about another outfit with the same equipment. Every flying unit thought they were better than the rest. There was a healthy competition among C-130 units, and that was fine. As long as it remained healthy.

"North Carolina ain't no Minnesota," said the colonel. "But who is? You'd best believe those guys talk about us too."

The C-130 was now within fifty miles of the air base, as Dana rolled slightly left to parallel the jungle-draped coast with its narrow trace of white sand beaches. The two pilots and the flight engineer were now immersed in their own assignments. There was a navigator on this air-drop mission too, but his seat in the right rear of the flight deck was empty. The navigator was back in the cargo compartment with the two loadmasters, their jobs complete after the air-drop. The nav was probably talking about the "go-home party" for his Minnesota troops that fell into his lap to plan. Halfway through their two-week rotation, it was time to think about going home. In deployments like this, you were never in one place very long.

In Dana's keen peripheral vision, he watched the coastline slip by, but he kept his primary focus on the flight instruments. The sea below was mottled with distinct sections of blues and greens, and even blacks, as scattered cumulus clouds cast shadows on the ocean. Pristine white clouds with flat bottoms and towering cauliflower tops contrasted against the brilliant blue sky. The sea was intermixed with milky reefs, nearly white sandy bottoms, and warm Caribbean water.

They flew on eastward in silence, following the coastline until they were over a hundred miles down the coast from their exit point from the jungle. But the colonel wasn't stopping Dana. It was still his airplane.

"How about a right three-sixty?" asked Dana, wanting another chance to practice his airwork while he had the chance before beginning the arrival route to the air base.

The colonel nodded, and Dana scanned through the right side window.

"Clear right," said Dana. He rolled the aircraft into the turn, forty-five degrees of bank this time, concentrating on the altimeter closely as he nudged the throttles forward to hold the altitude. The altimeter was pegged at fifty-five hundred feet as if riding on a rail. He dropped his gaze to the lower right side of the instrument panel, paying close attention to the vertical speed indicator, trying to hold the altitude precisely.

When his 360-degree turn was nearly complete, Dana again concentrated on the altimeter as he began his rollout. He eased the throttles rearward and simultaneously released the back-pressure on the control wheel. *Whack!* The C-130s own wake turbulence hammered the aircraft in a quick jolt. Right on the money – right on the altitude.

"You're getting a feel for this beast," said the colonel.

"Thanks. It feels good."

"Let's go home," said the colonel.

Dana glanced down at the chart that hung on the yoke clip in front of him. The arrival altitude for the Panama Canal low-level route was four thousand feet, so he eased the control wheel forward, leaving the throttles alone and picking up speed during the descent.

"I hear the Regulars want Volant Oak back," said the young flight engineer. "Or maybe the Reserves."

"Too late," said the colonel. "They both gave it up, and I can't see the Guard Bureau giving in to them now."

"Well, if you ask me, the Reserves aren't much different than us anyway," said the flight engineer. "Damned if I can tell the difference."

"The Guard works for both the Governor and the Air Force," said Dana.

"Sure," said the colonel. "In theory. Governors really need a fleet of C-130s, don't they?"

"In case Minnesota declares war on North Dakota," quipped the flight engineer.

The colonel punched his microphone button and requested an air traffic control clearance. He read it back to the controller with the ease of a man who had done this before – many times.

The canal entrance and the port city of Colón appeared off their right side, and Dana led the turn over it perfectly. The ancient city of Colón, with its military history of conquistadors and buccaneers, slipped behind. They were headed right down the Panama Canal, southbound now, a brief ride to the Pacific side of the narrow isthmus – a scenic cruise through the Canal Zone to Howard Air Force Base.

"It's hard to believe we're giving up the Canal," said the colonel. "By 2000, we'll be gone."

"They won't be able to figure out how to run it. The Canal, that is," said the flight engineer.

"I doubt that will be a problem," said the colonel. "The local government has been a major part of the Canal Zone for years. But things are pretty fragile here, politically. Hope it doesn't get worse."

Dana watched the Canal as it spread out in front of him into man-made Gatun Lake, a waerway formed by the construction of locks and the damming of the Chagres River. This was the center of the Canal's connection between two oceans. Beyond Gatun, ships could be seen grasped tightly within the locks. Ships of all nations, sometimes as wide as the narrow channel with only inches to spare, in their journey between the seas. Alongside the Canal, the trans-isthmus freight train was chugging away from Gatun, winding along the Canal as part of the well-oiled clockwork. Segments of twisting boxcars peeked around the mountains to the south.

"Politically, it can't get much worse," said Dana. "It's a scary country. Beautiful but scary."

Dana spoke as nonchalantly as he could. The view was awesome. The feel of the C-130 in his hands engrossed the part of him that wasn't captured by the view.

"It's gonna' get scarier," said the colonel. "The Cubans will love to see us go. But the U.S. can't solve all of the world's problems. Maybe we can enjoy this place a bit and solve just a few stumbling blocks in our own little way."

"It's hard to imagine we can solve much here," said Dana.

He was trying to talk with ease, but he was already dividing his attention between the scenery and the airplane. Lush greens of the jungle contrasted with the watery thread of the Panama Canal beyond Gatun Lake, a silver slice through the isthmus that was punctuated by the locks.

"You're right," replied the colonel. "We can't solve the big things. But we can help keep this crazy country moving forward. It's our job in fact."

"Some job," said the flight engineer. "It's tough to make a difference here."

"So just enjoy it then," said the colonel. "I do. And we're providing some stability to a region that's teetering on awfully weak legs."

The Pacific Ocean was in view now. The final locks slipped under the Herk. This canal was a historic feat of engineering, sliced through mountain and jungle by determination, but it wasn't a lengthy stretch of waterway. Now, off the nose, the high-rises of Panama City and the flat spread of the runways at Howard Air Force Base came into view.

"Cleared to land," greeted the control tower.

Dana eased the throttles back, let the nose of the aircraft sink, and marveled at the fact he was about to land a C-130. As the landing gear came down, he relished the view from his perch one more time, and then slipped into total concentration for the landing. All checklists were complete, and the cockpit was sterile-quiet.

They slipped past the white sand beach at the end of the runway, throttles coming back now, flaring, and touching down on centerline.

Reverse thrust, brakes, and the intense vibration of sudden deceleration.

When the props came out of the reversing negative pitch, the Hercules was slow enough to make the next turnoff onto the taxiway. Dana's body was overcome with a surge of relaxation.

All was well in paradise. How lucky he was to be sitting here, poised just a few minutes ago above the Panama Canal for reasons he didn't clearly understand – didn't really need to understand. But he was doing his job. A job that overwhelmed him with pleasure. He was at the peak of his life. And best of all, he knew it.

* * * * * *

As the C-130 pulled into its parking spot on the Howard Air Force Base ramp, a new day was settling over Panama. The heavy air was pungent with the smell of the surrounding jungle. The calls of exotic birds pierced the industrial hum of an American air base.

In the adjacent parking spots, Minnesota Air National Guard mechanics refueled North Carolina aircraft, preparing them for the long flight home. And out over the Gulf of Mexico, four C-130s – three California E-models and one "B" – were headed south as replacements.

Chapter 6

Go-Home Day

Shawna opened the center drawer of the desk and removed her favorite pen and a small blank notepad. Anyone looking at her desk, even in the middle of the duty day, would see an organized and nearly empty work area. Typically, she had minimal paperwork to attend to during the course of her shift. Most of her routine functions involved putting out fires, particularly the type that involved unique personalities. Those personalities were most often connected to the hot-line phones at the other end of her call-center phone. Her least favorite button was the one highlighted in red and labeled "Command Post." Most of the rest she could deal with on a daily basis without losing her composure. Of course, it was a lot easier dealing with shop supervisors and mechanics. They might sometimes be belligerent; but, by regulation, they still had to salute her.

In reality, almost no one worked for her. Maintenance Control was a staff function, empowered by the Chief of Maintenance to keep the flying schedule flowing. The supervisors and mechanics at the other end of these telephone lines had their own bosses, and Maintenance Control was nowhere in that chain of command. The only people who really worked for Shawna were right in this room. Yet, somehow the system worked, and the airplanes kept flying. Most of the time.

* * * * *

Grumpy was an understatement for the prevailing attitude in the grassy area just outside Base Operations. Everyone was about as negative as possible. The aircraft mechanics from North Carolina were in an unfenced holding area, having completed their Customs inspection. Their bags and bodies were now captured, awaiting the incoming C-130s from California – captives in a country they were eager to vacate.

The holding status of the mechanics in the grassy area was bad enough, but an intrusion by drug-sniffing dogs aggravated the situation even more. Every mechanic was bringing home a souvenir or two, and their favorite items included local artwork – framed native molas and carved wooden statues. The Customs inspectors used their waiting time to run the dogs through the holding area and to dismantle some of the wooden statues, redundantly looking for drugs and adding to the mood of harassment.

After two weeks duty in Panama, a delay on go-home day was unacceptable. To make matters worse, many of the mechanics had worked all night to prepare their aircraft for departure, and now they were trying to rest in the heat-sharp grass of this hot and humid country. Relaxing in a C-130 was difficult enough, but resting out here was nearly impossible. The only consolation? – they were going home.

The flight crews, of course, were in the air-conditioned comfort of Base Operations. The pilots would get the star treatment while the grunt workers got the shaft. It was always that way. If mechanics couldn't complain about the flight crews, something was drastically wrong.

Already two hours late, with another hour of delay expected before wheels-up, it was a welcome diversion for everyone to wonder where David Ricardi might be. The red-headed playboy must have experienced quite a night on the town, because missing a go-home flight was virtually unheard of. If he didn't show up soon, everyone from the shop chief on up would be in trouble. Of course, the mission commander was worrying about this too – from the air-conditioned comfort of Base Ops.

Box lunches arrived via pickup truck, and the grassy area prisoners finally had something more to complain about. Nothing like a warm carton of milk in the penetrating Panama heat. The lunches were unloaded by the First Sergeant, a fellow with more unusual tasks than anyone else on this mission. He too would have some explanations to make if Ricardi, the red-headed Romeo from the Hydraulic Shop, missed his aircraft.

Just as the box lunches were being distributed, the mission commander emerged from his air-conditioned sanctuary to announce that the first inbound C-130 was inside the arrival window, and departures were now authorized. That meant the mechanics, already hot and cranky, had to gather up their bags and just-opened lunches and walk across the hot ramp to their assigned aircraft. The task of dragging two or three bags and facing the hot ugly parking ramp was further enhanced when the flight crews' blue bus scooted past them at the mid-ramp point, headed for the four awaiting aircraft. The mechanics provided a few amplified one-finger salutes.

But it was go-home day, so the mood changed very quickly. The engines cranked faster than the checklist norms. The roar of sixteen Allison T56 turboprop engines bounced off the jungle canopy at the edge of the ramp and resonated across Howard Air Force Base.

A few minutes later, the four aircraft were airborne without Sergeant Ricardi. He would get to ride home in the comfort of a TWA Boeing 727. But there would be hell to pay when he arrived in North Carolina.

Chapter 7

Mushrooms

Shawna's nightmare didn't return again that week. But the poor start for the latest Volant Oak rotation didn't reverse its trend. Upon arrival in Panama, one of the C-130s was immediately grounded for a landing gear problem, a not-locked-down indication. The rumor was that the aircraft, 62-1801, had left home station in California with that same mechanical discrepancy, but the documentation for the squawk was suspiciously missing from the maintenance records. An inflight-check entry in the maintenance forms provided clear evidence of a recurring problem with the landing gear.

Jacking a C-130 on an open ramp wasn't any fun, but it would be necessary. There was only one hangar on the base that could fully enclose a C-130 airframe, and that hangar bay was currently occupied.

Another problem involved the cargo-loading equipment for the B-model. Many of these accessories were missing, probably the result of the quick switch of aircraft prior to departure from California. So now, here was a lame duck with barely enough fuel reserves (no exterior tanks) to fly to neighboring countries, and the same aircraft had to steal loading equipment from other C-130s when it was assigned a mission. Moving a cargo winch from aircraft to aircraft wasn't an easy task. The B-model and the troubled landing gear on 801 didn't herald a smooth start to California's rotation.

* * * * * *

The hot-line phone from the control room's entry door rang and flashed red. Shawna answered it from her seat at the rear of the room.

"Maintenance Control, Lieutenant Whitney," she said in her official voice.

"Major Tobia and Sergeant Rotella, California Air Guard." It was an official voice answering an official voice.

"Stand by, sir," said Shawna. "I'll buzz you in."

Hanging up the phone, Shawna avoided hitting the entry buzzer switch. These were unknown personalities, so she stepped down from her raised platform and glanced through the one-way glass in the window of the entry door. Standing within a few feet of the window was a major in informal blues, accompanied by a tall senior master sergeant in fatigues. The major was staring smugly into the mirrored one-way glass, pretending to comb his hair with his flight cap still in place, obviously expecting inquiring eyes on the other side. Shawna laughed to herself and then opened the door and invited them in.

"Come in, sir," Shawna said.

"Hi" was the jovial reply from the major.

He was smiling, looking harmless. The sergeant was more of a threat. Senior non-commissioned officers were a bigger problem than commissioned officers of any rank. Enlisted maintenance personnel always knew more about the mechanics of things than Shawna, and she seldom felt at ease around them.

The major and the NCO stepped through the doorway. Their eyes adjusted slowly to the darkness.

"Sure is dark in here," said the NCO.

Is he kidding?

"It's best to keep everybody in the dark," said Shawna. "Just part of our job."

"Like mushrooms," replied the officer. "Keep 'em in the dark and feed 'em shit."

An old line. Who in Maintenance Control hadn't heard that one? But it sounded crude when said by someone you don't know. Does he even notice he's talking to a woman?

"Very true, sir," replied Shawna without flinching. "Like I said, it's part of our job."

"I'm Brian Tobia, California Air Guard." The major offered his hand, and Shawna shook it. His handshake was firm and friendly. "And this is Jay Rotella, my line chief."

Shawna shook the hand of the NCO. He seemed disinterested by the visit, aloof from the moment.

"We're your problem for the next two weeks," said the major.

He seemed likeable enough. Crude, but obviously friendly. His line chief looked like the typical problem, most likely a very knowledgeable guy.

"Welcome to Howard Air Force Base, home of the homeless," said Shawna.

"Thanks," said the major. "Sorry we haven't introduced ourselves earlier. Been busy with those hogs, you know."

"They're all hogs to us," replied Shawna. "That includes the A-7s."

"Oh, those fighter pukes have got it easy," said the major. "Must be nice to have only one engine to worry about."

"Until it stops running," noted the NCO.

Another old joke, but both Shawna and Brian laughed.

"Looks like your aircraft are in pretty good shape today," said Shawna.

"Not bad," replied Brian. "Of course, you haven't really met 801 yet."

"No, I haven't had the pleasure," replied Shawna. "Should I be worried?"

"Nothing to get too excited about," said Brian. "But at home she's our hangar queen. There are more mysteries in that bird's landing gear system than any sane mechanic has ever been able to figure out."

"Great," said Shawna. "I'll keep that in mind."

"Just never let 801 into a hangar, or she'll take up permanent residence," said Brian.

Shawna caught herself as she was about to make a cutting reply, squelching some tempting comments regarding the general quality of Air Guard aircraft. She stopped short, knowing those around her often saw an overly critical and blunt female lieutenant. She seldom tried to shake that image. To mechanics, the quality of their aircraft was an extremely sensitive area.

A tour of the control room would be a way to avoid her standard foot-in-mouth problem. Already Shawna felt relaxed with this officer. His level of seriousness might not be very high, but it was nice to see a maintenance officer who was having fun. His sidekick NCO, however, didn't strike her as someone she wanted to deal with. He undoubtedly knew a lot more than she did about C-130s, with the typical resentment for officers, particularly female officers.

Shawna led them toward the front of the control room. As they approached the status boards, she spoke to the major as if the sergeant weren't present.

"What's your job back home?" asked Shawna.

She was fascinated by the concept. If she decided to get out of the Air Force, "weekender" status might be the way to go after her four-year hitch. Getting out was a more likely possibility every day.

"I'm a school teacher. High school math," said Brian. "Jay's an Air Tech, so he has to put up with these hogs every day."

"Air Tech is similar to the Reserves ARTS program?" asked Shawna.

She was really quite green to the concept of weekend warriors. None of her Air Force training had prepared her for confrontation with the Reserves. The Reserves, as a whole, were pretty much a joke.

Total Force. Now there was a farce. The military's leadership was spouting off about integrating everyone together when it came to military operations. The Army, Air Force, and the rest of the military were supposed to work in harmony, contrary to their differences in specific missions. But every time she saw Total Force in action at a Joint Chiefs of Staff exercise, it was every man for himself – women, too. The Air Force Reserve was about as friendly to the regular Air Force as the Air Force was to the Army. In other words, not pleasant partners. But the Air Force still preached Total Force, and it sounded good on paper.

"Air Techs are Air National Guard personnel who work full-time," replied Jay. "I like the Navy's name for us better. They call their full-time civilian employees 'station keepers', which is pretty much what I am as an Air Tech. Back home I'm a full-time line chief, getting Herks ready for the weekenders to fly and break."

"Must be nice to wear civilian clothes on the job," noted Shawna.

"Actually we don't," replied Jay.

That figures — this macho NCO has to correct the bumbling female lieutenant.

"I have to wear the uniform during the week," continued Jay. "That's one of the few differences between the Air Force Reserves and us. Other than that, the Air Guard and Reserves are pretty much the same concept. Of course, the Guard is better."

Lighten up, Sergeant. Even if you do know more than me, don't preach the facts, as if I care.

"Of course," said Shawna. "Sounds like a fun job."

"Not bad," replied Jay. "Except for rotations like this. No offense."

"No offense to Panama or to the schedule?"

"Both," replied Jay. "I'm not much on hot and humid, and even less on the middle-of-the-night."

The California Air National Guard had joined the Minnesota unit, each contributing four C-130s to the on-going Volant Oak mission in Panama. California replaced North Carolina, and everybody was on a two-week rotation. Minnesota still had a week remaining, so there was always an overlap that kept the confusion to a minimum. But there was still a lot of chaos. Who could blame them? It took at least two weeks to start feeling familiar with a new base. Just as soon as the level of comfort began to take hold, they were on their way home. And to add to the current situation, one of their airplanes was a B-model and another was a landing gear cripple.

"It's tough on a rotation like this, without any inter-fly," said the major. "California and Minnesota refuse to fly each others airplanes. Those fly-boys have their stupidity."

Brian wore maintenance officer wings above his left pocket, an emblem new to the Air Force. It was an attempt by the Air Force to add prestige to non-flying personnel. It didn't work.

"Heck, we even have a hard time getting our own E-model crews to fly our B's," said the NCO. "Fortunately, on this trip, they have no choice. But it's still a mess. Sorry about the B-model."

Sorry? Now that's a switch. This guy might not be so bad after all.

"Well, it's really not a big problem," replied Shawna. "We're getting used to the fact you always get your airplanes in the air somehow. Our Chief of Maintenance is afraid to ask how you do it."

"He doesn't want to know," said the NCO.

Jay Rotella was tall and very impressive, sporting senior master sergeant chevrons on his sleeves. Quite young too. Shawna guessed he was in his mid-thirties, not bad for his rank. In fact, the Guard and Reserves seemed intent on promoting their NCOs fast. That led to even more distrust from their regular Air Force counterparts. This guy was young and probably couldn't hold his own with a "real" sergeant in the regular Air Force's "top three" NCO ranks. But, still, he somehow earned the chevrons.

"Well, we just wanted to say hello," said Brian, paving their exit.

Like most Guard officers, there was an aura of informality about this guy. His hair was quite a bit out of regulation, so long that it curled upward in back, but Shawna wasn't about to challenge him. Jay, on the other hand, seemed exceedingly stiff. In fact, his hair was a short crew cut, and his fatigues appeared starched. Probably not the kind of guy to tackle on a technical matter, and most likely not an NCO to deal with on any subject voluntarily.

"Let me show you around a bit," said Shawna. She didn't want this officer to think she was pushing them out.

"Over here is the Volant Oak board," said Shawna. She led them to a white vertical board with a colored grease-pencil display. The four California tail numbers were in blue, sequenced under the orange Minnesota aircraft.

This was usually the way it started. The new rotational maintenance officer almost always introduced himself by a visit to Maintenance Control. He invariably pledged to work closely with the Howard Air Force Base permanent personnel, and then you never saw him again except during the colonel's daily stand-up briefing.

The permanent cadre at Howard were often lacking in enthusiasm about the air base, and temporary duty personnel seemed even less attached to the sprawling facility. Even with the base's idealistic history of trying to keep peace in an ever-insurgent Central America, the role of Americans here was winding down, as the Panamanians prepared to take over management of the Canal Zone. To many of the military residents of the base, it felt a lot like living out the last days in an old apartment that soon would be vacated, only to be demolished and replaced by an impersonal parking lot.

Now in front of Shawna, this particular Air Guard officer seemed friendly enough and quite harmless. He certainly didn't seem to take this assignment seriously. Major Tobia was probably a lot more of a school teacher than a military leader. But there was really nothing wrong with that.

Most of the Guard NCOs, on the other hand, were better off never seen again. This one seemed like typical trouble, only younger, less experienced, and with an ego to match a Van Nuys home on the edge of Hollywood.

* * * * * *

On the third day after the arrival of the California C-130s, all hell broke loose. The young senior NCO from the Air Guard was at the morning stand-up briefing, while a C-130 mission was rapidly approaching delayed departure status. To make matters worse, the A-7 fighter squadron from the North Dakota Air Guard had aborted a low-level mission the night before because of a still-undiagnosed engine problem, and their spare airplane had been a "vapor" tail number. There was nothing like a fake spare to get Colonel Penland's attention. He had an openly hostile attitude towards the Air Guard.

"What's the estimate for 755?" asked Colonel Penland. His tone was controlled and sounded respectful and sincere. His staff knew otherwise.

Except for the colonel's own line chief, Jay Rotella was the only other NCO in the room. Why the Air Guard's maintenance officer had chosen to send him to this briefing wasn't clear. A C-130 delay was in progress, and the Guard officer had sent his NCO. Either the maintenance officer was stupid or exceedingly smart.

"One hour plus parts," said Jay in a firm voice.

Jay Rotella stood tall in this room, at least an inch taller than anyone else, athletic looking and not the look of a maintenance manager. A California kid. If he was a bit younger and had a little more hair, he'd be easily mistaken for a California surfer.

"But we can get the fuel control off our spare engine," said Jay, "if Supply doesn't come up with one in the next few minutes. We plan to give them until nine o'clock, no later."

"Shawna?" The colonel turned his attention towards Shawna, and at first she wasn't sure why. Then it clicked, and she was quick on her feet.

"Supply says the fuel control isn't loaded in their inventory," said Shawna.

"Computer's down," stated the duty-shift supply officer, also a lieutenant. "We're making a manual check of assets right now."

The supply officer seemed less than confident his answer would be accepted.

"Figures," replied Colonel Penland.

The colonel's hefty body fit nicely in his form-fitted dress blue uniform. His chest expanded farther outward than his trim weight suggested, and the multitude of ribbons on his blue jacket demanded respect. The wings of a rated flight officer were the clearest emblem of his level of authority, even exceeding the tremble everyone in the room felt from the colonel's "chicken" insignia on his shoulder straps.

"Stinkin' B-model," said the colonel. "You'll never have her airborne by ten o'clock. It'll take an engine burp run after you replace the fuel control, probably a full engine run. Maybe we should switch to the spare."

It wasn't really a question.

"If you can live with ten o'clock, we'll have her airborne," noted Jay. He spoke confidently, contradicting the raw cynicism of the colonel.

"And if you miss, we lose the mission," countered the colonel. "You'll need an engine-running ops check before launch, and that takes time."

"Our flight crew will do it on the takeoff roll, retorted Jay. "We do it all of the time at home."

"This isn't home, Sergeant Rotella!"

"But it's our airplane and our flight crew, sir," said Jay. "Give us a chance, and we'll get her airborne."

Colonel Penland paused, appearing to purposely calm himself before speaking. This colonel seldom gave in. They didn't call him 'Colonel No' for nothing.

"Okay, Sergeant. You've got until ten o'clock. But one minute later and I'll have your ass."

"Thanks, Colonel. We'll have you an airplane. I'll risk my ass on it."

Shawna gritted her teeth and cringed. The room rippled with constrained chuckles. No one dared to laugh out loud.

The colonel glared at Jay. But when he responded, it was with a faint smile.

"So, now let's move on to last night's air abort," he said calmly.

* * * * * *

Ten o'clock came and went. And 755 didn't make it. The spare replaced the grounded B-model, but not before the delay window expired. Getting airborne at 10:40 didn't hack it. There would be hell to pay at the next morning's briefing. Shawna was looking forward to the action.

The hot-line from the Volant Oak office rang, and Shawna answered it.

"Lieutenant Whitney," she said

"Bet you're celebrating in there."

Shawn immediately identified the confrontational voice as that of Jay Rotella, but she wasn't about to admit she recognized him.

"Sir, what do you mean?"

She tried to act like she was talking to Major Tobia.

"Don't 'sir' me. Otherwise I'll 'ma'am' you," said Jay.

She preferred being called 'ma'am' over dealing with this surly sergeant.

"Sergeant Rotella?" she asked.

"Don't 'Sergeant' me, ma'am,"

Shawna laughed. This guy had guts at least. She had figured he wouldn't be heard from again today, and she doubted he'd show at tomorrow morning's briefing.

"Your colonel is a real Guard lover, isn't he?" noted Jay. "Heck, if nothing else, it provides a pleasant day for him. But when 'Colonel No' speaks, it's hard not to challenge him."

"Challenge him? Nobody around here challenges him, unless there's a mighty good reason. You might be wise to do the same. So you know about his nickname?"

"He's a bit famous with our guys over here," said Jay. "Why don't you pay us a visit, and I'll show you around our little empire. But you'd better let me know before you arrive. My boys will have to put away their girlie magazines and poker chips before an officer visits."

"How about your maintenance officer?" asked Shawna. "I haven't seen Major Tobia lately. I figure he sent you to the morning stand-up briefing to watch you sink."

Jay laughed and replied immediately: "Around here we treat our officers right. He's fishing on Gatun Lake. We like him too much to make him worry about Herks in delay. And he probably figures we can get the job done better without him."

"The loyalty of the Guard troops." Shawna regretted her words, winced her lips for a moment, and awaited the reply.

"You bet," replied Jay without a hint of anger. "We take care of our own. But that doesn't mean we can't play the game. We want those missions to go just as much as you do."

"I know. Sorry," said Shawna. "Officer Training School didn't prepare me for the Guard."

"OTS. That explains it. We've got a lot of 90-day wonders in the Guard too, but we have our own officer training academy. I'm afraid you wouldn't like how the Hollywood Guard gets things done."

"Hollywood Guard. That's a new one," said Shawna. There was a lilt in her voice.

"Oh, that's just our undercover name. We got the name originally because of our location near Los Angeles. Bob Hope always departed for his holiday tour of the Vietnam troops from our base in Van Nuys. So it was a natural name. But since then we accept the name 'Hollywood Guard' for less inspiring reasons."

This guy is different. Maybe I've misjudged him.

"Well, you got the spare C-130 going mighty fast once we made the switch," said Shawna. "Congratulations."

"Thanks. So when are you paying us an inspection visit, ma'am?"

Chapter 8

Roommates

In her year at Howard Air Force Base, Shawna hadn't once visited the Volant Oak C-130 maintenance office. Nor had she visited the Air Guard's A-7 office. It really wasn't necessary. If anybody worked for anybody here, the Guard worked for Maintenance Control. However, she knew the Air Guard felt it was the other way around.

This was her first assignment since Officer Training School, excluding her maintenance officer training in Illinois. Howard Air Force Base was certainly a learning experience, but she didn't regret she would be gone in another six months. On her dream sheet, her next assignment was Dover Air Force Base in Delaware. She probably could have received Dover right out of maintenance officer training, but it seemed too close to her home in Cheswold, Delaware. Join the Air Force and see Delaware. Join the Air Force and see Panama – not much better.

Panama, at first, sounded like an ideal assignment; lots of international flight activity and a personal chance to see both Central and South America. There were many opportunities to ride along on trips to distant countries, and Shawna thought she would be traveling a lot. So far, there had been one trip to Ecuador. The lack of travel was entirely Shawna's decision. The Volant Oak aircraft rotated in and out of South America almost every day, and it would be simple to secure a seat. But she always found an excuse for waiting until the next time.

Her hobbies hadn't prospered here either. She loved to play tennis, and there were plenty of tennis courts on base. But all of the available partners were male, and the few times she tried using her racket with them, she regretted it. Keeping up with a macho guy on the courts in this heat was a struggle. It left her merely worn out and sweating. She didn't like sweat.

Hiking was another hobby that remained behind her in the States. There were some exotic locations nearby, but the level of political safety when traveling off the air base was in doubt. And Shawna visualized snakes everywhere. She had heard those stories about giant pit vipers lying on the sidewalks at night, cooling themselves on the pavement. Yet in her entire assignment in Panama, she hadn't seen a single snake. Of course, she didn't frequent remote sidewalks at night, and when she had to walk on them, she walked very carefully. Her guidelines for walking after dark involved pavement like the flightline where the grassy areas were far removed and the level of human activity was high.

But she could ride her beloved bicycle around the base, and biking was one of her favorite hobbies. And she could read. Now there was a hobby that was geographically universal. And in Panama it was a necessity to keep her sense of orientation. Without her trash novels, she would be dead.

Thus, the future looked brighter. Nothing could look worse than this. Thoughts of a pending reassignment to the States kept her going, and Dover Air Force Base was the focus of her dreams.

Cheswold, Delaware, was a tiny town, and she had grown up there with the C-141s of nearby Dover vibrating through her childhood. During high school in the early 70s, the aluminum overcast of the new C-5s demanded her attention as they lumbered overhead on final approach to the air base, the loud piercing whine of the huge GE turbofan engines penetrating the solitude of the Delaware swamplands. She dreamed that someday she could be associated with something as important as C-5s.

High school was a bit too exciting, judging by her sexual experiences. But those were mostly experiences of the wrong kind. If her parents had even a hint of her promiscuous nature, they kept it far from the dinner table. Somehow she survived without her exploits becoming a family problem. If her dad had known about half of her adventures, Shawna would have been grounded for her entire senior year. Fortunately, she survived without getting pregnant or even being discovered. Everyone in her family thought she was an innocent angel. Her father called her "Princess." After discouraging bouts with high school boys, she planned to be more of an angel than a princess for the rest of her life.

Delaware State College wasn't much of a challenge, partly because it was just down the highway, but her parents were pleased she stayed at home for her education. The predominantly black population of the college gave her little attention, and it kept her love life in check. That was fine with Shawna.

By the time she graduated with her degree in history, Shawna was ready for a change in location. But she wasn't sure she could handle such a move. Maybe that was part of the reason for the Air Force. If it didn't work out, there was always the possibility of pleading for assignment to Dover and moving back in with mom and dad.

Not surprisingly, her friends at her first real assignment in Panama perceived her anti-male attitude as the marks of a lesbian. After all, she was a female who had chosen the Air Force, she avoided men, and she felt comfortable without being pursued by a guy. To discount such suspicions was counterproductive. If they wanted to consider her a lesbian, that was probably to her advantage.

But Melissa Henesie knew differently. Melissa had been Shawna's roommate since their simultaneous arrival in Panama, and Melissa was an open lesbian. Or at least she was as informally open as could be expected in the modern Air Force. Few asked, and even fewer told. It could only be taken so far, but there seemed to be few problems for Melissa. And she didn't give up on Shawna. Melissa could learn to love Shawna, perhaps already did.

As for Shawna, Melissa seemed surprisingly able to accept her as a friend, without expanding the relationship into a physical one. It's not that Mel wanted it that way, but she could accept it. The two of them got along amazingly well from the start, and Shawna's request to limit it to friendship seemed reasonable enough. It probably wouldn't have worked with another woman, but Melissa adapted to a platonic relationship, and Shawna was quick to follow. They simply cared too much for each other to mess it up.

Melissa was particularly attractive, driving men crazy when she repeatedly pushed them away. Her dirty blond hair touched the middle of her back when released from its Air Force bun. And when it was bundled in accordance with Air Force specs, it gave her face a full and supple look. She was a knockout for most men and some women. Mel had that encompassing softness of a woman. Soft, alluring, complex, vulnerable. These were traits Shawna loved, and traits that men craved.

After rooming with Mel for a few months, Shawna approached her after experiencing four repeated memories of the future. Melissa was prepared to be as helpful as possible, but she could offer only what her personality perceived as realistic.

"So go ahead and tell me," said Melissa.

"You'll think I'm queer, Mel," said Shawna.

"I wish you were queer."

Melissa wasn't only open; she was satisfied with who she was and where she was. Her biggest problem was the boredom of being a supply officer. Public relations had been her choice, but the needs of the Air Force came first. Yet Melissa believed in the military and was convinced her efforts to cross-train would pay off eventually.

By the time Melissa was promoted to major, she'd be on her way toward a specialty code change. In fact, she was counting on it. She had signed on the dotted line to continue beyond her four-year commitment, with a public relations slot as her declared goal. She was now almost eight years into an Air Force career, and still trapped in Supply.

"I've had a strange dream several times in the past few months," said Shawna. "It's always exactly the same, and when I wake up in the morning, it's more than a dream."

"More than a dream, meaning very real?"

"Not just very real," said Shawna. "It is real. It's more like a memory. In fact, it is a memory, just like I remember our dinner at the officers' club last night. All of the details; everything, absolutely everything, fits together."

"Realistic dreams aren't uncommon," said Melissa. "Of course, that's spoken by a roommate who can never remember her dreams."

"It's not a realistic dream. Nor is it a typical nightmare. It's a firm memory."

"You mean like a very realistic memory," said Melissa. "That's what the most realistic dreams probably feel like."

Melissa tilted her head to the side, a subtle gesture that usually made Shawna smile.

"What I'm trying to say is that it's a memory, Mel," repeated Shawna. "It's perfectly real in every respect."

Shawna paused. She wanted to convince Melissa she really believed what she was about to say, but she wasn't sure she believed it herself."

"It's a memory of the future," said Shawna.

"Of the future," Melissa said and then paused.

Melissa wasn't known as an empathetic person, and Shawna imagined her trying unsuccessfully to accept the concept of these memory episodes.

Melissa continued: "So that makes it a prediction you're dreaming about. A lifelike prediction."

"But that's just it, Mel. It's not a prediction. It's not at all like I'm foreseeing the future. I'm remembering the future, because it's exactly like a memory rather than a foreboding."

"But how do you know that?" asked Melissa. "If it seems so real that it's a memory, maybe it's a memory. Why couldn't it be part of the past?"

"Well, for one thing," Shawna said slowly, "you're in this nightmare, this memory. And you're a major."

"Minor detail," countered Melissa. "It doesn't take a lot of dreaming to know I'll be a major next month. I've already got my orders. Maybe you're confusing the two dreams. So what's the problem?"

"The problem is... Todd Chandler gets killed."

"Todd Chandler, your Maintenance Control nemesis?"

"He's not my nemesis," said Shawna. "I don't like him much, but he's not a problem for me."

Shawna recognized she could be overly critical of everyone around her. She questioned nearly everything and everybody in life, including Todd Chandler. At least Shawna admitted it.

"But your dislike of Todd could result in a dream, not particularly a nice dream," noted Melissa. "How does he get killed?"

"A C-141 rudder falls on him in Hangar Two."

"Nice way to go," said Melissa. "Poor rudder."

"Com'on, Melissa, be serious. This is a very graphic memory I'm experiencing. It's much more than a nightmare, and it's definitely in the future. The details are unbelievable. Not all of them make sense, but too many of them do."

"So what's a Maintenance Control captain doing in Hangar Two?" asked Melissa. "That's the Aerospace Systems hangar, isn't it?"

"We go in there once in a while," said Shawna. "This memory takes place in the middle of the night, and there's a transient C-141 that's undergoing a rudder replacement. The Aerospace guys drop the rudder from a Pettibone crane, and it kills Todd instantly."

"In your dream."

"In my memory."

"So where do I come in?" asked Melissa.

"I remember Todd's funeral, and I remember we sat there together. And you're a major."

"Shawna, I hear what you're saying, but maybe you're making too big a deal out of this. It's pretty hard to imagine a maintenance officer supervising a rudder change. And a C-141 doesn't make a lot of sense. I can assure you as a world-renowned supply officer that 141 rudders aren't a common failure item. Maybe it's the rudder of Todd's sailboat that falls on him."

Shawna was ready to give up. But she changed direction to see what would happen.

"Did you ever have a dream as a kid that came true?" asked Shawna.

"I don't think so," replied Melissa. "I don't remember it anyway. You mean a not-so-important dream that came true?"

"Well, I had one I remember," said Shawna. "I dreamed my grand-father died, and everybody was crying at his funeral. I don't like thoughts of funerals, and I hated them even more as a kid."

"And he died?" said Melissa.

"I know that isn't very surprising," said Shawna. "After all, he was pretty old. But it happened within a few days of my dream, and he wasn't even sick. They said it was a heart attack."

"So that proves it," said Melissa. "People never die unless you dream about them."

Shawna was sorry she had brought the subject up.

"Well, it scared me," said Shawna. "I thought I had something to do with his heart attack. I believed that for a long time, and I was always afraid to go to my grandmother's house after that. I just knew his ghost was in that house waiting for me somewhere. Scared the hell out of me."

"You were just a kid," said Melissa.

"Yes, just a kid. But this time the details are terribly specific. And it's a memory."

"Correction," said Melissa. "Memories are of the past. Your grand-father is a memory. A falling C-141 rudder is a nightmare and an improbable one at that."

"Thanks for being so understanding," said Shawna. "What a room-ie."

Chapter 9

Chevrons

The morning stand-up briefing was viewed with apprehension by most of those in attendance, as they made polite conversation, awaiting the arrival of the colonel. Sergeant Jay Rotella was, to everyone's surprise, taking part in the small talk with the officers. He didn't seem to be fearful of the obvious confrontation that loomed ahead.

As Colonel Penland entered the room, the First Sergeant called the participants to attention. Everyone stood tall as the colonel marched in.

"Carry on," directed Penland.

He strutted to the head of the conference table and leaned over to examine the two status reports lined up at attention in front of him. He quickly examined the papers, blinked twice, and promptly sat down. One boss sitting, twelve workers standing and listening.

"Chief, your report."

The home station line chief stared directly at the colonel.

"All's well, sir. Both A-7 locals are off on time. All three C-130 missions are on-schedule at this point. Tire change on 62-1801 is in-progress. No delays expected. A C-5 from Norton is due in at 0840, alpha status one. They have an A-7 spare engine on board. That's about it, sir."

"Thanks, Chief. Maintenance Control?"

Shawna glanced at her notes and started her report.

"Sir, two C-130s are not-mission-capable, but one is the tire change. The other NMC is 62-1833 for a Doppler cross-track problem. Parts are available in Supply, with an ETIC of 0930."

She continued with a similar report for the A-7s, the single transient C-141 awaiting departure (and ready to go), and the status of the ground equipment. All was well in paradise.

Colonel Penland turned his gaze to Jay. Everyone knew what was next.

"Well, Sergeant Rotella, where's your California boogie board this morning?"

"Back in the barracks, sir," replied Jay without a moment's hesitation or any sign of concern.

"Hollywood Guard," said the colonel, matter-of-factly.

"That's what we call ourselves," replied Jay, without a pause or any sign of embarrassment.

Colonel Penland seemed to be in a kidding mood, and that was a good sign. The colonel continued.

"I see you're brave enough to show up again today," said Penland. "Congratulations on the launch of the spare yesterday. After all of that confusion, you almost salvaged an on-time departure."

"But it wasn't on time, sir," stated Jay distinctly. "Nor was there any confusion."

Everyone waited. Colonel Penland wouldn't let this get by him.

"Well, Sergeant, a fuel control change that you so obstinately insisted on led in a late departure. Sounds like confusion to me."

"No, sir." Jay replied briskly. "We had a handle on it. But the TD amp just wouldn't mate up with that fuel control. It was nobody's fault, and my guys made a valiant effort. Sometimes it just doesn't work out."

"You're right, Sergeant Rotella," said Penland. "Sometimes it doesn't work out. But that's what we're paid to prevent."

"Count the numbers at the end of the month, sir. I promise you'll like them."

The room was perfectly silent and unconditionally tense. The colonel looked back down at the small pile of reports in front of him, but no one suspected he was reading anything. When he looked up, he was smiling, and it looked genuine.

"I look forward to that, Sergeant. It was a nice effort. I wish all of us could be so bold."

* * * * * *

This time Jay visited rather than called. Shawna recognized his voice immediately on the entry-door phone. She buzzed him in without leaving her desk.

"Hi," he said as he stepped into the dark control room. "I still think you should raise mushrooms."

He issn't challenging me. It's merely friendly teasing. This is a fellow I could come come to like. First impressions aren't always correct.

"Nice job with Penland this morning," said Shawna. "I think he's taken a liking to you."

"He's a nice guy. I like him. He just thinks he hates the Guard."

"It's all part of our professional jealously," said Shawna. "As far as I'm concerned, we're all doing the same job in this business. We're pretty competitive, that's all."

"So, Shawna, what makes you so gruff?" challenged Jay.

Give a guy some slack, and he takes advantage of it. And what about a little respect for rank? Just when she thought she was starting to like Jay, he tried to put her in her place.

Only her friends were supposed to see through her bluntness. All of her NCOs routinely addressed her by her rank or at least a passing 'ma'am'."

"Sergeant Rotella, I'll take that to mean you consider me by-the-book," said Shawna. "Sorry if that bothers you."

"No, Shawna, it doesn't bother me at all. In fact, I kinda' like it. You're different than any of our female maintenance officers."

Shawna! Where does he get off calling me that? Shawna! It's Lieutenant Whitney to you.

"I'm afraid to ask what you mean by that," said Shawna, as she tried to keep her composure.

Hold your temper. This disrespectful NCO will be gone in less than two weeks.

"It's a compliment, I can assure you," said Jay. "Not all women join the Air Force to pursue its mission, but you impress me as someone who puts duty first."

"Sounds like a bit of machismo on your part."

"Maybe. But at least I admit it."

For a brief moment, Shawna remembered something engrained in her military training but seldom emphasized. It wasn't something that came up very often. Quite infrequently, in fact, and never for her. Officers should keep their distance from NCOs, especially when it involves men and women.

Fraternization was never a problem for Shawna. NCOs scared her, and often she found herself detesting them. This young senior master sergeant was no exception. In fact, he reminded her of all she disliked in the relationships between officers and NCOs. The best way to describe her dealings with NCOs was professional but oftentimes artificial.

"We're still waiting for your visit to the Volant Oak office," said Jay. "My guys are quite harmless, and I bet they'd enjoy meeting you. Even if you don't want to meet them."

"I want to meet them."

"Really?"

"Almost really?"

"So stop by, anytime," said Jay.

"Lunchtime today?" asked Shawna.

She surprised herself.

"We'll do some house cleaning first," said Jay. "The atrium is a mess."

* * * * * *

As noon approached, Shawna found herself excited about the visit. Jay had sounded sincere, although unacceptably informal, typical of the Guard. Maybe he was really sincere and she was just too defensive. She could probably use some mellowing. But not for the benefit of this NCO. She was proud of how she could hold her own in a man's world.

But what she found in the Volant Oak office wasn't an all-man's world. When she arrived at the office, two of the five occupants were women. Shawna noticed that Jay introduced the women before the men, regardless of the women's lower rank. Mary was running the dispatch board and seemed to have a lot on the ball. Denise was an engine mechanic on her lunch break, visiting with Mary.

The office was barren; basically a dispatch desk, a rectangular table with a few metal chairs, and a soft-looking yellow sofa. A hinged accordion-style dispatch board sat on the dispatch desk. A standard gray radio base station, also on the desk, was topped by a plastic, purple dinosaur. A large gray standing microphone and a black telephone with a single row of buttons appeared to be the working end of the operation.

To Shawna's eye, the office seemed unexpectedly comfortable. Absent were the typical shiny-clean military floors that showed artificial attention. Instead, there was a taste of civilian life, including a flowered quilt across the top of the sofa and a framed seascape on the wall. The painting looked like an expensive artistic original. A large red-on-blue rectangular sign on the adjacent wall proclaimed: *We Guard America's Skies.* Taped on the inside of the closed door to the flightline was a bumper sticker: *C-130: Ugliness at its Best.*

Jay introduced her to Jake, his propulsion supervisor, whose snack lunch was spread out in front of him, and to Ken, the administrative NCO. Both were tech sergeants, but Jay referred to them by their first names. He introduced Shawna as Lieutenant Whitney, but then called her "Shawna" (twice!) in front of these enlisted workers. She felt uncomfortable about that, but it soon passed. She even slipped once and called him "Jay," immediately correcting herself – "Sergeant Rotella." The single upside-down chevron above Jay's other six stripes provided an impressive display of enlisted rank, and his chevrons looked even bigger on a fatigue uniform. Still, he wasn't an officer.

Where is everybody?

She had expected to find a bunch of greasy guys hanging out, playing cards and telling war stories. But nearly everyone was on the flightline.

"How about a ramp tour?" asked Jay.

"Sure," replied Shawna.

Jay grabbed a brick-sized radio from a drawer in the dispatch desk and the keys to a pickup truck from a rack on the wall.

"If you need me, I'll be *Maintenance Two*," he told Mary as he escorted Shawna out the door.

That implied *Maintenance One*, Major Tobia, might be somewhere on frequency, but it wasn't clear where. Or maybe Jay used his call-sign of *Maintenance Two* out of respect for his MO.

As their blue pickup truck approached the restricted entry-point, the permanent party Air Force security guard gave Shawna's line badge a much closer inspection than Jay's. Maybe she needed to get out of Maintenance Control a bit more often.

The flightline was bristling with activity. Everyone they approached in their truck waved or nodded to them. Many of the mechanics yelled "Hi, Jay!" which added to Shawna's discomfort. Jay called all of the mechanics by their first names or their nicknames. There was "Hooter" and "Stainless" and "Woody" and "Mother."

Jay slowed the truck as they approached the front of the C-130 parked in Spot 7. Angling the dark blue Air Force pickup truck parallel to the left wing of the airplane, Jay came to a stop, shifted into *Park*, and turned off the ignition.

The C-130 sparkled wet, with the olive drab camouflage paint-scheme echoing her power. From this vantagepoint, it seemed that a smile could appropriately be painted on the bottom of the nose radome. The four turboprop engines, each with four propeller blades, had been aligned by the crew chief so each lower blade was exactly vertical. The aircraft looked like it was ready for an inspection by the Wing Commander.

"Now there's a face only a mother could love," said Jay. "Ain't she a beauty?"

"Oh, yes, a beauty to be sure," retorted Shawna.

"I'm serious. This is the best C-130 in the Air Force."

"Oh, I believe you," said Shawna. "That olive drab paint-scheme is my favorite."

"How about you?" asked Jay. "Are you a real airplane lover?"

"I've come to appreciate them," said Shawna. "But nothing like the way some mechanics look at these machines."

"So you like airplanes?" asked Jay redundantly.

"Yes."

"How about guys?"

She was sure he was trying to catch her off guard, but she wouldn't give in.

"I'm not sure they're as reliable as airplanes," answered Shawna.

"How about girls?" asked Jay.

Now this was a direct threat to privacy. Was that the way he meant it?

It appeared that Jay was going to win the bluntness contest, and Shawna was supposed to be an expert at this game.

"Girls are also more reliable than guys," retorted Shawna, "But that ain't saying much."

Jay laughed. Maybe he was just kidding after all.

"Well, airplanes do win in my book when it comes to reliability," said Jay. "Let me tell you, I've been through hell with this bird. Quite literally. Spent many-a-night in the Lockheed Hilton."

"Hilton? Oh, I get it now."

"Just a sleeping bag in the cargo compartment, but at least it's dry," noted Jay.

He went on to explain that this aircraft, USAF tail number 62-1826, was the original aircraft he had been assigned upon entry to the regular Air Force in 1965. The airplane was almost new at that time, and Jay was her assistant crew chief. He followed 826 to Vietnam, a rather unusual request that was supported by a caring line chief at Forbes Air Force Base.

After crewing 826 throughout its Vietnam assignment, the aircraft came back to the States with Jay in tow. He remained her regular crew chief for several years until the aircraft was transferred to the Air National Guard. When he realized his airplane was going to California, Jay timed his Air Force discharge accordingly and applied to the 146th Tactical Airlift Wing in Van Nuys. There was a gap of only a few months between the release of 826 to the Air Guard and Jay's catching up with his dream machine in California.

He continued his career as a weekend warrior and the crew chief of 826 until eventually securing a full-time job as a civil service Air Technician. When he was later promoted to flight chief, the stipulations were that his assigned aircraft include 826. And so for three years, Jay remained as flight chief for four-of-sixteen California Air Guard C-130s. When promoted to line chief and senior master sergeant in 1980, 826 became one of his sixteen grandchildren. But this airplane was still his favorite.

"I guess it's no fluke that this C-130 is with you on this trip," noted Shawna.

"Not much of a coincidence, but it took some convincing for our Chief of Maintenance to buy it. Good ol' 826 was due for depot maintenance this month, but we managed to get it delayed four weeks."

"What happens when she goes to depot?" asked Shawna. "Heartbreak?"

Jay laughed. Depot-input generally placed a C-130 out of commission for several months.

"Well, I've agreed to let her go back to Lockheed for a visit, but you can bet it will coincide with my scheduled leave. I want to visit Georgia anyway."

"I'm sure you do," smirked Shawna.

How could the Air National Guard promote someone to senior master sergeant at such a young age? It is almost demeaning to the rest of the service. In the regular Air Force that rank is a goal seldom reached in less than twenty years.

"So how old are you?" asked Shawna.

"Miss Gruff."

"No, I'm just interested, if you don't mind."

"I don't mind," said Jay. "But it's the stripes, isn't it?"

"In part. We don't have any senior master sergeants in our wing as young as you."

"Thirty-six," said Jay.

"Oh."

To her, he seemed even younger.

"How about you, Shawna?" asked Jay.

"Whoa!" She felt shocked, and immediately expressed it: "As an NCO, do you ask all female Air Force officers their age? And be sure to use their first name while you're at it."

"Okay, so how old are you, Lieutenant?"

"Twenty-four."

"Getting pretty old."

"Oh, I get by."

"I suppose you consider me ancient."

"Young for a senior master, but otherwise I guess you're on the 'old' list. Age doesn't matter that much in this business. The Air Force makes all of us give up our jobs to young whipper-snappers before we get too old."

"That's what keeps the military young and vibrant," said Jay. "No regrets for me."

"And not many for me," said Shawna. "When did you decide to make it a career?"

"It just sort of happened. Chasing 826 all of these years caused some of it. What about you? Are you going to be a 'lifer,' too?"

"Probably not," answered Shawna. "Right at the moment, I haven't decided about a second hitch. If I stay in, I can probably get my dream assignment."

"And that is?" asked Jay.

"Dover, Delaware," said Shawna.

"That's not in many people's dreams."

"Born and raised near Dover," said Shawna. "But not certain I want to go back. Not sure I can contribute very much to the Air Force as a maintenance officer either. And I'm not convinced I wouldn't be wasting myself on this as a career."

"The Air Force needs women like you."

"Well, my age and sex aren't exactly held in high esteem in this Air Force. The age will take care of itself, but that solves only half of the problem."

"From what I've seen, you've got ideal leadership qualities, although you sometimes seem to try to hide them. Maintenance Control at Howard is one of the best I've ever seen, and I've seen a bunch. When an organization is so obviously superb, there's little doubt what's behind it. You're one of those quiet leaders, and I like that."

Jay let the words end. He paused for a few seconds, waiting for Shawna to respond, but she didn't. So he turned his head towards 826, scanning the aircraft from nose to tail. Then he turned back to Shawna, looking her directly in the eyes. She stared back at him, expecting him to challenge her again.

"Lieutenant, this airplane was born in 1962, so that makes her almost twenty," said Jay. "She's younger than either you or me, definitely female, and she might last longer than either of us. She never complains about anything in life, and she practically runs the Air Force."

"Wow, that's quite a woman," said Shawna.

"Sorry. I get carried away. But these airplanes really do have a personality of their own."

"I can see that," replied Shawna.

"I guess my point is that both airplanes and people are a critical part of what makes this business work," said Jay.

"Both are important, but you're right about 826. She's the prettiest of the bunch."

"You're mighty pretty yourself, Miss Shawna, and the Air Force can't afford to lose you either.

"Well, they might have to do without me," replied Shawna.

She spoke the words, but she was concentrating on the word "pretty" and trying not to blush. But she knew her face was already red.

"Too bad," said Jay, not appearing to notice Shawna's embarrassment. "Maybe I can change your mind."

Chapter 10

Girlfriends

Melissa had blown it. Her lighthearted reaction to her roommate's nightmare of the future led to Shawna's complete abandonment of further discussion. Shawna was frustrated with Melissa's put-down about the importance of the issue.

Mel regretted how she handled Shawna's openness on the subject. She could have done it differently. Shawna just wanted to be told that Melissa understood, even when she knew it wasn't so. Mel knew this, but didn't seem to have enough diplomacy to handle her girlfriend with anything other than truthfulness. Maybe Melissa simply cared too much.

* * * * * *

The next morning after her visit to the C-130 flightline, Shawna awoke to the exact same memory of the accident in Hangar Two. But Shawna also awoke thinking about Jay. That was quite a dichotomy, since the nightmare was so strong.

Shawna recognized she was beginning to like Jay. As she sat on the edge of her bed, getting ready to start her day, she preferred to think of him rather than Hangar Two.

Jay was an enlisted man, and he was a lot older. That led to two reminders. One was that fraternization could be the kiss of death for a military career, although enforcement seemed lacking. The other reminder was that the situation was traditionally in reverse. She'd seen lots of male officers pursuing enlisted females. That didn't seem to pose any real problems for anyone. But she'd never encountered a female officer involved with an enlisted guy? At least not that she could remember.

Why was she even thinking about this? She didn't feel physically attracted to Jay. And he was a much riskier friend than the men she normally avoided. His age was a problem in itself. And what did she know about him? He might be married. She had noted his lack of a wedding ring, but around airplanes this wasn't unusual. In fact, by regulations, mechanics had to take their rings off on the flightline. Military safety journals repeatedly displayed gory photos of lost fingers. It was worse than those gruesome high school driver training traffic accident photos, and it served the same purpose.

Shawna had two days off coming up, but first there was one more shift at Maintenance Control. She always looked forward to the last day of her work-week, until the final afternoon arrived. It was then that she faced the fact she really didn't like being away from work. Most of the time, after the first few hours of relaxation, there was little to do. Sometimes it was an all-out battle with emotions ranging from boredom to mild depression. The extra sleep was great, but everything else was usually a disaster. The next two days would probably be no different. Except for going to the latest film at the base theater with Melissa (and now she wasn't sure she felt comfortable to be with her), she had nothing scheduled.

Panama was a small environment, at least for military personnel. There were lots of off-base politically problematic places you couldn't visit, and many other places where you shouldn't go if you were a woman thinking about personal safety. What remained wasn't much. You could drive the three-hour road from one ocean to the other only so many times before it got old.

This morning Shawna enjoyed the luxury of sitting for a few minutes in her bedroom's reclining chair, just listening to the local classical music station before she left for work. Her room was on the opposite side of the quarters from Melissa, and she had plenty of privacy, including her own bathroom. Shawna and Melissa shared a common kitchen and living room, but they had separate entries to their bed-rooms. It was a step above normal for shared officers quarters.

Melissa was a good roommate most of the time. She did have a bad habit of not cleaning up after herself in the kitchen, and Shaw-na ended up doing most of the dishes. Things like dirty dishes upset Shawna's sense of organization, and she often caught herself cleaning up after Melissa in personal ways that would upset some roommates. But Shawna didn't mind the extra work, and Melissa just let it go, or maybe she simply appreciated the help with the household chores and the attention she received.

Melissa made up for her relative sloppiness in other ways. She paid for more than her share of the groceries and incidentals, never asking for reimbursement. And she kept out of Shawna's life most of the time, seldom asking questions. Shawna considered that an important blessing. And Shawna kept out of Mel's affairs too, and there were a lot more of them.

Shawna was in the mood for her blue Air Force blouse today, dress-ing more formally than anytime in the past week. Once in a while, there was an occasion at work that required it. Today she did it simply because it felt good. Those loose fatigues were actually cooler in the damp heat, but the blues were a lot lighter against her body.

Her clean outfit was devoid of nametag and insignia, so she found the blues she had worn last week and removed the maintenance officer wings, silver lieutenant's bars, and nametag. It took only a few minutes to get the blouse up to regulations.

She was early anyway, so she had plenty of time. That frustrating nightmare was awakening her too early too often. Surely it would go away eventually. The date of the future memory was rather specific, since it was set after Melissa was promoted to major, yet before the scheduled change-of-command ceremony. In this performance staged within her memory, the current wing commander was an important character during the aftermath of the accident. The commander was scheduled to depart within two months, so she concluded that the act of horror in Hangar Two was somewhere on next month's calendar.

* * * * * *

The day after her Volant Oak flightline tour with Jay, Shawna returned to the C-130 ramp. It was a slow morning, and the previous day's visit to the flightline reminded her of how refreshing it was to get away from Maintenance Control. It was easy to lose sight of why her control room was important. A close-up look at the aircraft on the flightline served as a fitting reminder.

Shawna pulled her pickup truck through the Security Police checkpoint with no delay this time. Maybe it was the same guard as the previous day, but probably it was because she was driving a recognized permanent party vehicle. The guard saluted crisply and waved her through.

Rather than cruise the rows of airplanes aimlessly, she looked for a C-130 with the most vehicles parked in front, and pulled up to that aircraft. A pair of fatigues in the left wheel-well caught her attention, and she waited for the mechanic to climb out. When he did, she boldly left the protection of her blue truck and approached him.

The mechanic was short in stature and looked a bit old for a tech sergeant. His hair was completely gray and considerably longer than 35-10 standards. He stopped in front of the left wheel-well and simply waited for her to arrive. No salute, but he did give her a warm "Hello, Lieutenant" as if he considered her a friendly force.

"Hi, Sergeant," she replied. "Are you the crew chief?"

"That's me," he said. "The regular crew chief."

Shawna smiled.

"I've always wanted to meet the regular crew chief," she said.

"Well, now you've seen him," replied the sergeant.

Like many NCOs, this one was a lingering threat. Shawna perceived that he knew a lot about airplanes. But he also seemed to have a down-home disposition that she appreciated. At least that was her first impression.

"So is this a preflight?" asked Shawna.

"I thought your maintenance schedule told you all about our birds," said the mechanic.

This fellow knows who I am. Or does he?

"Well, you Guard guys do your job so well that we hardly pay attention in Maintenance Control," said Shawna.

She wasn't used to reacting to NCOs with open pleasantness. But this fellow's friendly personality urged her on.

"Thanks," said the NCO. He sounded genuinely grateful for Shawna's comments. "Yes, this is the paradrop bird for four o'clock. The preflight is finished, but I haven't signed it off yet."

"So this is your bird," noted Shawna.

"Yup. She ain't much, but she'll get you to where you want to go. Almost always, and usually on time."

"How long have you been her crew chief?" asked Shawna.

"About ten years," said the mechanic.

"Unheard of, by Air Force standards," replied Shawna.

"I know," said the mechanic. "We don't move people around much in the Guard, and that's one of our biggest strengths. I know every inch of this airframe, including some inches I don't want to know."

"Must be fun. Being a crew chief, that is."

"It's a blast. Really, it is. But nobody has kept one of these Herks hostage as long as your buddy Jay?"

My buddy Jay? Is he just guessing?

Maybe she had met this mechanic yesterday, but she sure didn't remember him.

"Yes, I hear Jay had quite a history with one of your C-130s," said Shawna.

She was uncomfortable pushing the word "Jay" out of her mouth.

"Quite a history," replied the NCO. "We don't call him 'The General' for nothing?"

"The General?" asked Shawna.

"Well, some of us call Jay 'The Little General,' but that doesn't fit his size very well. He's just like Napoleon Bonaparte, only a lot taller. He struts around bragging about 826, just tempting you to test him."

"And I bet you test him a lot," said Shawna.

"You bet we do," said the smiling NCO. "But 'The General' just stands his ground, and 826 keeps coming through when we need her."

"But your bird looks ready for almost anything too," said Shawna.

She hadn't been this pleasant with an NCO in months.

"You bet she is, Lieutenant," replied the crew chief. "Wanna' go for a ride? Any friend of Jay's is a friend of mine, and a friend of 801, too. Besides, you're obviously not the average MO."

Now what did that mean? And how about the tail number? – 801. This was the aircraft with the landing gear problem she had been warned about. She hoped she didn't look surprised.

"You look surprised," said the sergeant, smiling broadly. "I can take it. My buddies give it to me all the time."

"Sorry," said Shawna. "Someone mentioned the tail number to me, and I guess I was a bit surprised to find myself out here today. She looks like a great airplane."

"You've got that right. And it's fun to prove 801 can hold her own when she needs to. This bird takes more maintenance than some, but she's easy to love, though she does have a bit of a personality."

"Don't we all?" laughed Shawna.

She grinned, nodded good-bye, and turned to walk away from the proud crew chief and his aircraft. She was feeling good about herself. And good about her job.

Shawna glanced back as the crew chief returned to his preflight chores. As she drove away, she saw the crew chief climbing a stepladder positioned behind the inboard engine, shading his eyes with his hand to peer forward into the turboprop's tailpipe.

This mechanic obviously associated her with Jay. Most friends of Jay were probably within his family of C-130 addicts, so this crew chief put her in the same group. And 801 was clearly a part of that family.

* * * * * *

Buck Sergeant Ricardi's reputation in the North Carolina Air National Guard wasn't exactly pristine. In fact, there probably wasn't another aircraft mechanic in his unit so well recognized as a supervisor's nightmare than this red-headed fellow from the Appalachian foothills. Only twenty-two years old, David Ricardi had substantial professional credentials, including a solid college background, an FAA airframe and powerplant certificate, and working on a private pilot license. Like many of his fellow mechanics, Sergeant Ricardi was dedicated to an aviation career, but sometimes it seemed he was throwing it all away. Today he was on the verge of losing his job in the Hydraulic Shop.

"So you think that riding home on a civilian airliner was quite a joke, do you?" asked the captain.

"No, sir, I don't," said Ricardi.

They sat in the captain's office at the North Carolina air base, Ricardi in a straight-back chair facing the officer's desk. He didn't know this officer very well. He was used to studying his opponent's character before waging battle, but now his expertise at maneuvering was being challenged.

"That's not what I hear," said the captain. "I hear you've been bragging about getting away with this. Screwing up without a scratch. Well, I'm here to tell you that ain't so."

This captain, the Squadron Commander's new assistant, was pushing it. No one outmaneuvered Ricardi. He could fall in horse shit and come out looking like he had discovered gold. Few sparred with him because few were up to the task. The rest simply didn't bother.

"If you must know, those TWA stews are cute," said Ricardi.

"Knock it off, Sergeant!"

This officer was taking him to task. Maybe it was time to give in. Even Ricardi knew when the odds were against him.

"Sir, I'm sorry about what happened. There was no excuse for my missing that flight. It won't happen again."

"You bet it won't happen again, Sergeant. In fact, I can guarantee it. Because I'm going to be keeping a real close eye on you. Do you understand?"

"Yes, sir. I understand."

It seemed like a watershed moment for David Ricardi. He had treated his weekender position with the Air National Guard too lightly for too long. And he knew it. Ricardi knew the truth. He was an intelligent late blooming adult who was on the verge of either criminality or greatness. Take your pick.

"I've heard about your antics, and let me go on record as saying they're over. I'll have your ass if you step out of line one more time!"

Ricardi was speechless. This guy was going to be his downfall if he didn't figure him out real quick.

"Any questions?" asked the captain, with amazing composure.

"No, sir," replied Ricardi.

The captain dismissed the red-headed sergeant. As soon as Ricardi closed the door behind him, the captain took a deep breath and went back to his daily attendance report. The only real question was whether this young troublemaker was even worth saving.

At that moment, Ricardi was thinking exactly the same thing.

* * * * * *

"**8**33 looks good for the Quito run," Jay said to Shawna, standing by her desk in Maintenance Control.

That down-country cargo haul and the paradrop mission were the full extent of the schedule for the C-130s today, and tomorrow's schedule was looking easy as well, with adequate spares and even an additional backup for each mission. Jay's visit to Maintenance Control wasn't to discuss aircraft considerations.

"Easy day for you, by the looks of it," said Shawna.

"How about you?" asked Jay.

"Oh, not bad. The A-7s are standing down for an engine inspection on the entire fleet. I bet the pilots are long gone. There's one A-7 on alert and a spare, and that's about it. And no inbounds on the transient board."

"You've really got a good handle on this, don't you?"

"I try. But it's merely organized chaos," replied Shawna.

"Which is exactly what they pay you to organize."

"Guess so. But not much to deal with today."

"Then how about lunch?" asked Jay.

"Sorry, I can't. My duty sergeant has a scheduling meeting that straddles lunch, so I really can't leave. Tomorrow's my day-off, so that will make up for such abuse."

"Where can we go for lunch tomorrow?" asked Jay.

"We?"

"Sure. I can get the time off, with the schedule so light. I need to let Brian get his baptism by Panamanian fire anyway. It'll do him good."

"Well, okay. Where?" asked Shawna.

"How about Colón?"

"A bit far for lunch, don't you think?"

"Not if I let you drive," said Jay. "I've never been to the Pacific side."

"Wrong, Sergeant. That's the Caribbean Sea and the Atlantic Ocean you're talking about. Everything is backwards around here."

"I'm always disoriented," said Jay. "The Atlantic isn't supposed to be in the direction of the setting sun. Who built this place anyway?"

"It's further to Colón than you think," said Shawna. "The road isn't one of those Los Angeles freeways either."

"Better yet, we'll leave in the morning and take the whole day for lunch," said Jay.

"You really want to eat lunch in Colón?" asked Shawna. "You obviously have a different idea about what to expect than I do."

"That bad? Or is it just the critical you speaking?" asked Jay.

There he goes again. Thinks he knows me. You haven't seen 'critical' yet, Sergeant.

"I may be critical," said Shawna "But there's a lot to be careful about around here, including Colón. Have you eaten lunch anywhere off base?"

"Not really," said Jay. "But I've been warned about the empanadas."

"They can be hot," noted Shawna. "Personally, I won't eat anything off-base, except in the better known local restaurants. Filthy, most of them."

"Well, you can pack us a lunch then." Jay's mouth was scrunched in a teasing smile. "Very domestic, don't you think?"

"That's me. Domestic," said Shawna. "And what if I don't have a car?"

"Do you?"

"Lucky for you. But it's only a get-around wreck."

"With air conditioning, I hope."

"Just barely."

"Sounds great," said Jay. "How about picking me up at eight o'clock, and we'll have breakfast first."

"I'm not too keen about picking you up at the Animal House," said Shawna. "How about the BX cafeteria for breakfast? I'll meet you there at eight."

"So you call it the Animal House, too," said Jay. "The reputation of such a fine abode gets around."

"It certainly gets around," replied Shawna as she looked down at her desktop calendar as a diversion. "I bet your wives and girlfriends love the stories you bring back about that place."

"My girlfriend would prefer not to know about such things."

Shawna thought of ending it right there by changing her mind about tomorrow. He had a girlfriend – or a wife – and Shawna should have guessed that. But she didn't end it there. Instead she felt an inward sigh of relief. The hovering burden of commitment was lifted.

"See you tomorrow then," said Shawna. "Eight o'clock at the cafeteria."

* * * * * *

"No problem about missing the movie," said Melissa. "What's up?"

"Not much. I'm going to Colón with the C-130 line chief."

"Wow. Now that's news. I met him at the general's weekly staff meeting. Talk about a young senior master sergeant."

"Not that young," said Shawna.

"I bet he's only thirty-five."

"Not bad. He's thirty-six."

"You just happen to know his exact age, huh?" said Melissa.

"Oh, come on, Melissa. It's just a drive to Colón."

"With an enlisted guy."

"It isn't a big deal," said Shawna. "Nobody pays attention."

"They might," said Melissa. "Be careful. If you have trouble getting him off your case, tell him about your roommate. Better yet, tell him about your dream."

That got Shawna's attention. What a thing to say. Not only was Melissa lacking in compassion, she could sometimes be a definite bitch.

"Just kidding," said Melissa. And judging by the smile on her face, she was.

"Well, don't kid me. I'm not in the mood."

"Tell your C-130 sergeant that," joked Melissa.

"Mel, how about laying off for a while. You can be a real pain."

"Everyone can be a pain for you," kidded Melissa. "For me, it's all part of the job of being a roommate. But you know, I'm a bit concerned about you, although running off with this NCO might be a step in the right direction."

"And just what are you concerned about."

"Your nightmare, for one thing. Not the nightmare as much as your reaction to it."

"And how should I react to it?"

"Well, try not taking it so seriously," said Melissa. "You act like this thing has to be real. At least admit to yourself that it could be your imagination. That's what dreams are."

"Look, do you think I'm interpreting this 'thing' as some kind of a Jesus moment?" asked Shawna. "Well, that's not the way I'm looking at it at all."

"So how are you looking at it?" asked Melissa.

"As something I want to understand before it drives me crazy," said Shawna, "The problem is that it's far from the typical dream."

"Because it seems so real?" said Melissa.

"Because it is so real."

"It won't be real unless something happens in Hangar Two," replied Melissa.

"Unfortunately, it will happen. And what should I have done in the meantime?"

Melissa stared at her friend, trying to show some compassion, but also attempting to break her out of this mood. When Shawna only stared back, Melissa broke her gaze. It was tough to stare at someone you cared this much about, knowing they were on the verge of being psychotic. And if it really was more than Shawna's imagination, there seemed nothing Mel could offer.

Chapter 11

Gatun Lake

It was raining when Shawna arrived in the Base Exchange parking lot. That didn't mean it would rain all day, since showers kicked off many of the mornings, even in the dry season. Shawna was usually attentive to the weather on workdays, since it could impact the flying schedule, but she had lost the habit of even checking the forecast on her days off. Each day was very much the same in the winter season – hot and humid. In the summer, more rain fell and maybe it was a tad bit hotter. But the weather could be described on almost any day as simply hot and dripping.

Jay was waiting for her in the cafeteria at a table by the window. He waved as she entered, nursing a cup of coffee in front of him.

This was the first time Shawna had seen him in civilian clothes. Very athletic looking – tall and thin, with long muscular arms, dressed in a dark blue tank-top T-shirt dangling outside his matching blue shorts. His dark brown hair, styled in a crew cut and already graying at his short sideburns, was topped with a baby-blue UCLA *Bruins* baseball visor. In his black basketball-style sneakers, he looked ready for a round of hoops. Here was a completely different guy from the olive drab line chief. He was informal in the flightline environment. Now he looked like a real troublemaker.

Of course, Jay hadn't seen Shawna in civilian clothes either. She suddenly wished she had dressed a bit more conservatively. And maybe a bit older. She wore black shorts with white side stripes. Her V-neck T-shirt was white with vertical blue stripes on the shoulders and more blue stripes at the "V." She hoped her bra wasn't showing through. And she hoped she didn't look like a kid, but she knew she did.

Shawna sported white sneakers with short, thick blue socks. She wore no makeup, and her hair was brushed back to emphasize its natural wavy appearance and bundled in a pony tail. If this was a basketball team, he'd be the pro center, and she'd be the young cheerleader.

"Lookin' good," said Jay.

"Feeling pretty casual," replied Shawna. "Hope you didn't have anything formal planned."

"Well, I've never been across the isthmus, but I doubt it's very formal. It will probably rain all day."

"That's okay with me. You get used to it around here," said Shawna.

"Are you ready for breakfast?" asked Jay.

"Not very hungry yet, but I did bring lunch for us. Want to wait until then?"

"Sounds good to me. Thanks for joining me. I bet it'll be a fun day."

"Bet so, too."

* * * * * *

And it really was fun. Initially completely negative towards Jay, Shawna was becoming enthralled with this man. She recognized it as it was happening, and she couldn't fight it no matter how hard she tried. In reality, she didn't try very hard. Yet in the back of her mind, she couldn't forget high school. It wasn't that long ago.

It had been at least a year since Shawna had been on a date, and this was a definite date. It didn't matter whether it was romantic or not. She was out with a man, and she was enjoying it. She was also surprised this man wasn't what she thought him to be.

The tradition of the Air Force dictated that education equated to rank. But Jay was a sergeant working on his master's degree at UCLA – in physics!

"Back home they call me 'Quantum,' but I try to ignore it," said Jay as they drove along the jungle highway. "I really don't like the nickname."

"From the quantum theory of physics?" asked Shawna.

"Close. It's actually short for 'Quantum Mechanic'. Now you see why I find it a bit embarrassing."

Shawna laughed. There was a macho aura that mechanics liked to nurture. "Quantum Mechanic" didn't fit too well.

Shawna was driving the old Ford she had bought when she arrived in Panama. Jay stretched out in the passenger seat as if he was ready for an all-day ride.

"Why physics?" she asked.

"Actually, I'm interested in science in general, but physics has always been a challenge."

"So where do you go from here?" asked Shawna. "With physics, that is."

"Well, it's really only a hobby. I just love the stuff. I've never seriously considered working as a physicist. I'm more of an applied kinda' guy. Aircraft maintenance suits me just fine."

"And you can apply physics on the job too," Shawna said.

She was trying to be agreeable, less blunt.

"Not really. I suppose a bit of it has some application to aircraft maintenance, but most of it is just theoretical. At least for me."

"You could become an officer."

"If I wanted to," said Jay. "No offense, but I really enjoy the flight-line work. You're lucky as a maintenance officer. But that won't last for long. They'll put you in a real office soon enough. I prefer the excitement of the ramp."

"I must admit I'm probably better off in an office," said Shawna. "I'm not very mechanically inclined."

"I've done mechanical things my entire life," said Jay. "On my days off, I work on small airplanes as a civilian mechanic. It's fun to be able to do an annual inspection on all the systems in a single day. You really get to know the airplane. On a C-130, the equivalent inspection takes several weeks, and no single person has the expertise to work on all of the equipment."

"But you do know C-130s, especially 826," said Shawna.

"True, but I still can't work on the electrical system or avionics. Nobody is trained for that except the specialists, to say nothing of legalities."

"Legalities?" said Shawna. "I thought you were in the Air National Guard."

Shawna gently bit her tongue. She really should let up a bit. She hardly knew this guy, and already was teasing him about his professional image.

"Thanks, friend," replied Jay, but he was smiling. "You know, I don't think many people understand the whole concept of the Guard and Reserves. They know we're weekend warriors, and they think it's just a game for us."

"It is a bit of a game, isn't it?" asked Shawna.

"We're the brunt of a lot of Air Force jokes," replied Jay. "But look at our experience level. I've been able to follow the same model of aircraft for over fifteen years, to say nothing of the same tail number. Try that with regular Air Force, where assignment changes happen every few years."

"You're right," said Shawna. "But I must admit I didn't understand the Guard at all when I joined the Air Force. In maintenance training, there was a captain from the Air National Guard cross-training from munitions. He was our class leader, a real personable guy, but no one understood him. He was a bank manager on weekdays and a maintenance officer on weekends. It seemed his weekends were for play. He had a saying about his fighter outfit's aircraft accident rate in Florida – 'One a day in Tampa Bay.'"

"Hopefully he was kidding," said Jay.

"Undoubtedly," retorted Shawna. "But it was hard to take that fellow seriously. He was simply having too much fun."

"Maybe that's what makes the Guard so different," said Jay. "You don't find many Guard bums who aren't there for the fun. And that pays dividends when it comes to a tough mission. We know we've got it good, so we're willing to give a bit extra when it's important."

"Crew chiefs seem to have all the fun," said Shawna. "And that's true of both the Air Force and the Reserves.

"Hey, Lieutenant," said Jay. "The Reserves are part of the Air Force."

"Sorry, you know what I mean."

"Sure," said Jay. "My bosses refer to you as the 'regular' Air Force, but most of us prefer to call you the 'real' Air Force. That's only because we know how good we are."

Shawna laughed. She wasn't going to get one-up on this guy, and that was okay.

"I get the point," said Shawna. "But don't you think crew chiefs have a fun job, universally."

"No doubt about it," said Jay. "There's nothing like having your very own airplane. I hear you met Bozo on the C-130 ramp. What did you think of him?"

"So that's what you call him," said Shawna. "Nice guy, and seems to be having fun as a crew chief."

Careful. Obviously the Guard is a small family.

"He does have fun, but did you notice how old he is? Bozo refuses to move out of his crew chief spot for a higher position. I really respect that, but he'll remain a tech sergeant longer than he should."

"I respect that too," said Shawna. "It's easy for a person to rise above their level of competence and their level of satisfaction."

"Agreed," said Jay. "Crew chiefs have got it made. It beats being a flight chief or a line chief. I can speak from experience. Only pilots have it better than crew chiefs, if you ask me."

"You could be a Guard pilot," said Shawna.

"Too old for that, even in the Air Guard," replied Jay. "But I would like to own my own Cessna someday, or maybe a Piper. The best part would be flying an airplane you maintain yourself."

"I'd go for a ride with you."

Shawna blushed at her boldness, kept her eyes glued to the road, and drove on towards Colón.

* * * * * *

On this rainy day, Gatun Lake sat in all of its splendor. As Shawna parked her old car in the small lot at the side of the road, the sun broke through for the first time that day. As they had traveled further northwest, the overcast thinned, partly due to the changing weather and partly because of the new location. The small country of Panama seemed to have a host of microclimates. It might be a sunny afternoon after all.

The boat dock at Gatun was deserted, with several small fishing boats unattended but ready to go, fishing poles and tackle boxes already loaded aboard. This was a favorite spot for the military during their days off, and the bass in this lake were reportedly huge. But Jay and Shawna had no interest in fishing. They chose to hike instead.

The available hiking routes were limited, with the lush jungle growth quickly reclaiming any seldom-used trails. But there was a well-maintained gravel path along the south edge of the bay, and they followed it. Jay donned a brown leather daypack that was bulging with who-knows-what, but apparently not very heavy. Shawn carried a small red, plastic cooler that contained the lunch she had prepared for them.

They walked, watched, listened. The nearby jungle was recessed far enough to give Shawna a sense of safety, but she would never try this alone.

They walked in silence, stopping occasionally to observe the lush plants steaming from the jungle heat. Bright tropical flowers, predominantly yellows and whites, made it difficult to believe this was a natural habitat. It could have been an arboretum tour.

After about a mile they came to an opening right next to the lake that signaled a break.

"Nice spot. I've got a blanket in my pack," said Jay.

"Okay. But this ground looks pretty wet."

"Everything is wet around here," said Jay. "The blanket won't soak through for awhile. Let's give it a try."

As they settled to the ground, the tropical sun poked between the trees, a sun that looked swollen and somehow closer than normal. Shawna thought for a moment about piña coladas and Panamanian ceviche, a tasty mix of fish and salsa. Neither was in the picnic of tuna sandwiches and orange soda she had prepared, now spread out before them. But the sandwiches and soda looked tasty. It was that kind of a sun. That kind of a day.

They ate slowly and talked about Central America, and their great country back home. Shawna packed up the lunch wrappers and the empty soda cans and stowed them in the small cooler. The blanket was a nice touch, but it eventually started to soak through. Jay got up and offered Shawna his hand. She used Jay's strong arm for leverage, grabbed the cooler with her other hand, and rose to her feet. But Jay didn't let go of her. He reached down and pulled the blanket into a pile with his other hand, tucked it under his arm, and led her back to the path. Only then did he release her hand. Shawna was ready to hold on a lot longer.

This relationship probably wasn't going to be simple. But she was suddenly sure it was something she wanted.

Chapter 12

Questar

That night, Shawna returned home during the evening twilight, having dropped Jay at the Base Exchange. That's where Jay suggested she leave him, and Shawna didn't offer to take him the rest of the way to the Animal House. Judging from the rampant prostitution she had heard about in the transient men's enlisted quarters, the reason seemed obvious. From what she knew about those outrageous accommodations, it wasn't a place she wanted to visit or even be seen. On the other hand, it might have had something to do with the fact he was an NCO and she was an officer. In the back of her mind, from a military code of conduct standpoint, she wondered how important that really was.

Nor did she invite him to her quarters. Except for the few moments they walked hand-in-hand at Gatun Lake, Jay hadn't made another advance towards her for the remainder of the day. She wished he had.

But the rest of the day had been wonderful – friendly, sincere, and a whole lot of fun. They talked for hours, and Shawna told Jay about her family back in Delaware. She didn't have much to tell and very little to hide. She even felt comfortable enough that she mentioned having some unpleasant teenage experiences with boys in high school. Jay didn't probe any further, and Shawna didn't offer more.

Jay talked a lot about his job with the California Air Guard at Van Nuys, but he didn't even mention his family or his girlfriend. And Shawna didn't ask.

* * * * * *

"**H**ow about a date tonight?" asked Jay over the telephone.

His tone didn't make Shawna uncomfortable. He sounded serious but not too serious. She felt bold, even talking to him here in her place of work. No one would know who she was talking to on the phone. They probably couldn't hear her conversation anyway, with all of the commotion regarding the latest A-7 air abort.

"Maybe," said Shawna. "Should I play hard to get?"

"If you want to," said Jay. "But I should warn you I'll show no mercy."

"I should at least ask what you have in mind."

"Less than you probably would guess," said Jay. "It's supposed to be clear tonight."

"Hot-diggetty," said Shawna in her least enthusiastic voice. "Just love those clear nights."

She waited.

"Well?" said Shawna.

"Well... Let's just say I'd like to show you the stars through my telescope," said Jay.

"Now that's suspicious. You brought a telescope all the way from California?"

Shawna knew the Air Guard was famous for traveling with cargo compartments full of personal items. One time she had crawled aboard a Reserve C-141 during a quick-turn and found a single-engine Cessna filling the width of the fuselage, wings removed and stowed behind it. What a private aircraft was doing aboard a military cargo jet passing through Panama was beyond her ability to even imagine. She was afraid to ask.

More recently, she had met an arriving Volant Oak C-130 and watched the Air Guard offload a parade of bicycles and golf clubs. She had heard there were two surfboards aboard the aircraft from California. A telescope was a bit of a surprise.

"It's a small scope," said Jay. "I want to see some of the southern objects that aren't visible from California. You can see all the way down to within ten degrees of the south celestial pole from here. That opens up a lot of sky I've never seen before."

"Okay, so now you're an astronomer," said Shawna. "I'm game. But I've got to go now. We're working an air abort on one of the A-7s."

"Those A-7 guys and their single-engine puddle jumpers. Call you later."

* * * * *

That night, in the middle of the parade field, Shawna gazed through the small telescope. This was a fascinating event for her. At first she thought it was a toy telescope in a camera-size carrying case. But Jay was proud of this instrument, one of the finest and most portable telescopes, he said. It did look well-machined, but the black tube had constellations painted on the outside, something she didn't expect in a precision instrument.

"Questars are way overpriced, but their portability is a great asset," said Jay. "The optics are the best available for this small size. Everything is hand-crafted."

The view in the eyepiece was far from spectacular, but the stellar images were sharp. The lights of Howard Air Force Base were taking their toll on the quality of the view. The current target was a dim gaseous nebula.

"The Orion Nebula is visible from the States, but it's still one of my favorites to show neophytes," said Jay.

"I thought I was a date rather than a neophyte."

"You're both," said Jay. "Right now you're looking at a stellar nursery. All of that wispy stuff is the birthplace of new stars."

"The longer I look, the more I see," said Shawna.

"Try looking towards the edge of the eyepiece's field of view. You can see more when using your peripheral vision."

Shawna was impressed with this telescope and Jay's knowledge of astronomy. Why he had chosen airplane repairs over a career in science seemed strange. He obviously had a sincere interest in science; more than a mere amateur.

But Jay was fumbling as he tried to point out some of the southern constellations. He admitted he had enough trouble with the familiar northern star groups, and even his star chart wasn't enough to ease the struggle.

"I guess this sky is just as simple as the one I'm used to," said Jay. "But I can't connect the dots very well."

"Better than I can," said Shawna.

They stood in the middle of the parade field, not a totally dark location, but darker than the inhabited parts of the base. The Questar sat on a tall tripod, and they had now stepped a few feet away from the telescope so Jay could survey the southern constellations.

Shawna had never been here at night. She'd heard stories about the snakes that gathered on the parade field in the darkness, but Jay had tried to convince her they were merely tall tales and that Panamanian snakes were actually quite harmless. She still wasn't a convert to that line of thinking. Every now and then she shivered in the warm night air and kept looking down as much as possible.

Jay stepped behind her and inched forward until his chest was barely touching her shoulders. He was a full ten inches taller. Her body quivered, and she hoped he didn't notice.

"Over there is Sirius and just below is Canopus," said Jay. His right arm was over Shawna's right shoulder, his hand pointing just above the southeast horizon. The two bright stars were easy to identify, but Shawna was having trouble concentrating on the sky. Jay lowered his arm, pulling it around her neck in a mock strangle hold. His forearm felt warm against her chin. He kept his arm there for what seemed like several minutes. She rubbed her chin against his arm, a bold move for her. He slid his forearm up and across her lips, paused briefly there, and then let go of her. They stood in silence, Jay still behind her, and it was minutes later before Jay backed away.

"Nice night," said Jay.

"Wonderful. I could learn to really like astronomy."

* * * * * *

Jay rotated onto the night shift with his maintenance crew, and the Rhode Island Air National Guard arrived to replace the outgoing Minnesota unit. Shawna didn't see much of the Rhode Island line chief or maintenance officer. That was the way it usually went.

Shawna couldn't push the memory of Gatun Lake or the night on the parade field from her mind. The whole day at Gatun, in fact, was a day that excited her in ways she had never previously experienced. In ways she cherished. And, when she thought too much about it, in ways she feared.

Jay checked with Shawna each evening as he came on shift and she was preparing to leave. One evening they met for dinner off-base, but that meant Jay had to change into civilian clothes in the middle of his shift, since local military regulations banned uniforms in town. He seemed to put up with the inconvenience willingly.

At a small restaurant under the towering Balboa Bridge, they talked as they drank after-dinner coffee. Shawna was feeling particularly intrigued by Jay this evening and more than a little inquisitive. Jay sat next to her in the crescent-shaped booth. He could have sat across from her instead, but he didn't.

His crew cut had grown out a bit in only a few days. Jay's hair looked darker now, with a perfectly rounded hairline across his forehead. His mouth caught her attention, wide lips that were set, as usual, in a half-smile. Youthful dimples were barely evident.

"Saturday's go-home day," said Shawna.

"Yes. I'm gonna' miss you," said Jay.

"I'll miss you too. But at least I won't have to worry about the Security Police catching us eating dinner together. Those fraternization police are tough, you know."

"You could just tell them I'm with the Air Guard, and they'd walk away shaking their heads."

"Probably true," said Shawna.

Shawna was dressed in her standard informal outfit, a heavy T-shirt, light gray with a dark green V-neck. Her hair was loosely curled, spreading outward in wind-blown fashion to the sides. Her naturally dark eyebrows, long and narrow, were set above deeply recessed eyes. She didn't wear makeup very often, but tonight was an exception. It made her look even more alluring, maybe a little older. Older and softer was better tonight.

"You've eaten here before," said Jay.

"It's one of the few off-base restaurants I trust."

"What's for the next intercourse?" said Jay.

He's trying to catch me again. Trying to see if he can make me flinch. Or is it just friendly teasing?

"All guys are the same," said Shawna.

"I hope not. Give me a chance."

"I can be pretty demanding," said Shawna.

"I noticed," said Jay. "But at least you admit it. There's nothing wrong with questioning things."

"I do that a lot," said Shawna.

"And I like it."

Shawna could feel herself blushing, and she liked the feeling. But she didn't want to dwell on it, so she changed the topic.

"Tough questions are my specialty," said Shawna. "What's up when you get home?"

She thought about how that might be interpreted, but the words were already out. She forced herself to relax, but Jay seemed comfortable with the question.

"Well, the big deal is to get caught up at UCLA. Disappearing from school for two weeks this early in the semester will be tough to make up. I'm taking only two courses this semester, on purpose because of this trip, but it'll still be tough."

"Both are night courses?" asked Shawna.

"Late afternoon classes. My boss gives me lots of latitude at work."

"That's why they call you the Hollywood Guard."

"True," said Jay.

Jay paused, apparently done with his answer to her question. Thus, he had ended an inquiry that probed into his personal life without even mentioning his girlfriend or anyone else who might constitute a family.

"What about you?" he asked. "What are your plans for the rest of the month?"

"Oh, just a bunch of guys who are always hitting on me. Generals and stuff."

Jay laughed. "I'd hit on you, if I were a general."

Shawna liked to hear it, but she turned away as her face reddened.

"Actually," said Shawna, "I need to get busy with plans for a visit to Dover Air Force Base. Decision time is approaching for me, and I want to get another look at Dover before I give my choices to Personnel Headquarters. I've lived in Delaware practically my whole life, but I've only been on the base once since I joined the Air Force."

"If I want," she continued, "I can probably complete my four-year commitment right here in Panama, but I'd like to get another perspective on the Air Force with a different kind of assignment."

"I bet you'll get Dover, if you ask for it. The Air Force won't want to lose you," said Jay.

"I think you're right, but probably not because the Air Force cares about me. Personnel Headquarters has almost promised me Dover, but I'm not sure an Air Force career is what I really want. Visiting Dover, now that I know a little about military bases, might help me decide."

"I hope you decide to stay in," said Jay. "You're good. A lot better than you think."

Coming from this line chief, the vote of confidence in her work meant a lot to Shawna. They'd spent quite a bit of time together in a very short while, but she really didn't think he had noticed her performance as a maintenance officer.

"Dover and California are linked pretty conveniently by those C-141 east-west shuttles," said Jay. "You never know who might step off one of those Starlifters."

Shawna had thought of that, more than once. Direct flights between Dover and Norton Air Force Base in California were on the schedule twice weekly, the closest thing to an airline route in the Military Airlift Command. If she were stationed in Dover, she wouldn't mind a visit from Jay. Her mind immediately began fantasizing. As she looked into Jay's eyes, she couldn't stop the thoughts. So she bit her lower lip purposefully, and tried another probing question to bring herself back to reality.

"What about things at home? The ol' homestead must have slipped a bit these past two weeks."

"Not much to worry about," said Jay. "It's a condominium, a townhouse really. As long as the payments keep flowing, the lawn gets mowed."

"And your family?" Shawna wanted to know, but she was afraid of the answer.

"Nobody to worry about except my girlfriend and Rough Rider, and they pretty much take care of themselves."

Shawna's mind was racing. A girlfriend was less clearly defined than a wife, and could mean almost anything.

"I hope Rough Rider is your dog," smirked Shawna.

"Close. My cat. He's been through a lot of cat fights and a lot of vet bills."

"What's your girlfriend's name?"

Shawna felt the words come out like bullets, so fast it probably didn't even sound like a sentence.

"Irene. Her friends call her 'Ire', but I prefer 'Irene'."

"So do I," said Shawna. "Pretty name."

Shawna was trying to stay calm, but she could feel her heart pounding, and she was starting to sweat.

"She's a CPA," said Jay. "Has a small office in Woodland Hills near where I live. Does taxes mostly, but she has a few big-buck clients."

"How long have you been going together?" asked Shawna.

The questions were agonizing for her. Just piecing together the words "going together" made her feel foolish.

"Almost five years, but I've known Irene for over ten, ever since I joined the Guard. She's a bit older than I am."

"So 'a bit' is how much?"

Shawna felt her questions were ridiculous, but Jay seemed to take them in stride.

"About eight years older than me. That makes her... forty-four... no, forty-five now."

"That's a bit," said Shawna. "Looks like you enjoy women of all ages, some older, some younger."

Now that was harsh. It made her sound jealous. But too late – the words were out.

Jay merely smiled.

"There's nothing wrong with enjoying women," said Jay.

Shawna let it pass. She was feeling very uncomfortable now, but still wanted to know more.

"How'd you meet?" asked Shawna.

She could feel her voice changing. Those last words were crisp and almost evil sounding – as if she was questioning a person who she despised.

"At the Guard. She works for Aerial Port as a weekender. She's a master sergeant now. Specializes in load planning."

"Must be nice having something like that to share with your girl-friend."

Shawna was sure it sounded mean. She meant it to be.

"It's nice to be able to discuss Guard stuff," said Jay. "But I get plenty of that at work anyway. And if you want to know the truth, I always feel uncomfortable referring to Irene as my girlfriend. She's too old to be a girl, but what better word is there?"

"None that makes any sense," replied Shawna. "Do you have a photo of her with you?" asked Shawna.

It was another question that seemed inappropriate and contributed further to her self-imposed tension.

"Sure," said Jay.

He pulled his wallet from his back pocket and withdrew a photo of Irene. It looked like a photo that had been cropped from a bigger print, now small enough to fit in his wallet. It was a picture of his girlfriend in a flower garden, and she was wearing a large brimmed hat. Most of the brim was in the front of the hat, so it was difficult to see her features clearly in the shadows. Her hair was short and dark, mostly covered by the hat.

"Pretty," said Shawna.

"Yes. It's my favorite photo of Irene. She loves her garden."

"Your garden too," corrected Shawna.

"No, it's hers. Oh, I didn't mean to indicate we live together. Irene has her own place – a nice house a few miles from me."

It may have been devious, but that's exactly what Shawna was trying to determine.

"Divorced?" asked Shawna.

"Her or me?"

"Either, I guess," said Shawna.

"Her – yes. Me – no," said Jay.

Jay's voice was starting to harbor a deeper tone, like he was tired. It sounded like he wanted this to end. Shawna did too, but she had a hard time not asking more.

They drank their coffee, and the conversation was over for now. But Jay seemed to have the knack of smoothing things over quickly. When she drove him back to the flightline after dinner, he kept her laughing with tales of the Animal House. How Jay managed to change the subject so smoothly was amazing to Shawna. He gave her some of the lurid details of the open prostitution in the men's transient barracks. It was a topic that fascinated Shawna because she had heard the rumors since arriving in Panama, but she was always afraid to ask for details.

The name "Animal House" had been adopted years ago, but there had been a terrible dose of reality the previous month when a prostitute fell to her death during Georgia's Volant Oak rotation. Whether the woman fell, jumped, or was pushed remained undetermined. In any case, activities in the Animal House were now reduced considerably because of the tragic incident. For the first time, Security Police visited the Animal House on a regular basis. Previously ignored by all, the transient barracks were getting administrative attention. But still the women rolled in every evening. They ranged from beautiful to terrifically unattractive. Their dark, smooth Latin bodies appealed to many of the Volant Oak men.

The biggest Animal House news of this rotation, according to Jay, involved the A-7 unit from North Dakota. A female A-7 munitions loader who resided in the female enlisted quarters was visiting the Animal House regularly. She seemed to be in competition with the local prostitutes, although she fucked for free. There was supposedly an incident in the community bathroom where she rode a guy in one of the toilet stalls. A crowd of interested observers gathered in the bathroom to witness the event, which consisted of listening to moans behind the toilet petition. The consistency of their reports was convincing, but the accuracy of such accounts was open to dispute. Jay couldn't confirm it by first-hand knowledge.

Shawna found herself paying close attention as Jay spoke. It wasn't only her interest in the situation at the Animal House. She was trying to determine Jay's attitudes relative to the prostitutes. It seemed nearly all of the NCOs were taking advantage of the Panamanian whores during the Volant Oak rotation, but Jay seemed uninterested in these women. Maybe it was simply what Shawna wanted to believe. Besides, regardless of their discussion of prostitutes, the word "girlfriend" had a more stinging sound to it.

* * * * * *

Two scary dreams overwhelmed Shawna that night. The most horrifying was the exact same memory about Todd and Hangar Two. The other dream was about Jay, and it was frustratingly sexual. When she awoke, both dreams lingered in her memory. It's hard to say which bothered her the most.

* * * * * *

"**M**aintenance Control, Lieutenant Whitney speaking," Shawna spoke into the telephone as her shift was about to end.

She hoped it was Jay.

"Hey, Lieutenant, your C-130 rascals have another tail number change."

Jay was his normal self.

"You change tail numbers as quickly as we can post them, Sarge. Can't you just schedule those beasts and then make them fly."

"Around here we refer to such decisions as 'schedule improvements' rather than changes," said Jay.

"Okay, whatcha' got?" asked Shawna.

"Oh, I lied. No schedule changes. Just a line chief looking for his favorite officer."

Shawna's heart thumped. He kept doing that to her. She had to keep control of herself. To let on how she really felt could end this relationship in tragedy.

"Well, here I am. Same time, same station," said Shawna.

"I've got an idea," said Jay.

"I know about your ideas. They're dangerous."

"And this one could be too," said Jay.

When Shawna didn't reply, he continued: "How about hopping a ride home with us on Saturday afternoon? We get into Van Nuys on Sunday at about one in the morning, or nearly four o'clock if we have to stop at Kelly Air Force Base for fuel. I could take you to Norton from Van Nuys, and there's a shuttle to Dover on Monday afternoon."

Shawna was caught unexpectedly. She hadn't even considered the possibility. It sounded wonderful.

"But I don't have any leave scheduled. I bet Colonel Penland would really go for that."

"Hey, let me talk to him," said Jay. "Colonel No and I are ol' buddies."

"I can use that kind of help," said Shawna sarcastically.

Shawna was laughing now, but she really did wish it was possible.

"Think about it," said Jay.

She did. She thought about it a lot.

Chapter 13

Hercules

The noise was deafening, even at low-speed ground idle. Shawna had flown on a C-130 only once before, and it was even louder than she remembered, even with her blue ear-defenders that made her feel like Mickey Mouse. Although this was survivable, what would happen after six hours at cruise power en route to Kelly Air Force Base? Then four more hours to Van Nuys.

The cargo compartment of the Hercules was densely packed. Thirty maintenance troops were only part of the problem. Two very full pallets, a jeep, and two rolling-stock ground power units made the cabin claustrophobic.

For about ten minutes, they had been waiting in the run-up area for their departure clearance. The Herk's cargo compartment was filled with the downward flowing fog from the aircraft's hefty air conditioning system. The white vapor pumped out of the overhead vents that ran the full length of the cargo bay. The aircraft's water separator simply couldn't handle all of the humidity, and the fog poured out in thick ribbons. It was damp, but at least it was cool.

She sat with her metal-to-metal seat belt buckles pulling her against the red cloth side seat. Leaning back made her head rest uncomfortably against an oxygen walk-around bottle. Even when she didn't lean into the obstacle, her upper back whacked against an equipment support bracket. Not exactly first class.

Jay sat beside her. Both of them wore ear-muffs, so they were unable to converse except by a combination of yelling, lip reading, and hand signals. The airplane started to ease forward out of the run-up area. Time to go.

The sound actually smoothed out as 826 picked up speed, props in synch, lumbering at maximum gross weight down the long runway. At rotation, the wheel-wells behind their seats creaked, the aircraft squatted one last time with the weight shift onto the rear wheels, and the C-130 broke cleanly airborne.

Considering their cargo and passenger weight, along with eight full fuel tanks, the Herk still climbed purposefully. She might be a face only a mother could love on the ground, but she was beautiful in the air, even under stress.

As the aircraft settled into the climb, Shawna peered over her left shoulder, looking out the small circular double-pane window behind her. It was an awkward angle, but good enough to catch a glimpse of the ground. The white sand beach at the end of the runway slipped by in an instant, and then they were in a gentle bank. The dark green jungle reappeared in the small window, lush green trees that bordered the blue ocean. As the turn continued, she saw the runways at Panama City's civilian airport. When the C-130 rolled out of the turn, the green was replaced by dark blue ocean, interspersed with scattered cumulus clouds, now well below them. It was a beautiful day for the start of a flight home to the States.

Shawna rolled her head away from the window, and caught Jay's intense blue eyes staring back at her. She pushed her shoulders back and slightly to the side, into a more comfortable position, as good as to be expected in a C-130 troop seat. From the corner of her eye, Shawna could see Jay still gazing intently at her. For a moment she ignored the stare, but then she shifted her head to the left and stared up at his face. He didn't flinch, nor did she. It was a magic moment, and capturing it in 826 made it all the more special for both of them.

For the rest of the noisy climb to 22,000 feet, there was little to do except stare at each other. If you couldn't talk by normal means, you might as well use your eyes. It worked for them.

When Shawna adjusted her position to lean back against a different portion of the seat webbing, her head rested on one of the cross-straps. Jay leaned his head back, too, their mutual gaze broken.

As the C-130 leveled off in cruise flight, Shawna's mind began to drift. She imagined the entire load of military passengers examining them. What could these mechanics be thinking? These were Jay's troops, and she was the only outsider in the airplane. And she was a woman. Worst of all, she was an officer. Surely they must be imagining the worst. Or maybe the best.

But when she looked around quickly, trying to catch the passengers gawking at them, she found no one paying the least bit of attention. Maybe they had noticed but had since turned away. No one sat in the seats mounted on the center stations directly across from them. Looking further through the red center-aisle webbing, there were several mechanics directly across the fuselage, all of them with their eyes closed, heads propped in a variety of positions that would probably result in stiff necks.

Towards the front of the cargo compartment, the loadmaster was settled on the opposite side of the fuselage. He was scanning a magazine, rapidly flipping the pages. There was something about a C-130 that lulled its passengers into private thoughts – quiet thoughts in a noisy airplane.

Jay motioned for Shawna to join him as he headed for the cockpit. But they had to move rearward first to get behind the row of center-aisle seats and around the contorted occupants. Those who were awake moved their legs to let them pass, but they had to step over those slumped in near or deep sleep. Finally, they passed the loadmaster who looked up, smiled and then returned to his magazine.

The galley floor had been lowered, so there were no flight deck stairs up to the cockpit. They had to pull themselves up four feet, using the strength of their arms, to the metal floor that led into the small galley. Jay climbed first, landing on the upper floor on his hands and knees. He offered a hand to Shawna but she shrugged it off and arrived unceremoniously on the flight deck floor on her stomach. She ignored Jay's extended hand once again and stood on her own.

This was Shawna's first time in the cockpit of a large aircraft in flight, and she was amazed at the roominess. The cockpit had always seemed a bit cramped on the ground, especially when full of mechanics working on equipment and subsystems. But now all of the flight crew were in their seats, and the cockpit seemed spacious. Sunlight streamed in from all angles, including through the spacious windows to each side of the pilots.

The aircraft commander's seat was pushed aft on its rails, with the pilot's feet propped up on yellow footrests. The co-pilot was in flying position, but his face was down, studying a chart. The flight engineer rode in a forward-facing seat just behind and between the two pilots. His head was reclined on his headrest, eyes gazing upward at the overhead systems panel. Interphone cords dangled everywhere.

The navigator's seat on the right side of the cockpit was empty, with its normal occupant sitting on the crew bunk at the rear of the flight deck. The navigator was already engrossed in a thick paperback novel, with the front cover wrapped behind the pages. He looked up long enough to motion Shawna toward his vacant, high-backed crew seat.

Shawna sat down at the navigator's station and leaned her head back against the headrest, the top of her head barely touching the bottom of the pad. The seat was locked in position, currently angled nearly directly forward and away from the navigator's panel. Through the lower side windows, Shawna could see the ocean ahead and below. Scattered towering cumulus clouds topped with flat anvils formed a backdrop for the pilots and the flight instruments in front of her. The weather radar at the top of the instrument panel was sweeping smoothly through its arc.

It was amazingly quiet here, at least compared to the cargo compartment. Shawna took off her Mickey Mouse muffs and stretched her neck left and right. It was nice to be less confined. The noise was best described as "uncomfortable" here, a big improvement from "deafening."

Jay took off his muffs too and directed Shawna's attention to the nearby navigator's panel.

"Omega," he said, pointing to the small rectangular avionics display on the lower right side of the panel. She could hear the word without having to strain, a nice change of pace.

Jay glanced at the navigator and seemed to catch his attention on-cue. The navigator raised his eyes from his book and nodded his approval before returning to his reading.

Jay rotated the Omega rotary knob to display a variety of flight parameters.

"Quite an improvement over our old LORAN equipment," said Jay, still on the boundary of shouting. "LORAN was a maintenance nightmare."

"And Omega is more accurate," chimed Shawna.

"You bet," replied Jay. "But nothing like INS and GPS. We don't have them yet, but we'll be upgrading to an inertial navigation system soon, and I bet we have satellite nav in a few years."

Jay walked a few steps to the other side of the flight engineer's raised seat. The engineer pulled the left ear-cup of his headset back so they could converse. It was more like yelling than speaking. At her distance of only six feet, Shawna couldn't understand a word.

Time stood still, or so it seemed. There was no connection with reality. Or was this reality? And if this was reality, what was all of that drudgery they had left behind on the ground. Shawna found it difficult to identify where she stood within the temporal patterns of the earth below. It was pure detachment, and it was wonderful.

The air was so smooth that the slight trembling of the altimeter's pointer-hands, ten feet in front of her, was distracting. The altimeter vibrator was flicking the hands just enough to make certain the instrument didn't stick. The air was that smooth.

Shawna looked at the back of Jay's head as he talked to the flight engineer. Every few moments, Jay would turn his head slightly as the heated discussion continued, and Shawna could see them both laughing and smiling.

She felt far removed from the routine of Panama, now doing what the Air Force was meant to do – fly. And she was headed for the States, now level at twenty-six thousand feet above the Caribbean after their step-climb. A guy who practically owned this airplane had invited Shawna on this amazing trip into the atmosphere. And if it hadn't already happened, she was falling in love.

Chapter 14

RGB

Their Herk was the last plane out. The other three C-130s were spaced in front of them at thirty-minute intervals. Their aircraft, 826, had acceptable UHF radio range for communication with the airplane directly in front of them, 801. Farther in front was 833, and in the lead was 755, the B-model, pulling ahead slowly. All things considered, the B-model was the fastest of the C-130s without the extra drag of external fuel tanks.

All four aircraft were in good shape. 801 had a quirky nose landing gear shimmy the past few days, but it was troubling no one but Bozo, the crew chief. Permission for overflight of Mexico hadn't been received, so they didn't have enough fuel to make it to California nonstop. Thus, they would deviate to the east, landing at Kelly Air Force Base in San Antonio. It was always difficult to predict when the Mexican government would approve overflights. There were supposed to be a maximum of three U.S. military overflights per day. But, in reality, permission didn't seem to be related to anything except at-the-moment quirks of the Mexican government. C-130 flights that deviated around Mexico were a bit too close on fuel reserves. And a B-model's fuel capabilities were more limited, making a nonstop flight to California out of the question, even with the best of winds.

After returning to the cargo compartment, Shawna found a position comfortable enough to doze off, using the opportunity to lean against Jay's shoulder. They were both bundled in their fatigue jackets, while huge overhead vents and underfloor heating ducts warmed the cool air at altitude. But it seemed only two temperatures could be achieved – too cold and too hot. Too cold was a lot more appealing than too hot on a long flight, so everyone was bundled up, and no one was complaining.

While resting against Jay, Shawna watched him reach across the aisle and grab a wool blanket from an empty seat. He slid closer to Shawna, and placed the blanket over their laps. Now Jay's hand was resting gently on Shawna's thigh below the blanket. Tingles of excitement raced through her. She wished this airplane could stay up here forever.

Before she could fall completely asleep, Jay was shouting in her ear, trying to get her attention. When she sat upright, Jay was saying something inaudible and pointing toward the far side of the airplane.

"Look outside," he said in a raised voice.

"Outside? What?"

Jay pointed towards the row of windows on the opposite side of the fuselage and slightly rearward. The wing and one engine were barely visible through one of the small oval windows. At first everything looked normal, and then Shawna noticed that the blades of the propeller on the inboard engine were clearly in view. The blades weren't rotating.

"They shut down number two," yelled Jay. "Didn't you feel it?"

Shawna heard most of what Jay said, but asked him to repeat it, and the second time he used the term "bagged the engine" and indicated he was going up to the flight deck.

Shawna pulled away from Jay so he could get up. She watched him circumnavigate the center seats, climbing over several still-sleeping mechanics. Some of the mechanics were clearly aware of the feathered propeller and were pointing it out to their buddies. Shawna knew propellers might be feathered on a C-130 for a variety of reasons, many of them not directly related to the engine's condition. A common cause was generator failure. On the new C-130s, the H-model, you could disconnect a generator in flight and leave the engine running. But on the older models, you had to shut the engine down when a generator failed or risk damage to an expensive turboprop powerplant.

In a few minutes, Jay returned, and his report wasn't good. The RGB, the reduction gear box connecting the propeller to the engine, had suffered a loss of oil pressure. Since the gear box changes the high jet engine RPM to a more reasonable rotational speed for the propeller, the engine was now useless. On the C-130, swapping out the RGB could take longer than changing the entire engine, especially if it had to be cannibalized from another engine. This airplane wasn't going to make it to California tonight.

Jay told Shawna their aircraft would continue to San Antonio. Their flight crew was attempting to relay a message to the other three aircraft ahead of them. There was a spare engine aboard 833, two aircraft in front of them, but that was too far for direct communication. The aircraft directly in front of them, 801, was attempting a communication relay to 833, and 833 would be advised to wait for them at Kelly Air Force Base. The preliminary plan was to off-load the spare engine from 833 and have that airplane wait for 826 at Kelly. Once the engine was changed, the old engine could be loaded back aboard 833 and both aircraft could head for home.

It was a fortunate situation to have a spare engine, carried to Panama and back without being touched, and an aircraft full of C-130 mechanics. But it would still be a lengthy delay. The engine mechanics would have to work all night, and it would take two shifts to complete the work in the best of circumstances.

Jay made his way through the cargo compartment, briefing his men and establishing a plan for expediting the engine change. There was nothing for Shawna to contribute, since she wasn't a C-130 expert, but she noticed the coordination skills Jay exercised. He was taking suggestions from the mechanics to improve the engine change plan. Jay eventually made his way back to the cockpit, and this time he was gone at least half an hour. When he returned, he briefed her on the details.

The propulsion shop supervisor was aboard 833, so that solved the problem of technical supervision for the engine repairs. Jay's role in the engine change was primarily to organize the troops. But he'd still have some supervisory duties regarding the engine removal and replacement, if that turned out to be the best solution. With a spare engine available, it was simpler and quicker to change the whole engine rather than swap out the RGB. He'd be busy during his short stay in Texas, probably spending the night in 826. The C-130 wasn't called the "Lockheed Hilton" for nothing.

As they approached the south coast of Texas, the loadmaster started through the cargo compartment, spraying government-issued silver cans of bug spray into the already musty cabin. He held two cans over his head, waving and spraying them simultaneously as he moved towards the rear of the airplane. Shawna gave Jay an inquisitive look.

"Keeping the Agriculture folks happy," yelled Jay. "It doesn't prove a thing, but it keeps those Ag guys placated."

"No smart bug would ride on this thing," yelled Shawna.

"Hey, you're talkin' about 826."

The mood was jovial throughout the airplane. Their trip home wasn't complete, and they had a major delay ahead of them, but they were back in the United States.

During the descent, Jay brought his mouth close to Shawna's ear and spoke slowly in a raised voice so he wouldn't be misunderstood. He told Shawna he would join her for the party at the visiting officers quarters within a few hours after landing. She wasn't sure if he was kidding.

* * * * * *

The engine was already being rolled off 833's cargo ramp as 826 pulled into the parking spot next to it. It was approaching eight o'clock, Texas time, and it was sprinkling. The Customs inspector climbed aboard 826 as soon as the last engine shut down. He seemed in a good mood, and the clearance procedures for immigration and customs were cursory. The inspector was gone in only a few minutes.

When they finally exited the Herk, small cold drops of rain were reflected in the beams of the light-all carts positioned near 826. Everyone was tired from the long flight. Baggage drills were never a pleasant exercise. Those who weren't directly involved in the engine repairs were in charge of getting everyone's bags to the transient quarters.

"See you there," said Jay, as Shawna headed for the waiting bus.

As an officer, she was expected to ride with the flight crew to the visiting officers quarters. She hastily grabbed her bag, waved goodbye to Jay, and climbed aboard the crew bus. Jay obviously had a lot to do in the next few hours. She doubted she would see him again until just before takeoff. Hopefully, that would be tomorrow afternoon, if all went as planned.

* * * * *

Her assigned room was adequate but rather bare. There simply wasn't a visiting officers quarters that felt like the Sheraton. The television screen was bigger than Shawna had ever seen, but it sat in a room with little personality.

She read two chapters in her tag-along book, but she still wasn't sleepy. She clicked on the TV in an attempt to finally wind this day down. When the middle-of-the-night news was nearly over (a repeat of the earlier 11 o'clock Eyewitness News), she watched the national weather maps cycle across the screen. It looked like a major winter storm was just pulling out of Southern California, headed their way. If they departed by tomorrow evening, they should beat the brunt of the storm arrived, but they still would have to fly through the cold front. Getting high enough to fly over a major weather system in a C-130 was unlikely.

Settled in for the night but still not yet ready to sleep, Shawna watched the opening credits for a techno-thriller that replaced the weather maps. She sat on the couch, drawing her feet up under her thighs in the lotus position. In the first scene, the bad guys were getting ready to blow up a building.

A knock at her door startled her. It was nearly two o'clock in the morning.

She heard Jay's voice before she got to the peep-hole. She opened the door part way, standing back far enough to keep her pajamas mostly out of sight.

"Hi. What are you doing up so late?" said Jay.

He was wearing drenched fatigues, looking like he'd been in the rain for hours. A new storm might be moving in soon, but this one still hadn't left.

"Me? How about you? I thought you'd be sound asleep on top of that engine by now."

"Are you kidding? That's why they created shop chiefs. Guys like me just get in the way."

She thought for a moment before speaking.

"Come in. The party just broke up," said Shawna.

She opened the door farther, and he walked casually into the room. Shawna felt naked in her pajamas and bare feet.

"Great. I could use a good night's sleep. How's the shower?" asked Jay.

"My shower is just fine," said Shawna. "Hot and wet. How about yours?"

If Jay had been to his room, he hadn't washed his face yet, and he certainly hadn't changed his clothes. There were streaks of oil across his forehead. He stomped his feet just inside the doorway to shake off the water. Raindrops clung to his crew cut and his wide lips were shiny wet.

"Everything looks good out there except the weather," said Jay. "The engine shop has already disconnected all of the horse-collar hoses. They'll swing that engine off well before sunrise. Connecting up the new engine is what will take some time."

"Great," said Shawna. "The flight crew was pretty grumpy on the ride over here. The co-pilot says he's going to lose a major business contract by getting home late."

"Poor baby. That's the life of a weekend warrior," said Jay.

"Where's your room?" asked Shawna.

"I'm in it," said Jay without hesitation.

"I don't think so," said Shawna. "This is the officers palace."

"Some palace," said Jay. "The Senior NCO quarters are probably at least as exciting, but personally I'd prefer to stay with you."

Shawna wasn't prepared for this. She hadn't expected Jay to sleep anywhere tonight, certainly not here. She floundered for words, wondering what she really wanted to say. Maybe if she just started talking.

"The bedroom has only one bed, and we hardly know each other," said Shawna.

"Maybe that could change," replied Jay.

Shawna didn't know whether to keep kidding with Jay or divert the conversation in a different direction. Standing there in her over-large pajamas and bare feet, she turned away from him, walked to the far side of the living room, and plopped down on the sofa. It gave her time to think.

In that brief walk, she thought of many things, most of them negative. As much as she liked Jay, and as much as this seemed so easy, she was afraid of the consequences. Perhaps she knew what the result would be, and it would be more than a temporary night together.

Shawna felt vulnerable, complex. These were feelings she didn't know how to deal with under the best of circumstances.

"Jay, are you serious about wanting to stay here tonight?"

"Very serious. I want you to invite me to stay."

"Well, I don't think so," said Shawna. "For one thing, you're in the officers quarters."

"You're right," said Jay. "But then again, I'm already here."

"This can't be," said Shawna in a resolved tone.

"It's all a matter of whether we want it to be," said Jay.

"We hardly know each other," said Shawna.

"But I want that to change," stated Jay. "Don't you?"

Shawna bit her lower lip gently, exposing her upper teeth and hoping Jay could see she needed to think this through. He had caught her by surprise. But how long could she dwell on something that had no answer?

She remembered those bastards from high school. They had treated her like dirt. They had hurt her bad, and it could never be forgotten.

"You've got a girlfriend," she said.

"Yes, but there are details you don't know about. Probably now isn't the time."

"What do you mean by that?"

It was Shawna's most probing voice. A voice she didn't like, but there it was. This felt like a showdown. Because it was.

"I think it would be best to talk about that some other time. Couldn't I just say, for now, that my relationship with Irene is one of convenience.

"Convenience?"

"That's the best short answer I can think of for now."

"Short answer? Right! You do this regularly, don't you? Other women, that is."

Her voice was biting now, more than critical.

"Not regularly. Not regularly at all," said Jay.

"So occasionally."

"Shawna, don't," said Jay. "I'm not an angel, but I don't take advantage of women."

"So what's this?" asked Shawna.

"This is an attempt to explain that I care about you. Yes, I've got a girlfriend at home. We both know it, but that's not the topic."

"And it's happened like this before," stated Shawna.

"No, not like this," said Jay. "Please, leave it alone. I like women. Don't you like men? The point is, I'm crazy about you. That's what this is about."

Silence. Neither spoke. Shawna curled her legs beneath her on the sofa, thought harder and more critically than anytime in recent memory. Jay stood next to the sofa, staring down at her, his combat boots planted firmly, his clothing soaked from head to toe. Finally she replied.

"Sorry for the interrogation. I just keep wondering if this is really so different for you."

"Different?" asked Jay. "Yes, very different. Shawna this is important."

"Important? Maybe," said Shawna. "But probably headed for lots of trouble."

"Could be."

Jay waited, and finally Shawna raised both eyebrows, seeming to ponder the situation deeply.

"You need some sleep," said Shawna, "But not here. I'm sorry, but I just don't feel comfortable about this, and I need you to go. It doesn't mean I don't like you, 'cause I do. It's just that I can't do it this way."

"Do what?" Jay asked, with a less than innocent smile.

"Sure, what? I suppose you just want to use my shower?"

"That too," replied Jay, again with that silly grin.

"Hey, you've got oil all over your face," said Shawna. "And we both need to get some sleep. You in the Senior NCO quarters, and me here in this sad version of Hotel Royale."

She paused as Jay wiped his face with the sleeve of his fatigues.

"Okay, I can take a gentle hint," he said. "But let's make another date that ends differently sometime soon."

"Might happen," she replied. "I guess you really never know."

Chapter 15

Hollywood Guard

The next morning, Jay called and invited Shawna to join him for breakfast at the Base Ops cafeteria. When Shawna heard his voice on the other end of the phone, she was immediately relieved of a tension that had plagued her all night. It hadn't been easy to send Jay back to the enlisted quarters, and she agonized over whether it would bring their relationship to an immediate halt. The telephone call renewed her faith in being straightforward and accepting the results.

They were both dressed in their fatigues as they ate a breakfast of overcooked scrambled eggs, bacon, and toast. Their relationship hadn't missed a beat, which amazed Shawna. Then they headed to the flightline.

It was a short walk to the controlled entry point, but 826 was parked quite a distance farther down the ramp. The Security Police sergeant at the entry insisted on calling Base Ops to provide them with a ride. A step-van arrived within a few minutes.

The number two engine on 826 was already hung, with three mechanics finishing up the connections under the cowling and in the horse-collar.

"Hi, Jay. Morning, Lieutenant," yelled the one of the three mechanics on top of the wing, a young-looking staff sergeant who must be barely out of high school. "She's almost all buttoned up. We'll be ready for a leak run before noon."

The four-striper was clearly in charge of things at the moment, and he seemed exuberant with the chance to assume the leadership role, however temporary. The propulsion shop supervisor had gone to his quarters, and all was under control. These mechanics had just rotated onto duty and were fresh from sleep. Everything was pretty much on schedule.

"We can't do power runs here," said the staff sergeant. "Maintenance Control says we'll have to tow it to the blast fence over there."

He motioned to a high gray metal fence on the far side of a line of C-141s.

"I wish we could taxi her to the fence, like at home," said Jay. "But I doubt they'd like that here. So I'll arrange to have the flight crew come out once you've towed 'er to the fence."

"Probably about two o'clock, after our leak runs," said the sergeant. "It'll take a while to make adjustments. We should have everything signed off by late afternoon."

"That would be great," said Jay. "There's a storm headed this way that would be nice to avoid."

"Well, why don't you and the lieutenant go check out the River Walk downtown, and we'll take care of your baby. She's in good hands."

"River Walk?" said Jay. "Do you think that's all maintenance supervisors have to do while you grunt your way through an engine change?"

"It may not be all you have to do, but it looks like you would enjoy it."

Jay raised his eyebrows at the young sergeant and turned to Shawna with an embarrassed smile. Then he looked back at the sergeant on top of the wing.

"Does it show that much?" asked Jay.

The staff sergeant's response was immediate: "Believe me, it shows."

* * * * * *

The River Walk in downtown San Antonio was a relaxing interlude to a unique return to the States. For Jay and Shawna, it brought their relationship up a notch from where they had left it the night before. They had only a few hours, but they took advantage of every minute.

Shawna let her hair blow in the breeze. Not once did she reach for her hairbrush, but every once in a while she'd push flailing strands back with her hand. She had the feeling Jay liked it that way.

Over lunch, Shawna told Jay she had thought she hated San Antonio.

"Doesn't have anything to do with Officer Training School, does it?" asked Jay.

"Probably," said Shawna. "Lackland Air Force Base has to be the most depressing military base around, probably because it is so rigid as a training base. It brings back a flood of bad memories."

"If you were like me," said Jay, "you never got to see anything of San Antonio while you were at Lackland."

"No, I hardly got off the base the entire time. I guess basic training was similar for you."

"Similar, but not as gentlemanly. Sorry, gentle-womanly," said Jay. "It was just one of those things you had to put up with."

"I would never have guessed San Antonio could be so beautiful," said Shawna.

"It's influenced a lot by the company you keep," replied Jay.

"Agreed," said Shawna with a laugh. "I sure like you a lot better than I did when you arrived in Panama with that damn B-model."

* * * * * *

The C-130 broke into the wall of clouds as Fort Worth Center handed the aircraft off to Albuquerque. It was going to be a bumpy ride. The cold front had dissipated a bit from the original forecast, but it still challenged the Herk. The threatening cumulonimbus clouds extended upward to almost 40,000 feet, and that was well above the flight ceiling of the C-130.

From inside the cargo compartment, it was difficult to tell if the white flashes in the darkness were lightning discharges or the aircraft's own strobe lights bouncing off the clouds. Since pilots routinely turn off the strobes when flying in clouds to prevent flicker vertigo, those in the cargo compartment with some knowledge of flying knew the answer.

For Shawna, one of the lightning flashes was especially disturbing. At the instant it illuminated the cargo compartment, all of the details of her repeated nightmare of the tragedy in Hangar Two spilled over. It all entered her brain in an instant, concentrated and compressed for the brief moment that the nearby bolt lit the cabin. When the lightning flash disappeared, her memory of the tragedy began to fade. Not instantly, but her mind cleared quickly.

She latched violently onto Jay's arm, grabbing it with both hands as the lightning bolt and the horrific memory struck simultaneously. Jay flinched in surprise from the strength of Shawna's grasp. She hung on tight for several seconds after the lightning disappeared.

"You okay?" Jay yelled loud enough for Shawna to hear through her ear-muffs.

"Okay now," said Shawna, loosening her grip on his arm. This was no time to explain.

* * * * * *

The ride was rougher in the cargo compartment than up front in the cockpit. Shawna and Jay sat at the wing root, near the aircraft's center of gravity, and that helped, but it was still a physical battering. Several of the mechanics were severely airsick, but they refrained from throwing up where their friends could see. The smell of vomit caused a chain reaction of more sick mechanics, and the full-blast underfloor heat didn't help.

Everyone knew the flight crew was busy. This wasn't an easy situation for the plane's 1960s technology, including the autopilot, even though the cockpit was superficially updated to meet 1980 standards. The best way to handle such turbulence was to simply ride through it, hand-flying the aircraft to keep the approximate altitude and heading that were required. Chasing the instruments would only lead to additional stress on the airframe.

Shawna held onto Jay's arm very tight, letting go only during the brief moments of smooth air between the gusts. She wasn't prone to fear of flying, even in the worst conditions. Nor was she on the verge of airsickness. She simply enjoyed hanging on. Jay seemed more distressed by the violent bumps than Shawna.

The blasts of turbulence continued all the way to Tucson, and then 826 broke out on top of the remaining clouds. For a few minutes, moderate turbulence continued to rock the aircraft. But then it smoothed considerably. The solid cloud layer below the C-130 started to dissipate, and soon the lights of desert towns broke through, rivaling the stars above.

Jay recovered enough to read a book he pulled from a gray cloth bag stored under his seat. He slowly flipped through pages of *The Key to the Universe*. As he read, he would often pause to turn the pages back to review photos and diagrams. When he progressed to the next chapter, Shawn glanced at the book from her semi-dozing position and noted the chapter's title: "Sunfire."

Shawna sat silently, dozing with her head pressed back against the cloth seat webbing. And now she worried about how this trip would end.

* * * * * *

The airway, J-65, took them northwest towards Palmdale, but the lack of air traffic late at night allowed air traffic control to pull them off the airway, with a radar vector directly towards Van Nuys. The C-130 passed just north of Palm Springs, through Banning Pass, propelling the Herk and its homeward bound passengers past the remaining line of mountains and into the Los Angeles Basin. Now the ground was a continual wall of lights all the way to the Pacific Ocean. In beautiful clear air behind the cold front, city lights stretched until they suddenly stopped at the ocean's edge.

They began their descent just north of Riverside, paralleling Victor 186, one of the main east-west airways across Southern California.

The landing gear came down as they approached Burbank. Approach Control vectored the Herk into a middle-of-the-night visual approach with a broad left turn to line up with Runway 16 Right at Van Nuys.

Touchdown. As reversing props tried to thrust everyone in the cargo compartment towards the front of the aircraft, all of the mechanics had a firm grasp on the webbing of their sideway-facing seats. Noisy squeaking of brakes, and the aircraft slowed to taxi speed. The C130 exited the runway adjacent to the control tower and started back north on the parallel taxiway towards the Guard Ramp. As they taxied, both outboard engines were shut down and the inboards went into low-speed ground idle.

The loadmaster cracked open the cargo door, stopped for a moment, then continued to full open. As they continued towards the military outer ramp, he began lowering the ramp. The fresh California night air, cold by Panama's standards, swept into the cargo bay. The noisy GTC ignited in the wheel-well pod, and the overhead lights flickered as the air turbine motor, powered by GTC airflow, took over the electrical load.

The follow-me truck led them past the outer ramp and over the Bull Creek taxiway bridge to the inner ramp. The follow-me drew them to their parking spot, where a marshaller awaited with outstretched orange-lighted wands. The aircraft swung around in a 180-degree turn, brakes squeaking, and came to a stop.

The inboard engines were shut down, and the ground crew connected the auxiliary power cart. Now the GTC could be shutdown, and only the sound of the surging power cart filled the cargo compartment. By comparison to the last few hours, the noise was over.

* * * * * *

Jay and Shawna walked to Base Ops together, their bags following on the baggage pallet. As they approached the end of the aircraft parking ramp, Jay spoke.

"You know, I'd be glad to have you stay at my place tonight. Or I can give you a ride to the hotel near here that we recommend for transient flight crews."

Shawna was pleased how he put it. It sounded like Jay really understood her apprehensions, and he seemed ready to rest with her decision on the matter. Somehow she knew he wouldn't challenge her if she decided to stay alone. Quite unlike last night in Texas.

"I'd love to stay at your place," said Shawna.

"Great!" replied Jay, an immediate answer that made them both feel more comfortable.

"Isn't Irene waiting for you?"

This time she tried to say it like it was a concern for him, rather than a confrontation.

"No, I won't see her until tomorrow. And I want to give you a tour of the Guard base in the morning. Then, of course, I need to take you to San Bernardino."

"Look, I can make it to Norton Air Force Base on my own," said Shawna. "I can take a taxi."

"A taxi?" laughed Jay. "Do you have any idea how far it is to Norton from here? I think you need a loved one who wants to drive you there."

"So now you're a loved one," said Shawna. "Don't go getting cute on me?"

"Believe me, you have a loved one, my dear," said Jay.

* * * * * *

That night, Shawna was able to once and for all drive away those lingering concerns from her high school days. For Shawna, her first night in bed with Jay was simultaneously gentler and more explosive than she could have ever dreamed. But as wonderfully comfortable as she felt here with Jay, she fell asleep in his arms thinking about Irene.

It was a terrible time to think about a woman she didn't know, but when Shawna tried to change her train of thought, she found herself fixated on something even worse – her memory of the future and the lightning flashes in the C-130. Good or bad, it was a memory she didn't understand. That lack of understanding frightened her more than anything else, including Jay and Irene.

Rather than brood further over it, she tried cuddling even closer to Jay. Her mind immediately left those thoughts of Hangar Two and returned to the luxury of the moment. But she knew her memory of the future couldn't stay away for long. It was almost time for it to come true.

Chapter 16

Backwards Arrow

Shawna slept well that night and was awakened by Jay, curled up behind her, lips on the back of her shoulders. Gentle kisses she refused to acknowledge out of fear he would stop. Finally she rolled over to hold him, and they clung to each other as the sun's early rays poked through the edge of the curtains.

"Don't you need to call anyone?" asked Shawna.

It was a question that broke the silence and the mood of the moment. She regretted her words immediately.

"Not really," said Jay. "I'm not missed that much."

"You sure?"

"Sure," said Jay.

"Would you think I'm an idiot if I admitted something to you?" asked Shawna.

"Here it comes," said Jay. "Is this one of those tough questions?"

Shawna rolled over to face him. She propped herself up on an elbow.

"You mean like a girl thing? No, it's nothing like that," said Shawna. "It's sort of a statement of weirdness."

"Well, weirdness has got to be better than a girl thing." said Jay.

"Maybe you'll change your mind when you hear about my strange nightmares."

"How strange is strange?"

"Pretty strange, to me." replied Shawna. "You'll quickly see I'm a nut case, but let me tell you about my memories of next month."

"Memories are generally of the past rather than the future," said Jay.

"Not these," replied Shawna.

Jay listened as Shawna described her recurring nightmares of Hangar Two. He didn't intervene at all until Shawna mentioned the experience during the lightning storm aboard the C-130 the previous night.

"It seemed to coincide with a lightning flash?" asked Jay.

"Just as the cargo compartment lit up, the memory hit abruptly. It was piercing. That's when I grabbed your arm."

"Has it happened any other times like that when you've been awake?" asked Jay.

"Twice before," answered Shawna. "Both times were in Panama at Maintenance Control, in the back room where we store our personal stuff."

"What's the room like?" asked Jay.

Shawna gave a description of the storage area behind the control panels and told him how the occurrence of the memory seemed to relate to the UHF radio transmissions.

"How close were you standing to the radio?" asked Jay.

"Well, it was on the other side of the wall, but that wall is so thin you can easily talk to someone through it. I'd say about three or four feet between the radio and me."

"Sure sounds electrical, doesn't it?" said Jay.

"But that doesn't explain my nighttime dreams," noted Shawna.

"Is there anything electrical near your bed?" asked Jay.

"Now what kind of a question is that for the girl of your dreams?"

Jay laughed and continued: "You know, a clock radio going off when the memory hits, something like that."

"Sure, I've got a clock radio," said Shawna. "And a lamp on the nightstand, but this has happened when both are off."

"Not when the clock radio's alarm goes off?" asked Jay.

"No. Typically the memory flashes into me right at the moment I wake up, without an alarm. Or maybe it's the nightmare itself that awakens me."

Jay was obviously thinking, so Shawna said nothing until he responded. His attitude, so far, seemed to be much more receptive than Melissa's had been. Then again, he could hurt her, in a moment, with a lot more power than Mel ever wielded.

"Try to describe again why this seems like a memory rather than a foreboding," said Jay.

He was speaking slowly now, lying propped on one elbow, looking directly into Shawna's eyes.

"Let me give you an example," said Shawna. "Last night, I remember the lightning bolt. It was very real, backed up by the fact that I remember the reactions of your mechanics immediately after things lit up."

She paused, but Jay didn't say anything, so she continued: "I remember many of the details, even though I was trying to deal with the terrible flash of memory at the same time. There was a time sequence to everything. I remember what happened in the C-130, the exact order of things, including the sudden memory of the future. I wasn't imagining it."

"But you're talking about a future moment in time that's mixed with the present," said Jay.

"True. But that's exactly how this nightmare plays out in my mind. There are details, all appropriately sequenced, and they never change. It's a well-organized memory."

Once again, Jay paused in thought. Shawna appreciated his concentrated attention. His comments were probing, but they didn't reveal lack of acceptance of what she was saying. It seemed a lot like how she wanted to handle life – critically probing, demanding solid answers, and never accepting that some answers might not exist.

"Your arrow of time seems momentarily reversed," said Jay.

"I guess you could say that."

Shawna expected him to say more, and she waited patiently. Finally, Jay sat up in bed, squinched his mouth into an almost-pout, and held the pose for a few seconds. Shawna couldn't help but laugh.

"What's wrong, Mister Scientist? Are you bothered by lack of information about witches."

"Nothing wrong with the concept of witches," said Jay. "But that's not what I'm thinking."

"So what are you thinking?" asked Shawna.

"I'm thinking that electrical pulses and your nightmare are related, but your brain is also revealing the memory at night in a relaxed state."

"Yes, but so what?" asked Shawna.

"Well, biology and brain waves are a topic far from my expertise. But computers work, in certain situations, in ways similar to what you're experiencing."

"Meaning...?"

"Meaning there might be a specific stored memory that can be accessed by normal methods, like self-interrogation of your brain during sleep. But it can also be accessed by a short-circuit, of sorts."

"Thanks for the compliment," said Shawna. "So I'm a robot rather than a witch. Hey, maybe you can just call me an 'electronic fucking machine'."

Jay laughed and retained his smile as he spoke: "Nothing wrong with that, as far as I'm concerned. But I keep thinking about the concept of the arrow of time."

His smile vanished, replaced by a look of seriousness.

"You mean the direction of time?" asked Shawna.

"Exactly. One of the challenges of theoretical physics involves a problem regarding the lack of distinction between time running forward and backward."

"But it always runs forward," said Shawna.

"Yes, at least as far as anything we've ever observed," replied Jay. "But neither Newtonian mechanics nor relativity theory prohibit time-reversal. One of the big mysteries is why the arrow of time always goes in the same direction."

"So...?"

Shawna wasn't bored with this discussion, but she thought this was getting pretty far afield. Maybe Jay was trying to placate her.

"Irreversible processes should be clearer than that," said Jay. "Even time travel is possible under various theories of physics. Yet, scientists agree that thermodynamics prohibits the arrow of time from reversing. And you don't monkey with thermodynamics."

"Thermodynamics," said Shawna. "That's pretty heavy. I know thermodynamics is more than just heat flow, but I don't see the relationship."

"The point is that people seem to have memories only of the past, with no conscious knowledge of the future. But nothing prohibits it."

"So this could be a real memory?"

"Theoretically."

"But you don't believe it, do you?"

"I believe you have experienced it," said Jay. "And I know, at least in theory, there is no reason to prefer one direction in time over another. If the arrow of time reversed, even for a moment, we would remember the future but wouldn't have a clue about the past."

"So it's possible that's happening to me."

"Possible, yes," said Jay. "But why the arrow would reverse for you now – specifically you, and specifically now – is beyond me."

"It's beyond me too," said Shawna. "And it's scaring me all to hell."

* * * * *

Jay called the Guard base from the condo, asking for Base Ops rather than the maintenance squadron. As far as Shawna knew, he hadn't called Irene since they arrived, and she had been with Jay nearly the whole time.

It didn't take long for Shawna to learn what prompted Jay to call the operations side of the house. He was asking about diverting a local flight into Norton Air Force Base. That was an unheard-of request from her knowledge of the regular Air Force. It smacked of personal favoritism. Then again, this was the Air National Guard.

When he hung up the phone, he was smiling.

"It worked," he said. "Get ready for one more ride on the noise maker."

"They're diverting a flight to Norton?" asked Shawna.

"Sure," said Jay. "It's a local flight anyway, just going out to practice instrument approaches. They can practice as easily at Norton as anywhere else."

"Well, it's a pretty nice taxi service," said Shawna. "Can you go with me?"

"Of course. I wouldn't miss it."

"And after today?" asked Shawna.

She wished she hadn't said it, but it certainly was occupying her mind.

"That depends how much we want to be together," said Jay. "As for me, I want to be with you a lot."

"It's gonna' be complicated," said Shawna. "And I'm not sure if I can take complicated."

* * * * * *

Jay rushed Shawna around the Van Nuys Air National Guard Base. There wasn't a lot of time before the 11:15 local flight departed, but he wanted to show her the airlift wing he was so proud of. They briefly toured Maintenance Control, but it wasn't very impressive compared to regular Air Force operations. Everywhere they went, the base appeared to be a cozy operation. Everyone knew Jay, and everybody wanted to talk, but they kept moving as fast as they could. Shawna's bags were in the back of the pickup truck, and they kept a close eye on the clock.

At the flightline office, they looked out over the aircraft ramp and awaited the arrival of their aircraft. Since the airplane was already flying on a local mission, this would be an engine-running crew change, with the aircraft scheduled to pull into Spot 4 and change flight crews without even shutting down its engines.

Through the wall of windows in the flightline office, the inbound C-130 loomed on the northern horizon and grew all the way to touchdown on Runway 16 Right. It arrived nearly simultaneous with the landing of a single-engine Cessna on the parallel left runway. This was a very busy airport, and the mix of civilian and military traffic seemed hazardous to Shawna, like an accident waiting to happen.

It was a short walk to Spot 4, but Jay accepted a ride from one of the flight chiefs. Shawna's two bags were transferred to the rear of the pickup truck. A few minutes later, they watched the C-130 pull into its parking spot. Also awaiting the aircraft was the outgoing flight crew, huddled in a step-van parked nearby.

Jay waited for the crew exchange to be nearly complete before approaching the aircraft. Then he led Shawna up the front entry-door steps and straight ahead to the flight deck stairs. Shawna glanced to her right as she entered the C-130, noticing that the cargo compartment was completely empty. The interior of the aircraft looked a lot bigger in that configuration.

Within less than fifteen minutes of arrival, the C-130 was taxiing back for takeoff. As they settled into the cockpit, Jay handed Shawna an interphone headset and plugged it in at the jack above the crew bunk. There was an electrical crackle and then a mixture of cockpit voices, with air traffic control in the background. The aircraft was poised now in the run-up area at the end of Runway 16 Right. Clearance Delivery was already issuing their departure instructions.

"Coach 32 is cleared to Norton Air Force Base via the Glendale Two Departure, Burbank Transition, Victor 186, as filed. Climb and maintain niner thousand. Burbank Departure Control is 135.05. Squawk 3125."

The co-pilot read back the clearance, switched to tower frequency, reported ready for departure, and off they went. It happened quickly. No engine run-up or delay of any kind.

From the cockpit, the view of the takeoff was exciting. The C-130 leaped off the ground in less than a thousand feet, the aircraft nearly empty today. The deck angle during the initial climb was exceptionally steep. From the rear of the flight deck where Jay and Shawna sat on the crew bunk, the ground could barely be seen out the C-130s lowest windows near the pilots' feet. They leveled at nine thousand feet in less than seven minutes.

It was a short flight, about twenty minutes. Jay sat beside Shawna on the bunk at the back of the cockpit. He took her hand as they began their descent into Norton, oblivious to what the flight crew might say regarding an NCO holding the hand of an officer. Maybe in the Guard they wouldn't say a thing. The crew's eyes were busy looking for air traffic anyway. They had more on their minds than the political issue of military fraternization.

* * * * * *

They were down, props reversing, pushed forward in their seats. The C-130 made the first high-speed turnoff to the main taxiway and the next turn onto the ramp. Now stopped, engines still running in low-speed ground idle, Shawna was being ushered out the entry door by Jay. He walked with her past the front of the whirling props, carrying both of her bags. He led her to a waiting blue Air Force station wagon parked just forward of the wingtip.

In the noise of the four idling turboprop engines, Jay yelled "Love you!" loud enough that the driver of the station wagon could probably hear, and then he kissed her right there in front of everyone. There was little question that the C-130 pilots saw this goodbye kiss quite clearly from their elevated scenic view on the flight deck.

Shawna didn't hesitate to reply: "Love you too!"

Jay smiled, and then he was gone.

At the C-130's forward entry door, the loadmaster stood waiting for Jay, his interphone cable serving as an umbilical cord to the cockpit. As soon as Jay returned, the loadmaster followed him up the steps, pulled the door lanyard from the inside, and the aircraft was sealed shut.

Then they were gone.

Gone was the C-130. Gone was the noise. Gone was Jay.

Chapter 17

Starlifter

It had always been her favorite aircraft, the C-141 Starlifter. Built by Lockheed, this airplane shared its design with its short, fatter-looking cousin, the C-130. This aircraft was long and slim, particularly since a fuselage plug had been added to most C-141s during the previous decade, the mid-70s. Those four jet engines, noisy in their own right, shrieked power.

As Shawna gazed down the row of Starlifters at Norton Air Force Base, parked in precise alignment, she knew she was going to stay in the Air Force. Now approaching two years of service, she would be able to exit the Air Force without question in two more years. But this was where her heart was, and she knew this is where it would stay.

Dover, Delaware, had lots of Starlifters, and she expected to get her base of choice. In her case, Dover was ideal, just full of C-141s and ten miles from her parents' home in Cheswold. Of course, the C-5 was at Dover too. But big didn't intrigue her as much as sleek and efficient. She would probably be involved with both of these aircraft in whatever job she was assigned at Dover. But best of all, she'd be at home with the Starlifter.

Shawna walked back into Base Ops, hitting a blast of air conditioning on a warmer-than-normal winter day in Southern California.

The lobby was almost empty. The east-west shuttle, flown by a Star-lifter, carried more aircraft parts and paperwork than it carried people. But it ran on a regular schedule. She couldn't help but remind herself that such a schedule could tie her and Jay together in a few months, if they were willing to put up with the five-hour journey. The big question was whether their relationship was important enough for that. Or whether it would last.

She was troubled by Jay's level of seriousness. No, "seriousness" wasn't the right word. In many ways, Jay was more serious about this relationship than she was. How long it would last was the bigger question. They had been together enough in the past two weeks to know they were both interested in pursuing this relationship. Over the past three days, they had devoted time to each other almost constantly. But now they were apart for only an hour, and it already felt fragile. She wondered if their strong ties could survive.

It would be another hour before the Starlifter departed for Dover, so Shawna sank into a soft leather couch in the waiting area adjacent to Base Ops. She was lost in her thoughts when she grabbed a copy of *Time* magazine from the table beside the couch. Halfway through the magazine, she fell asleep to the gentle thrum of the air conditioner.

She awoke after what was probably only a few minutes nap, feeling relaxed and content. A phone was ringing on a desk behind the long counter. She saw a female staff sergeant in formal blues pick up the receiver, listen for a few moments, and then say: "I think so. Let me check."

Then she heard her name, here in California, thousands of miles from both Panama and Delaware.

"Lieutenant, are you Shawna Whitney?"

She knew who it was, and she already had the answer to her own question.

* * * * * *

The Starlifter was configured almost exactly the same as the C-130 — the same red-webbed troop seats, the same gray padded insulation.

Three other military passengers rode farther to the rear. It was strangely lonesome inside, and it was a long ride to Dover.

There wasn't a lot to do, but there was a lot of time to think. It was the kind of thinking that could get her in trouble. Shawna was so obsessed with memories of Jay that she couldn't concentrate on her worries about Panama's Hangar Two, even when she tried to. Until, that is, the landing gear started down.

She had sat near the front of the nearly unoccupied cargo compartment for most of the flight. But as they approached the East Coast, she wandered rearward and settled into a seat adjacent to the right main landing gear wheel-well. And when the Starlifter's engine power was retarded towards idle and the landing gear went down, a sharp flood of nightmarish memories caught her by surprise. In only a few seconds, all of the details of Todd and Hangar Two and the falling rudder were rammed into view.

When it was over, she had a piercing headache. And the landing gear was down and locked.

* * * * * *

Dover wasn't as she remembered it. The C-141s and C-5s were there, and everything was where she had recalled them to be as a teenager. But something just didn't feel right.

Maybe it was the nearness to her mother and father and her childhood home. She was an adult now, defending her country as a full-time occupation and involved in a career traditionally technical and even more traditionally male. She wasn't a child any more, and it would be impossible to live in this house and not feel she was stepping backwards.

Her parents were superb people and very excited to have her home, however temporary it might be. Her father still called her "Princess" more often than not, and it didn't embarrass Shawna in the comfort of their home. But being an only-child had certainly spoiled her. In her teens, she had served as the official under-age bartender for her parent's home social functions. She had been raised in a world of adults. Shawna had turned out quite well for a spoiled child.

To think their Shawna might be coming home to stay for a while, assigned to Dover Air Force Base, was enough to make Shawna's parents bubble with joy. But they too questioned whether this would be the best decision for their daughter in the long run. And when they questioned the pending assignment, Shawna was surprised. She had simply assumed her parents would want her to move back in with them, and that there could be no other way.

Over dinner, Shawna's father, a wiry and fragile looking fellow of forty-seven, started the conversation by asking if Shawna was considering an off-base apartment of her own or was thinking about living on the base. Shawna was shocked, and at first a bit hurt. Then she realized her parents had thought this through with more logic than she had. They even asked if she was sure she wanted to come back to Delaware at all.

Once the shock of the matter wore off, Shawna realized her parents were even more wonderful than she gave them credit for. She had some thinking to do. There were other places in this world that had Starlifters.

And so, for nearly a full week in Delaware, she pondered the matter, making several trips to the air base to get a feel for the atmosphere. It was a decision that took a lot of mental energy, but not so much that she forgot about Jay. Or Hangar Two.

* * * * * *

Jay called several times that week. Her father kidded her a bit, and then he realized she wasn't ready to discuss this relationship. Her parents gave her the privacy she needed, and she promised to tell them more when there was a real story.

On one of the days that Jay didn't call, she called him in Van Nuys. There was a possibility of flying through Norton on the way back to Panama, but it would take her quite a ways off the most direct route. In the end, the east-west shuttle didn't connect to anything headed for Central America, so she took a direct flight to Panama that was already on the schedule at Dover. Jay accepted the decision, but she enjoyed it when he pouted profusely.

In the end, before Shawna left Dover, she was able to come to an equitable decision with her family that seemed to work for everyone. She wasn't going to request Dover, but she would still have that option for an assignment later in her career, if there was a career. That didn't lock her into anything, and it was a way to get her plans moving. She would ask for a Military Airlift Command base in California, one with Starlifters. And she would be near Jay.

Chapter 18

Hangar Two

The disturbing memories didn't return again. There was a time, before the nightmares ended, when Shawna considered telling Todd about her premonitions, just in case. But not once after returning to Panama did the nightmares resurface.

* * * * * *

When Melissa was promoted to major, she asked Shawna to pin on her new oak leafs. It was a private ceremony, and Shawna cooked an elaborate dinner for the two of them, refusing to let Melissa lift a finger. Shawna dressed more formally than normal that evening, wearing a plaid summer shift, softness reserved for her special roommate. It was pampering that she knew Melissa craved more often than Shawna was willing to offer.

The dinner turned into an evening of quiet reflection, a night to consider their individual and mutual achievements. It was a celebration of their friendship as much as recognition of Melissa's promotion. They talked and laughed together, revealing their vulnerabilities and standing their ground on plans for the future. They had enough wine to regret it the next day, but the private party meant a lot to Melissa, and Shawna was pleased to be an important part of the moment. It was a celebration of spirit.

* * * * * *

The new wing commander arrived in a more formal setting, marking an important change of command. On a very hot and humid Panama day, Shawna and Melissa wore their dress blues for the ceremonial parade. Standing at attention on the moist parade field, Shawna remembered the starry night with Jay near this same spot.

Near the conclusion of the speeches, it began to rain. The ceremony was rushed to its finish but not before everyone was drenched. Many of Shawna's peers noted it might be an omen for what was ahead under the leadership of General Bruce Curto. He came to Howard Air Force Base with a reputation for shooting from the hip, and his arrival coincided with a time of little optimism for most of the military personnel.

For Shawna, the change of command ceremony was reason to celebrate. Her memories of Hangar Two hadn't returned, and the timeline of her original foreboding had clearly indicated the accident would occur after Melissa's promotion but before the new wing commander took charge. The time of crisis had passed, and the expected future hadn't arrived. It was a tremendous relief, although it made her wonder how something that seemed so real could evaporate before her eyes.

Right after General Curto took command, there was an incident that caused Shawna to shiver every time she pondered it. While she was off-duty one rainy night, a C-130 was being backed into an outside fuel cell repair facility, marked laterally by a row of tall floodlights. The Volant Oak tow team from Alaska was groping in the dark in an unfamiliar part of the ramp, and they clipped the rudder on one of the towering lights before the tail walker could signal for brakes.

Everything came to a halt in the fuel cell area, while the wing safety officer was summoned to the scene. General Curto showed up too, and everyone was quite frightened by his ranting and raving, including the safety officer. After several hours of discussion and filling out reports, the aircraft was released back to Volant Oak. The line chief from the Alaska Air Guard requested permission to move the aircraft into Hangar Number Two, since that was the only facility tall enough to house the complete empennage of a C-130.

The rudder change would have to be accomplished as quickly as possible to meet the week's flight schedule. There would probably be no C-130 rudder in stock within the Air Force supply system, so the Alaska Air Guard was already planning to cannibalize the rudder from an already-grounded C-130. The weather forecast called for continual rain for the next two days, so only a covered hangar would suffice for the rudder swap.

Since Shawna wasn't on shift, she wasn't notified until she returned to work. Captain Melissa Henesie learned about the rudder first, when she arrived at her office in Base Supply before Shawna showed up at work. When Melissa sat down at her desk, her first telephone call was from her assistant NCO who declared the C-130 rudder a not-mission-capable-supply component.

Although this was a C-130 rather than a C-141, Melissa immediately remembered Shawna's foreboding. The supply system order form sitting on top of her inbox showed a delivery destination of Hangar Two.

Cannibalization was a legal way to handle a situation like this, and there really was no other choice. Another Volant Oak C-130 was also listed as not-mission-capable due to landing gear structural cracks that required a depot-level repair team, and no such team was expected from the States for several weeks. The decision was made to cannibalize the rudder from that grounded C-130.

If all went well, the damaged rudder would be off by 10 am and the aircraft pulled out of Hangar Two. Then the other grounded C-130 would be brought into the hangar for removal of its serviceable rudder. After once again swapping these two aircraft within the limited hangar space, the replacement rudder would be hung.

Hopefully, this could all be accomplished by early evening. That time estimate included flight control rigging and multiple tow movements to reposition the two aircraft. This time-consuming procedure would make one good aircraft out of two cripples. Even then, the task wouldn't be finished. Flight control replacement would require a test flight before the aircraft could be released to the Command Post. For good reason, cannibalization was considered the last resort, always forcing double work, as a minimum.

It was a long night for the Alaska Air Guard mechanics, and the beginning of a long day to follow. When Shawna arrived at Maintenance Control in the morning, she went forward to the weapon controller's status board for a self-briefing regarding the on-station aircraft. When she saw the rudder change in red grease pencil, it sent a shiver through her, even though it was a C-130 rather than a C-141.

But Captain Todd Chandler was now going off duty from his beloved midnight shift, a schedule that allowed him to fish nearly every day. And he wouldn't be back until midnight tonight. By then the rudder swap would be complete.

Shawna tried to ignore the coincidence or at least call it just that. A rudder change was rare on any airplane, but they did occur. All day, Shawna closely monitored the progress. She considered visiting Hangar Two, but thoughts of the scene sent spikes of fear through her.

The rain pounded throughout the morning. At approximately 9:30 am, the rudder removal was complete, and the C-130 swap in Hangar Two began. By noon, the rudder was removed from the second C-130 and that aircraft was on its way back to the parking ramp. By 2 pm the Air Guard team was beginning the rudder installation on the hangared aircraft.

Hangar Two was the home of the Aerospace Systems Shop, a facility now on-loan to the Air National Guard for the rudder change. The shop's Pettibone crane was needed for the repair, but it was considered too precious to allow Air Guard personnel to operate it. So a permanent party NCO was assigned to assist the Guard mechanics. The sole purpose of this NCO was to assure that an inexperienced operator didn't damage the crane.

At precisely 3:37 pm, just as Lieutenant Shawna Whitney was thinking about placing a long distance call to Van Nuys, her telephone rang. It was the squadron's maintenance supervisor, Chief Jackson. He was extremely distressed.

During replacement of the C-130 rudder, the crane's boom had suddenly jammed as it approached its highest limit of extension. The C-130 rudder swung wildly from the apex of the boom. Then the rudder came loose. It crashed to the hangar floor, narrowly missing two mechanics. No one was killed, no one was injured, but someone could have been badly hurt. The shop supervisor requested that the safety officer be contacted and immediately dispatched to Hangar Number Two. An irate General Curto beat the safety officer to the scene.

* * * * * *

The next day, while driving an older model pickup truck filled with fishing gear along the wet road from Gatun Lake to Balboa, Captain Todd Chandler lost control of his vehicle and crashed head-on with a car traveling in the opposite direction. Todd Chandler died at the scene of the accident.

Waiting

The camouflaged hulks sit lifeless.
These bodies blend with the jungle.
The asphalt ramp steams from the tropical heat,
And night engulfs the flightline.

Inside the line shack, mechanics await the last aircraft,
Inbound from Peru and overdue.
The report from Maintenance Control is that she's broken,
With radios so bad she missed her last position report.

Relaxed, hot, and sweaty,
Vision fogged at the edges.
Damp curly hair hidden under a fatigue cap,
The air conditioner unable to keep pace.

The phone rings.
She's worse than expected,
Stumbling home crippled from Lima.
Without radios, it must be lonely in the dark.

A landing light flickers to the south.
The sky is quiet, but noise is approaching,
As the last bird slips down final,
Towards her place of recovery on the ramp.

She touches down gently, and the props reverse.
The jungle awakens from the sudden noise.
The camouflaged hulk turns toward the empty parking spot.
The last bird is home.

Our Year 1985: Distant Planet

4 Years Later

Every bodily process is pulsing to its own beat within the overall beats of the solar system.

Michael Young (Rockefeller University)

Chapter 19

The Minds

After all this time, nothing. There had been absolutely no hints of success since the experiment began. Progress was moving ahead on related projects regarding stability of the transmission signal. But the communication issues had been left far behind. Exploratory capabilities of transmitting matter as well as messages were in an advanced stage. But what good would this investment be, if there no intelligence was present to receive the messages? The first step was to get someone's attention.

On the distant planet, the experiment was considered a failure by most. But a small group of scientists, called simply the "Minds," refused to give in to those who called for termination of the project. They had designed this experiment with all of the problems taken into consideration. That included patience.

To date, nothing. If the first signal had been received at the target light years away, it hadn't been acknowledged. Technicians maintained a listening watch in all segments of the electromagnetic spectrum, even the visual frequencies. The signal had been locked onto the initial target long enough for the dialogue to intensify. The debate even questioned whether it was actually an intelligent being that was targeted. There was evidence that a receptor had received the signal, but the lack of a reply indicated either ancient technology or a lack of will. Either would lead the experiment to total failure.

The density of intelligent life in the universe was completely unknown. So the argument continued, with many pressing for a change of target. Those arguing for patience, including the small group of scientists called the Minds, were still in charge. But their dominance couldn't last long without some success to report. So far there was none.

To change the target now could lead to a quick termination of the experiment. Turning away when the proper destination might be right around the corner was unacceptable to the Minds. They would fight it to their death. But other leaders were calling the budgetary shots. Without their support, there would be no further engineering progress, regardless of the importance to science and society. But the Minds weren't talking to these bureaucrats. So the budgetary forces weren't listening.

Getting the attention of an intelligent being on this distant watery world might be a dead end. But it could also bring new life for all.

1985: Earth

Henceforth, space by itself, and time by itself, are doomed to fade away into mere shadows, and only a kind of union of the two will preserve an independent reality.

Hermann Minkowski (1908)

C-130 Turboprop Engine and Horse-Collar

Chapter 20

Travis

The phone rang her awake. Shawna reached to the nightstand and pulled the receiver to her ear. She thought about the Reforger launches as she identified herself.

"Captain Whitney."

"That's pretty official. Must have been expecting me."

It was Jay, and that put a smile on a very tired face.

"Hi! Nice way to wake up."

"Sorry to call so early. I'm leaving Van Nuys in about twenty minutes. The flight is about an hour and a half, so let's estimate my arrival as 8:40. Thought I should let you know."

"Thanks," said Shawna. "We'll roll out the red carpet. Or at least the follow-me truck."

"White coveralls please," said Jay.

"You really like those, don't you?"

"They look good on you," said Jay. "And that one-piece zipper in front is my favorite. No underwear preferred."

"Just remember where you are," replied Shawna.

"Where I'm going to be in a about two hours is Travis Air Force Base.

"But still remember where you are," repeated Shawna.

"With you."

"I'm glad," said Shawna.

* * * * * *

Shawna sat in her Air Force pickup truck and was dressed in her white transient maintenance coveralls when the C-130 pulled into the parking spot at Travis Air Force Base, just north of San Francisco Bay. She watched the marshaller, in his matching coveralls, give the "chocks in" signal to the aircraft commander, and the four turboprop engines spun down in unison. As the props stopped, the external power cart was already plugged in and the connected "T" hand-signal flashed to the cockpit. In another few seconds, the gas turbine compressor in the C-130s wheel-well spun down, and it was a lot quieter.

Shawna stepped out of the pickup truck, lowered her blue ear-muffs into a stowed position around her neck, and walked towards the crew entrance door on the left side of the aircraft. She stood a few feet in front of the nose radome, as she waited with the marshaller for the door to open.

The loadmaster was the first one out, still connected to his interphone cable. Four passengers came down the steps next, and the loadmaster waved them towards the waiting bus. Jay exited after the passengers, stopped in front of Shawna, and popped a precise salute. Shawna returned the salute with a quick raise of her right arm.

"Captain, thanks for taking care of us this morning," said Jay.

He had to raise his voice to be heard over the sound of the roaring power cart a few feet away.

"Anytime, Chief," said Shawna with a broad smile.

The flight crew was exiting now, and Shawna gave the aircraft commander, a major, a quick salute. He replied with a friendly wave of the fingers of his right hand. The Guard was different. She had learned to like them.

Jay was carrying a soft-leather briefcase and a tan cloth shopping bag.

"Yours," he said, handing the bag to Shawna.

"Thanks. How was the weather?"

"Bumpy," said Jay. "Santa Ana's down south. Not bad up here. So, are you wearing any underwear?"

"This isn't the best place, Sergeant. Let's wait awhile."

"If you insist, Captain," replied Jay.

They started toward the pickup truck as the aircraft commander debriefed the transient maintenance NCO on the status of the aircraft. Jay turned and waved to the major as they walked away. The major wiggled his fingers as a goodbye, and Shawna thought she saw a wink.

* * * * * *

Inside the Transient Maintenance building, the level of activity was intense. Jay stood to the side of the display panel as Shawna got a briefing by the shift chief on the latest Reforger departures, C-141s on their way to a European exercise. Everyone except Jay was dressed in traditional white transient maintenance coveralls with Military Airlift Command patches on their right chest pocket. Jay was wearing olive drab fatigues with a MAC patch and chief master sergeant insignia on his upper sleeves, two upside-down chevrons above all the rest.

"No more C-5s on this ramp," said Shawna.

"Try to tell that to Maintenance Control," said the shift chief. "They say the main ramp is full."

"They're idiots," replied Shawna. "Tell them that for me."

Jay laughed and interrupted: "So soon we forget."

The shift chief, a tech sergeant, reacted to Jay's comments, probably appropriate when a chief master sergeant spoke. You didn't see many of those around this place.

"Chief, our captain is able to hold her own with those guys in Maintenance Control. And she's right, they are idiots."

That got a laugh from everybody, including the buck sergeant who was shielding the telephone as he tried to talk with Maintenance Control.

"Your captain can be a bit critical," said Jay. "But she always asks plenty of questions, and in this business that's important."

Shawna was feeling too much the center of attention, so she intervened quickly.

"Well, we've got to make room for the McChord Reforger departures," said Shawna. "It's our top priority. Those base C-5s are second fiddle, and they take up too much ramp space."

"Yes, ma'am," replied the tech sergeant.

Shawna excused herself. "Be right back, guys," she said as she left the room.

Everything returned to normal. Phones were ringing, and there weren't enough people to answer them promptly. The hot-lines got first priority. Jay thought about answering the ignored off-base line, but decided he would be more of a hindrance than a help.

Just as quickly as chaos had broken out, things returned to quiet. The tech sergeant turned to Jay, probably out of respect for his top NCO rank.

"Well, Chief, where are you from?" asked the NCO.

"Van Nuys, near Los Angeles," replied Jay. "We've got an Air Guard base there. It's a civilian airport with sixteen C-130s to add to the traffic pattern."

"Sounds a bit messy. I thought the C-130s were at Point Mugu."

"That's our new base, we hope," said Jay. "If all stays on schedule, we'll be moving out of Van Nuys soon, before something bad happens. The air traffic mess in Los Angeles and the C-130's wake turbulence have produced a lot of close calls. We're hoping for a move to Mugu, but it isn't official yet."

"I might join the Guard when I get out," said the young buck sergeant sitting at the aircraft locator display board. "Got any openings?"

"We're always looking for crew chiefs and specialists," replied Jay. "You don't have to have the turboprop suffix. We have our own field training."

"Still have another year," said the young sergeant. "How do you know our captain?"

The shift supervisor shot the buck sergeant a glance that indicated "Shut up," but Jay answered cheerfully.

"Met her in Panama a number of years ago. She was just a puppy then."

"Still is," replied the tech sergeant.

* * * * * *

Shawna's apartment in Fairfield was wonderful. Jay always loved it there. Secluded, quiet, with modern styling. He felt at home.

"How's Irene?" asked Shawna.

It always sounded bitter to Shawna when she said it, but it was bitter in an indirect way. It wasn't her tone of voice. She tried to control that. Perhaps it was the suddenness with which she launched the question, as if to catch him off guard.

"Better," replied Jay. "She's home a lot more these days, but she can do most of her work from there. She's bought a computer with a modem. Some of her financial coordination can be done from her house. It's really catching on."

"Sounds expensive," said Shawna with genuine interest.

"Not really. But many of the financial wizards refuse to adapt to the new technology. My tax accountant hates it."

"I hope her doctor gets things resolved soon," said Shawna. "Is there a date for the operation yet?"

She was sincere, but doubted she sounded that way.

"No, it's nothing she's hurrying. Her doctor wants to give the medication a second chance. He thinks keeping her off her feet might even solve it."

"Hope so," said Shawna.

She did. And she didn't.

Chapter 21

Pain

Against the doctor's orders, Irene Bennett was on her knees in the garden, working on her patch of daisies. It wasn't very demanding on her body, just pulling weeds and loosening up the soil with the hand trowel.

As she stood up, she felt the ache in her back and tried to ignore it. At the age of forty-eight, everyone probably ached now and then. But the pain was more common these days, and it didn't take much exertion to set it off.

She stood in the warm sun, stretching her body to its full upright position. Her tall frame was dressed in blue jeans, white sneakers, a loose-fitting T-shirt, and no bra. She wouldn't be seen in public this way, but her backyard was very private. Even dressed in her garden attire, Irene looked every bit prim and proper. The dirt kept its distance.

The Santa Ana winds could be felt distinctly here, as the air moved up the north side of the Santa Monica Mountains from it's funnel-like flow through the Newhall Pass. The wind was minimal, but the dryness of the hot flow was evident. It didn't help her sinuses.

Irene loved her home, and she loved her life. She hoped it could go on without further illness for a long time. What she had now wasn't so bad – a stab of pain now and then, but nothing to get excited about.

Her general practitioner overreacted to nearly everything. The special-ists seemed to think this was a routine case.

And so her home and her life were in nearly perfect order. So was her job, such as it was. At least she didn't have to work very hard at it. Most of her work came easy, and now much of it could be done from her oh-so-comfortable home. It would be hard to ever return to the daily commute, regardless of her health.

What wasn't so perfect in Irene's life was Jay. He was increasingly aloof in the past year. He was just turning forty, eight years younger than Irene. It should have made a bigger difference when they first met in 1976, he at thirty-one and she at thirty-nine. But for some reason it seemed like a bigger gap now, and growing.

Maybe it wasn't age at all. Maybe it was the seven-year itch. It had been about that time when she began to notice the difference. Their relationship had never been much more than a union of convenience.

And she had been through this before. This was her third major relationship, two of them resulting in marriage and divorce. None of her relationships had lasted as long as this one, but none of them had been this easy either. Jay wasn't difficult to get along with, just not a sensitive person. He lacked sexual drive, especially in recent years, although all of his macho friends would have guessed otherwise. She had the drive but no longer the energy. And it wasn't the important part of things anyway. In fact, looking down at her beautiful daisies, Irene thought, for that moment, there was much more to life than her relationship to Jay. For example, there was her beautiful garden.

* * * * * *

It had been a long day for Shawna. The Reforger launches had their share of problems, and her hopes of getting away early were dashed in the bud. Jay had taken her car and gone to the apartment. She liked thoughts of him alone in her apartment while she worked. But thoughts of her being alone with him brought an even nicer image.

Shawna called her apartment at five o'clock, letting the phone ring until the answer machine picked it up. When Jay heard her voice, he answered immediately. She felt wonderful telling him to pick her up at six o'clock. It was an enticing image to think of Jay waiting for her in the Transient Maintenance parking lot in her ugly green Volkswagen Jetta. Going home with Jay!

It was 6:15 when she finally left the building, but the sun was still beaming on the northern rim of San Francisco Bay with temperatures in the eighties, warm for this place.

She actually caught herself skipping as she took the last few steps to the car. In the doorway of the small Butler building labeled "60th MAW Transient Maintenance," Senior Master Sergeant Ron Strickland, her shop supervisor, was taking a break in the retreating sunshine. As he watched Shawna depart, his trademark wooden toothpick was being shuttled from one side of his mouth to other. This was one of the youngest senior master sergeants in the regular Air Force, but not by Air National Guard standards. His wavy blond hair, brushed back on the top and sides, was already well en route to gray, maybe precipitated by the struggles of his rank. He hadn't made that rank by ignoring officers.

* * * * * *

Shawna awoke in a dream – a good dream.

Jay was lying on his side, facing away from her, and she rolled over to hold his naked body from behind. As she pressed up against him, he moaned in a satisfied tone. She snuggled closer, kissed the back of his neck, and felt him shiver. She could smell his hair. Its faint fresh odor was one of her favorite memories. She could smell it while driving alone on back-country roads with open car windows blasting fresh air all over her.

Jay rolled onto his back, and she immediately pulled off the covers and climbed on top of him, her legs spread, hugging his thighs. Then she sat up, inching her knees forward to place her weight right over his waist. Shawna felt alluring, soft, and far from vulnerable at this moment.

It was going to be a beautiful morning.

* * * * * *

Irene Bennett thought about pain that morning. It wasn't entirely negative notions. Instead, it was a personal analysis of how unimportant pain was in a nearly perfect life. Nothing was completely perfect, and pain fit in where it needed to fit.

As she sat now in her favorite chair, watching the noon news, her back was throbbing, but the medication would kick in soon. And the physical pain would be gone.

There was mental pain too. And that wasn't so easily controlled. There was no medication for it, and it wouldn't be gone soon. Worst of all, she didn't understand it. It was simply there.

* * * * * *

One of the perks of being the Transient Maintenance Officer was the ability to skip parade ceremonies. Transient Maintenance was one of the few functions on the base that simply had to be manned, even during parades. Today there was a specific purpose for the ceremonies – the arrival of General James Larkin, the four-star head of the Military Airlift Command. General Larkin's visit was in recognition of the 60th Military Airlift Wing's recent earthquake relief mission in Mexico City.

General Larkin was expected to be the aircraft commander on the inbound C-5. This aircraft was a transient aircraft, so Shawna's small unit was in charge of handling it.

The rest of the base personnel were all decked out in their dress blue uniforms, standing at-ease on the ramp, but expectantly uncomfortable, as they awaited the arrival of the general's aircraft. It was a hot day, in the upper 80s. During the earlier practice at-attention drill, two airmen had passed out from the heat on the apron, hauled away by the ambulance that waited at the side of the ramp for exactly this reason.

To enchance the ceremony, an actual red carpet was laid out for the predicted location of the C-5s forward ladder. Next to the red carpet were the VIPs, officially aligned according to military and civilian rank. The Governor of California, George Deukmejian, joined the Travis Wing Commander, Brigadier General Tom Eisley. They stood at the very front of the line, engaged in idle talk and a few political jokes.

In her pickup truck, dressed in her white coveralls, Shawna had one of her two radios tuned to the Command Post. The communication she was listening to was a bit unusual.

"Command Post, this is General Eisley."

"Go ahead sir."

The voice was ready to react to any order Eisley might provide. This was the big boss.

"What's that C-130 doing on the taxiway?"

Except for Shawna and her Transient Maintenance team, the C-130 was the only sign of activity near the runways, unless you counted the mass of uncomfortable troops standing at ease in the heat.

"Sir, the C-130 is awaiting ATC clearance."

A C-130 can be a loud noise within any silence. And the general apparently found this one particularly annoying.

"Get him moving," said the general over the radio.

"Yes, sir," replied the voice from the Command Post.

The C-130's four turboprop engines continued to drone unabated, in low-speed ground idle. Sometimes ATC clearances take more time than seems reasonable, particularly on a clear day with lots of recreational aircraft in the area.

"Command Post, this is the Wing Commander."

"Go ahead sir."

"I thought I said to get that aircraft out of here."

"Yes, sir," said the voice.

There was a hesitation from the officer in the Command Post, as if there was no other possible answer, but further words were added anyway.

"The control tower says the clearance should be coming from Oakland Center any moment."

"Get that TAC trash out of here!" General Eisley voice was now raised in obvious anger. "No excuses!"

Shawna, listening to this on-the-air conversation, was enjoying the show.

TAC trash? Doesn't the general know that's an air rescue bird from Moffett? Worse yet, he must not know it's an Air Guard aircraft. That would really pop his buttons.

"Yes, sir. We'll get him going right away."

"Not soon enough," said the general. "Shut him down right there."

"Sir, I'm sure we can get him out VFR right away," said the voice.

"Shut him down, I said!"

Clear enough. Only a few seconds passed, and Shawna visualized the communication relay to the control tower and the cries of "Oh, shit!"

In unison, all four engines of the C-130 spun to a stop. The aircraft sat there on the taxiway, engines off, for the remainder of the parade ceremony.

As if on cue, the C-5 appeared overhead, crossing from right to left in a high-speed low pass. The screaming-pitch of C-5 engines is unequalled by any other aircraft of any size or shape, and the sound today was enhanced as it passed nearly directly overhead.

All eyes from the ramp were focused upward, as the C-5 under command of General Larkin circled back to the right for another low pass, this time with landing gear and flaps extended. A low-speed pass in a C-5 is even more impressive. The aircraft floated by at a velocity that seemed below freeway speed. Then the giant airlifter banked steeply to the downwind leg for Runway 21 Right.

The wind was gusting from the northwest, and Shawna knew General Larkin, even with his extensive flight experience and a very capable co-pilot, had his hands full with this aircraft. As the C-5 lined up on final approach, the wind could be seen working the wingtips of the aircraft as the huge aircraft bounced into alignment with the runway.

Then for the first time in her life, Shawna saw an airplane crash. At least that's what she thought she saw, as the C-5 caught a sudden gust and hit hard and short of Runway 21 Right. A ball of smoke engulfed the aircraft for several seconds, and she knew it was over for all aboard the giant plane. Then the C-5 came rolling out of the cloud and down Runway 21 Right, having hit the gravel overrun at the approach end of the runway. Shawna immediately remembered that C-5s have 28 tires and that she owned this aircraft today.

The VIP's were stirring now, probably wondering how to handle this unceremonious and nearly tragic arrival. But they quickly regained their appropriate positions as the C-5 pulled up to the red carpet. Shawna's marshalling team directed the aircraft to a stop within a few inches of the predetermined spot necessary for the carpet to perform its intended function.

After a few seconds, the engines were shut down, and the lofty crew door opened. The huge access ladder slid down. The first person to appear at the two-story-high crew door was General Larkin in his customized light blue flight suit and red ascot. The general started down the tall steps, approaching the awaiting VIPs.

Shawna and her small crew were already in the left main landing gear wheel-well, surveying the damage. No structural problems were immediately visible, but several of the tires were torn to shreds. The smell of rubber permeated the wheel-well.

General Larkin was at the bottom of the stairs now, but he avoided the red carpet, turned away from the governor and the other VIP's, and started directly toward the wheel-well. Shawna, peeking out between the wheels, saw what was happening and felt a sense of panic. The MAC Commander was headed directly for her.

"Hey, guys," she said in a hushed voice.

The mechanics now saw who was coming and scurried out of the wheel-well. Shawna followed quickly.

"Attention!" called Shawna.

"At ease," replied the general immediately. "I want you to notice I haven't greeted the governor and your wing commander yet."

"Yes, sir," said Shawna, still in a pose that closely resembled attention.

"They can wait," said General Larkin. "First, I need to apologize to you. I've sure messed up your day. I bet you have several tire changes on your hands."

"No problem, sir," said Shawna.

Her heart was pounding. She wanted to cry, but certainly not in front of the general.

"There's no excuse for what you just witnessed," said the general. "But I'll offer a lame justification. We're still figuring out how to land this airplane. You sit three stories up, and it's a strange perspective from the cockpit during the flare. This is a great bird in all phases of flight, but I'm not the most current C-5 pilot around."

"Yes, sir!" said Shawna. "No problem, sir!"

Her heart was still pounding, and she felt the tears welling up. But she held her ground and tried to look as military as possible.

"Well, let me shake your hands," said the general. "Then I'll go back and say hello to the rest of those folks."

General Larkin reached out to Shawna and grasped her hand firmly, clasping her wrist with his other hand. It was a very sincere handshake. Then he shook the hand of each of the three enlisted mechanics who stood with her. They were all smiles, and now the general was smiling too.

"Good luck," said the general as he walked away. "Put it on my tab."

"Yes, sir!" yelled Shawna.

It went on a tab, but it wasn't the general's. And Shawna would never forget the day the handshake of a general convinced her the Air Force was the greatest fighting force in the entire world.

Chapter 22

Arrow

The Navy side of Point Mugu wasn't a place that put Jay at ease. He wasn't in control here, merely a visitor. Even when he drove the quiet road to the Aero Club, he was nervous about being stopped by the military police. He felt like an imposter in a strange land. It was probably similar to the way Irene always said she felt when they traveled through a military gate, any military gate, other than at her own Air Guard Base.

Jay was counting on Point Mugu. Construction was already started on the new Air National Guard Base, a complex that would be connected to the main naval base via a taxiway leading to Mugu's longest runway. They even had their own street entrance. It was a military dream, almost come true – a new military base during a time of nationwide base closures. That made it even less likely to become a reality, but by now millions of dollars had been sunk into the new construction, so it seemed a sure thing. Not necessarily so.

Jay and some of his co-workers from Van Nuys had already moved to the Mugu area, trying to get a jump on escalating real estate values. But it made for a long commute to Van Nuys until the move was official.

Maybe jay would always feel like an outsider on the Navy side of the base, even after the Air Guard moved in. But today it was worth that minor tension. This would be his final flight in the Piper Arrow before being released for solo. It wasn't a difficult aircraft to handle, and its relative simplicity made Jay comfortable. But military flying clubs had their own high standards, and he needed one more flight prior to solo.

The ink on his instrument rating was still fresh, but Jay had already logged the minimum amount of time needed for his next license, commercial pilot. What would he do with that? All he really wanted was a way to get to where he was going in comfort. The Arrow was similar to the Piper Warrior he had learned to fly in, but it possessed a bit more speed with retractable landing gear and a constant-speed prop. It was a very stable airplane, and had a cockpit laid out almost exactly like the Warrior.

The Arrow would be the perfect cross-country machine that Jay wanted. This one had a complete flight director system, extraordinary for such a small airplane. The Mugu Aero Club was a quality military organization. Unlike many typical civilian flight schools, all of the navigation equipment worked.

As he pulled into the parking lot, Jay saw his flight instructor's car parked in the front row. Most of the instructors were Navy pilots, earning a few extra bucks for some simple flying. He noticed most of them flew the Arrow with a bit of disdain. For a Navy pilot, teaching an Air Force NCO how to fly was considered the lowest form of financial necessity. The fact that Jay was actually a baby-faced Air Guard chief master sergeant made matters even worse.

* * * * * *

The next week, he was finally alone in the cockpit, now signed off by his flight instructor for unlimited solo. Jay leveled the Arrow at ten thousand feet, pulled the prop control back to 2350 RPM, and reduced the fuel flow to slightly less than ten gallons per hour. Then he fine-tuned the exhaust gas temperature for peak performance. He made a complete scan of the engine gauges, reached down to his right side and swung the rudder trim knob two turns to the left to center the ball. He began to relax. With his limited flight time in Arrows, this airplane was a lot to handle in solo flight. But it was getting more comfortable every day.

Jay liked to fly high, above the summer convective turbulence, and just to make sure it remained smooth, he flew the coastal route. It wasn't that much further to San Francisco via Victor 27, and it was a lot prettier. When the San Joaquin Valley heated up to over 100, this cooler route with its coastal stability kept the turbulence under control.

The flight director and autopilot were engaged, and the airplane was in altitude-hold mode. Using the nav-coupled capability of the autopilot, the workload for a solo pilot was considerably reduced. Just keep ahead of the airplane and you were okay.

His destination today was Nut Tree Airport in Vacaville, his second flight to visit Shawna in a private airplane and his first solo cross-county in the Arrow. This airplane simplified a short-notice rendezvous. Airline access, Burbank to Oakland or San Francisco, was a hassle, especially at the north end of the route, and C-130 travel was pretty limited. In fact, if he needed to get to Shawna quickly, a private plane was the fastest method possible. On these longer summer days, he could depart after work and be at Shawna's apartment by sunset. And he could still be home the next morning in time for a fashionably late arrival to work.

Everyone at home was getting used to this, including Colonel Main and Irene. No one asked any questions, but everyone made their assumptions.

Shawna had been a bit secretive about wanting to see him today. She even sounded a bit desperate. Jay was glad to comply, and he got a nice flight in the Arrow as a side-benefit.

His guess was that Shawna was having recurring memory episodes, similar to the Hangar Two incident in Panama. She had mentioned it on his last visit, but she didn't seem very upset about it then. The Panama incident had come and gone, and that meant it had been over four years since her last upsetting nightmare.

Jay needed to call Irene as soon as he landed. He had been in such a rush to get away from the base that he hadn't told her he wouldn't be over to her house tonight. But Irene was used to his unusual schedule, and she wouldn't be upset. It was only an if-I-can date anyway. Unfortunately, Irene's legs were bothering her a lot lately. In that condition, he hated to leave her alone for too long.

* * * * * *

Irene Bennett knew she wouldn't find the energy to prepare dinner tonight. Jay would understand. Since he hadn't called yet today, it was possible he wasn't even coming to dinner. She chose to ignore his hard-to-guess-when visits, instead being thankful to have him when she did.

They had their own lives, and she cherished her privacy. The life she had chosen was increasingly secluded, but it suited her as a time of reflection. Irene had spent her whole life trying to please others, and now was her chance to please herself. This illness would pass, but for now she was enjoying the chance for some private time.

Not having to trudge to the office every day was a luxury. She could do almost everything she needed to accomplish by telephone. She had a separate business phone line, and Jay bought her a fax machine, a technology she had resisted at first. But the fax had become her savior. Most of her clients didn't even know she was working out of her home. When the business phone rang, she could answer it with the proper formality, and no one ever questioned where she was. And the fax kept communication with customers even more businesslike.

Most of all, this private time in her life gave her a chance for the one thing that had always been in her dreams. She was writing a book. Writing was her biggest joy in life, and she had twice started a manual of financial planning hints for the general public. That was her professional specialty, and it was what she wanted to write about.

She faithfully absorbed every self-help book about writing she could find, each of them reminding her to "write what you know." She knew financial planning, and she loved wheeling-and-dealing with clients on the subject. When Irene met someone for the first time, you could tell if she liked the person; if she didn't probe into their long-range financial plans, she was probably unimpressed. It gave her a feeling of contributing to the world. This was a subject she understood, and she enjoyed assisting others and watching them meet their financial goals, maybe even more so than her own dreams.

But her latest attempt at writing wasn't about financial planning. In fact, it was a novel; a romance story set in the early 1900s. Write what you know – Irene was certainly not successful in romance, but she was having a lot of fun with this manuscript. She hadn't given up on her financial planning book, but no publisher seemed interested in rushing it to press. So in the meantime, she wrote about what she really didn't know – a lasting relationship between a man and a woman.

Throughout it all, each day, she awoke to pain. Irene could push it aside, turn on the fax machine and the Apple IIe computer Jay had bought for her, and crank up WordStar. She had all day to attend to her loves; her garden, her financial customers, and her romance writing.

So if Jay didn't make it to dinner tonight, it wasn't of particular concern. He had said he wasn't sure he would be able to make it. Besides, Irene certainly wasn't in the mood to cook or, even less, drive to a restaurant. A bowl of canned soup here at the table in the kitchen nook was just fine.

Jay wouldn't simply forget their planned date. If something came up, even if it was late, he would call and apologize for his absence, for he loved her in many important ways. For the moment, there was no pain sitting here, and she could spend the evening by herself, with a cup of tea doing what she loved most – writing.

Chapter 23

Daymare

As Shawna awaited Jay's arrival, she was definitely excited. She could hear the airplane whistling on downwind, the distinctive sound of airflow whistling through the landing gear. It was impossible to sneak up on anyone with an Arrow. When Jay had taken her for a ride during her last visit to Southern California, she could hear the whistle from inside the cockpit after the throttle was reduced for landing. Today that noise excited her as it passed nearly directly over the parking lot at Nut Tree Airport. The Arrow swung around to the left and entered downwind for Runway Two-Zero.

* * * * * *

When Jay stepped out of the airplane, Shawna was waiting for him on the parking ramp.

"Air service. I love it," said Shawna.

"My little RSP," said Jay.

He often called her that when he knew she was in a loving mood. The term "recreational sex partner" started as a joke. Shawna first used the phrase when she was trying to describe her frustration with their relationship. RSP was a term that attempted to hide the seriousness of what they felt for each other, and it helped keep things on a simple note. This wasn't a simple relationship.

"How was the flight?"

"Nice," replied Jay. "Unfortunately, no clouds, but nice anyway. I could have used some real-weather practice on the instruments."

As Jay tied down the Arrow, now a few minutes after sunset, the airport's rotating beacon swung past them in quick arcs. Orange sky blazed to the northwest. Jay retrieved his only bag, his brown leather daypack, from the airplane, and they started towards the small terminal building.

"I need to make a phone call first," said Jay.

"Of course," replied Shawna.

She was used to this.

"Then how about some dinner?" asked Jay. "Want to go to Branigan's?"

"Can we pick something up on the way home instead?" asked Shawna. "I don't want to waste our time, because I know it's limited. I want to talk in private."

"Private it is. My little RSP deserves private."

* * * * * *

They cuddled in the corner of the L-shaped sofa. The radio was playing softly in the background, tuned to a classical station. This was an ideal environment for love, but first things first. Jay's visit tonight was Shawna's attempt to discuss fear.

"It never happens when you're asleep?" asked Jay.

"No. It's different this time," said Shawna. "I can feel it coming on, and it's a slow process. But I know it's a memory as soon as it begins. And it's always during the daytime."

Shawna squirmed in Jay's arms, repositioning her thighs to straddle his left leg.

"How does it begin?" asked Jay.

"Usually, I can feel it coming on as a gentle flood throughout my body, similar to a tranquilizer. I know it's there, but I can't find any way to resist the flow of the memory, even though I know it's coming and won't be pleasant. It's a soft, relaxing feeling at first, followed by a stream of nightmarish memories of the future, a few years from now, I think."

"How do you know it's that far away?" asked Jay.

"I'm not certain," replied Shawna. "But there are airplanes involved, and I recognize all but one of them. There's a stealth fighter too. That's the one I've never seen before, but it's a lot like the drawings that have been in *Aviation Week* lately. The aircraft has pyramid-shaped fuselage panels like nothing I've ever seen. You know, the F-19 that's suppos-edly already flying."

"I'm sure it's flying, maybe even operational," said Jay. "It's in your dream?"

"Yes, but it's always during the daytime, not when I'm asleep. In my memory, an Air Force pilot gets killed in a terrible accident. Wreckage is scattered everywhere, and the fire keeps burning and burning. It's right along a river, and rescue workers are battling the flames to no avail for hours on end. There are gases given off by the blaze, or some-thing that makes the burning debris worse than normal."

"The Russians might be interested in you," joked Jay. "Or *Aviation Week*."

Shawna laughed and continued to describe the details.

"There's a blue Air Force pickup truck, and the side-door registra-tion number indicates it's a 1986. There's also a television news story about the Stealth Fighter, publicly unveiling its existence. The news has other stories too, unrelated to the accident. They make me think it's 1988 or 89.

"What seems to set off this flood of details?" asked Jay.

"Like before, sometimes it occurs when I get close to a powerful electrical source. Yesterday, it happened when I stepped near a C-5 that had just arrived. The crew chief was hooking up the power cart. I heard the cart surge as he switched to external power, and I immedi-ately felt the memory sequence beginning to build."

"But never at night?" asked Jay.

"Thank God, no."

Shawna cuddled up closer to Jay, clawing at his body, craving to be a part of him. She was done with her story and needed his thoughts. But it could wait until after they made love.

"We're gonna' figure this out," said Jay.

Shawna snuggled against him – clutching, demanding. But be-yond the sensual desires she felt this moment, there was an even more important reason to be thankful for Jay. He believed her.

Chapter 24

Reversibility

The next morning Jay was up before dawn, calling someone on the telephone. Shawna stayed in bed until he returned.

"I've got some ideas to run past you," he said.

"You're always full of ideas. But don't you have to get going?"

"I do. But those C-130s can wait a bit. I'll call Colonel Main as soon as the squadron wakes up. No problem for today."

"I need to be at work by eight o'clock," said Shawna.

"Well, let me tell you my ideas," said Jay.

He sat down on the edge of the bed and reached for Shawna's hand. He held it as he talked.

"If time is reversing for you, I think it's possible that it's a case of deterministic chaos, a sort of predictable randomness. Maybe it's caused by something involving a communication medium we don't understand."

"As in mental telepathy?" inquired Shawna.

"I suppose. But I was thinking more along the lines of something even more energetically powerful, something built by man or able to focus human communication."

"Built by man," repeated Shawna.

"Yes. The electrical sources that are needed for you to experience the memory seem to point in that direction."

"Big voltage means big technology," said Shawna.

"Precisely," replied Jay. "A voltage big enough to promote chaos in the scientific sense, with the possibility of a momentary reversal of the arrow of time."

"Back to the future!" kidded Shawna.

"Cause and effect could get reversed, but if it was more than momentary, you couldn't function in this world."

"Sometimes I wonder," said Shawna.

"Time is really a primitive quantity, not easily defined in physics," said Jay.

"Even for you, with your master's degree from UCLA?"

Shawna marveled at Jay's drive for more formal education. He had completed his degree and was still taking courses in more advanced aspects of physics and astronomy. Yet he described his demanding class schedule as something he did for "fun."

"Physicists still struggle with time reversal," said Jay. "Not because it's far-out, but because it seems so natural. Yet, we never see that reversibility around us."

"Hey, physicist, maybe here's your first nut case," joked Shawna.

"Not a nut case, as far as I'm concerned," said Jay. "The speed of light is the limiting factor for most things in physics, but now we're beginning to realize there are ways to keep that limit as part of our theories, without ignoring the flow of time."

"Faster than light communication?"

"Not just for communication," said Jay. "Maybe even for the transport of matter."

"But getting back to the chaos thing," said Shawna. "What's the deterministic part you're talking about? Do you mean somebody might be controlling this?"

"That's exactly what I mean," said Jay.

"So, who?" asked Shawna.

"Maybe somebody who needs a critical person, like you. If they need someone who questions things and is fond of organizational details, they've found the right girl."

"Another loving compliment," said Shawna. "Do they also need gruff?"

"Now don't get excited, my little RSP. I'm confident nobody on this world has such a process available, at least not yet."

Shawna reflected on that for a moment, and then she said what she knew Jay was thinking.

"So whose world are you talking about?"

* * * * * *

Senior Master Sergeant Ron Strickland swung his combat boots up onto his desk with a solid *Plop!*, right in front of where Shawna was sitting. She stared in disbelief. Part of her mind reflected back to Officer Training School where such an obvious disrespectful action by a senior NCO was never even contemplated. It was assumed that any sergeant capable of making it into the "top three" could be accepted as obedient of officers without question. And usually that was exactly the way it was. But accepting Sergeant Ron Strickland was an entirely different matter.

Strickland continued to chew on his trademark toothpick, shuttling the tiny twig from one side of his mouth to the other. It seemed obvious he was in a testy mood. He hadn't invited Shawna into his office to compliment her.

Where the fuck do you get off, Sarge. I'm the Transient Maintenance Officer. You work for me.

"Lieutenant, this won't look good at the stand-up briefing," said Strickland. "Now you and I know this isn't your fault, but the Chief of Maintenance will see it differently."

"He didn't even mention it today, Ron," said Shawna.

Put your feet up on your desk in front of me, and I'll kill you with kindness. Bet you hate it when I call you Ron.

"Well, wait 'til tomorrow."

The toothpick swung from left to right and back again. Strickland looked angry, but there seemed to be little here to get excited about.

"Our weekly departure statistics are the bottom line," said Shawna. "Colonel Clay might huff and puff a bit, but we're okay as long as there isn't a trend."

"Maybe so," said Strickland. "But if I were you, I'd be ready to cover my ass tomorrow when he sees two C-141 deviations on the report. And both for refueling delays."

"But we were maxed out on the night shift when they dropped in on us," said Shawna. "Besides, they were pretty much no-notice arrivals. Clay will take that into consideration."

Cover my ass? Sarge, you're just waiting for me to blow, aren't you?

Ron Strickland smiled at Shawna's remarks – that broad worldly smile that was another of his trademarks. And it always looked so fake. But he acted like he knew something Shawna didn't understand.

Maybe he did.

* * * * * *

"Captain, there's an F-16 coming in, engine-out," said the excited tech sergeant as soon as Shawna answered the hot-line in her office.

"Be right there!" said Shawna.

She didn't bother closing the filing cabinet where she had been hunting for the monthly logistics summary. Shawna grabbed her hat and headed immediately down the hallway towards the Transient Maintenance control room.

When she stepped into the room, the tech sergeant was on the telephone to Maintenance Control. He motioned for Shawna to pick up the extension.

"Captain Whitney is listening now, sir," said the tech sergeant.

"Shawna," said the deep male voice, "Major Teal here. It's an F-16 from the Fresno Air Guard, engine-out, and should land in just a couple of minutes. Can you see the fire trucks rolling?"

Looking out the double-bay window to the flightline, Shawna saw flashing lights everywhere.

"You bet, sir. They're headed out now. Is he completely dead-stick?"

"Don't know," replied the deep voice. "It could be just partial power, but he declared a 'May Day.' We don't have any more information yet."

"I'll be in my truck," said Shawna. "Call 'Tango Ten' if you need me."

* * * * * *

Shawna stopped her pickup near the fire trucks parked alongside the runway, waiting for the action. In the distance, there was a tiny dot on final for Runway 21 Right, plenty high and dropping fast. She didn't have a UHF radio in her truck, so she couldn't hear what was transpiring between the F-16 and Travis Command Post. She bet it was exciting.

As the aircraft grew in size, it seemed to be on an especially high but adequate approach for the runway.

Keep it high. Don't undershoot that runway. I bet an F-16 without an engine drops like a rock.

The F-16 touched down hard, smoke popping from the main landing gear tires. She heard the double-screech. It looked like a good landing, firm and near the approach threshold. The fire trucks rolled out, chasing the F-16 down the runway. Other emergency vehicles waited at other taxiways farther down the apron. Shawna picked up the microphone.

"Maintenance Control, Tango Ten."

"Go ahead Ten."

"The F-16 is down and looks fine. He's rolling out on Runway 21 Right."

"Thanks Tango Ten," said the deep voice. "Command Post says he has minimal engine power, but should be able to taxi. It was low oil pressure, but his throttle is responding now."

"Roger, Control," said Shawna. "Where would you like us to park him?"

"Echo-Three would be fine."

"Roger, Echo-Three."

On Shawna's right was the follow-me truck, and the driver in white coveralls nodded his head, indicating he had been listening to her on his radio and heard the parking assignment. The truck sped away, headed for Echo-Three. Shawna followed.

The buck sergeant jumped out of the follow-me at Echo-Three and slammed the door. The truck sped away again, rushing to meet the F-16 at the runway turnoff, to lead him to the parking spot.

Soon the sleek fighter was on the parallel taxiway and headed towards them, canopy already open. The low engine inlet scoop made the jet look like a formidable predator. The fire trucks fell into formation behind the F-16, lights still flashing but no sirens.

As the fighter pulled into its spot, everything looked normal. The follow-me vehicle pulled all the way through the parking spot and handed the aircraft off to the white-clad marshaller. The F-16 came forward the remaining few feet, nodded its nose with its brake application, and stopped. Immediately the engine of the fighter dropped to idle and then shut down.

The marshaller rolled a tall, scissor maintenance stand to the left side of the forward fuselage. It probably wouldn't be the kind of exit this pilot was used to at home, but it would get him down. The pilot was taking off his helmet, standing up in the cockpit, his blond hair matted in drenched sweat. He exited the aircraft rather quickly. Shawna had never handled an F-16 before, but this pilot sure seemed to be in a hurry.

As the pilot swung his leg over the side of the fuselage onto the awaiting maintenance stand, his flight suit displayed lieutenant colonel insignia. He bounced down the steps, the stand springing in resonance to his quick gait. Shawna was waiting for him when he reached the ramp. She popped a crisp salute that seemed to catch the pilot by surprise. The lieutenant colonel ignored it.

"Welcome to Travis, sir," said Shawna.

Now that must sound stupid. He has just lost his engine, made an emergency landing, and now a woman in white coveralls is trying to act like all is normal. Welcome to Travis?

"Can you get me to a telephone?" the pilot asked curtly.

"Sure, Colonel. Let's go."

She led him to her pickup truck as the marshaller watched. Pilots always gave the receiving maintenance NCO a debriefing, no matter how condensed. The marshaller looked concerned. He had inherited this aircraft on an air abort and didn't even know what was wrong with it.

"As fast as possible," said the pilot, loosening the straps of his g-suit as the truck continued across the ramp.

"Of course," said Shawna. "Hell of a day, huh?"

He looked across at her, loosening his stern face a bit and smiling. He pushed his shoulders back in the bench seat of the pickup truck and relaxed visibly.

"I need to call my airline," said the lieutenant colonel.

"Your airline?" said Shawna.

"United," replied the pilot. "I go out on a three-day trip in a few hours. I can't be late."

Oh, the Air National Guard. This guy has just lost his F-16 engine and aborted into an airfield he's probably never been to before. How often does a fighter pilot land an F-16 dead-stick? And now he's worried about his real job.

Shawna was smiling now.

"What about your airplane?" asked Shawna.

"Don't worry about it," said the pilot. "I'll call Fresno right after I talk to crew scheduling at United. They'll send some of our guys to take it off your hands."

"Yes, sir," said Shawna.

Take it off your hands?

This wasn't exactly how transient maintenance normally handled aircraft. It was up to her outfit to get the airplane operational, even change its engine, if necessary. Then again, this was the Air Guard.

* * * * * *

That afternoon, just as Shawna was walking to the parking lot to leave for the day, she noticed a blue Air Force pickup truck hauling a jet engine driving past. The truck was being escorted towards the aircraft ramp by a Security Police sedan.

The two vehicles pulled up to the ramp entry gate, and the guard waved them through. They were headed for the F-16 parked in Echo-Three. The fellow in the right seat of the pickup truck was dressed in a turquoise civilian T-shirt and was wearing a very large white cowboy hat. As they pulled through the gate, the cowboy waved his hat out the window in broad strokes, yelling something that was too far away to hear.

He had come to take the F-16 off their hands.

The next day, when Shawna returned to work, the F-16 was gone.

* * * * * *

Front Page
Los Angeles Times

Panama's Noriega Accused of Drug Charges and Murder

General Manuel Noriega, commander of the Panamanian Defense, has been accused of blatant and brutal murder of a vocal political opponent, Hugo Spadafora. General Noriega is considered the dictatorial power behind Panama's civilian figurehead president.

The U.S. State Department has provided evidence of Noriega's laundering of drug money and his sale of restricted American technology and information. Concerns regarding the imminent transfer of power in the Panama Canal Treaty make Noriega's recent actions of particular of concern to U.S. officials.

Under General Noriega, the size of the Panamanian army has significantly increased since the death of the prior Panamanian dictator, General Omar Torrijos, in an airplane crash. Noriega has closed all newspapers, radio, and television stations that oppose his wishes. The Panamanian military now runs the country's post offices and many other enterprises that were previously state-run. More ominous is Noriega's reported involvement in narcotics traffic in collusion with Colombian cartels.

* * * * *

Tech Sergeant Irene Bennett didn't like all of the personal attention. But it was traditional and not that big of a deal. Her going-away party at Aerial Port was meant as much for the rest of the squadron as for her. But usually it was "going-away" for a different reason, almost always retirement and occasionally for a transfer to another base. This afternoon she was being pushed out.

It was no one's fault. Irene's medical condition had deteriorated to the point where she couldn't make the weekend drills. She had tried, but her energy level expired before the day's work ended. Her squadron commander had tried to help, reassigning her to a desk job, but that only made it worse. She still couldn't make it through those weekends, and the importance of it all seemed further obscured by sitting behind a desk.

So she had given in to her doctor's request. She was separating from the Air National Guard after fourteen years of service, missing the minimum retirement requirement by six years. The retirement pay and benefits weren't that important. Jay had his own retirement guaranteed, having just passed his twentieth year of service. And regardless of all that she knew was true about Jay, Irene also knew he would never leave her behind financially. It was a quiet comfort in a moment like this.

The guests were there mostly for the camaraderie and the beer. A silver keg was excuse enough for an early finish to the workday, and they enjoyed the chance to wind down. Most of her Air Guard friends were right here in this hangar. Jay had arranged to have the party in the C-130 aircraft inspection dock, with plenty of room for both the airplane and a party. The hangar doors were closed snuggly around the tail of the aircraft because of today's rain and wind, and imparted an echoing loudness to the party. No one was very rowdy, but everything reverberated in this metal and concrete enclosure. The overhead mercury vapor lights cast an orange glow on her small group of friends.

The C-130 as a party decoration was a nice touch. She silently thanked Jay and her own squadron for a party she really hadn't wanted.

"Enjoy your free weekends, Irene," said Colonel Tobia, Jay's boss.

The colonel was a weekender too. But like Irene, he was an involved guy who often showed up mid-week to assure things were on track in his area. Irene didn't know him well, but what she knew, she liked.

"I will." said Irene.

She lied, but this party was really not for her anyway.

"I'll try to keep Jay under control," said the colonel. "Of course, nobody really can do that."

"Don't I know," kidded Irene.

She didn't want to control Jay anyway. Nor did she want him to control her. There was a quiet peace to their relationship, which is what she wanted the most right now. There had never been a high level passion that supposedly existed in some relationships. But that had never had been what she needed from Jay. In many ways, he was the perfect partner. And Irene possessed a quiet understanding of those things in Jay's life she didn't want to question.

"Jay and I are going up to Travis together next week," said Colonel Tobia. "I've got to take two days off from school to make the trip, but it should be fun."

Jay hadn't told her about the trip. No big deal, but it seemed like he was making trips to Travis a lot lately. She might ask politely tonight, but she really was afraid to ask too much.

Colonel Brian Tobia didn't need to make light talk with Irene, but he was a sincere fellow. It was obvious he was here to celebrate the departure of someone very important to his line chief. Irene tried to return the favor by keeping the conversation going.

"Join the Air Guard and see California," said Irene. "Travis is too busy a place for me, Brian."

Once in awhile she liked calling officers by their first name. It reminded her this was the Air Guard.

"Never been there," said Tobia. "Jay goes there a lot, so I'll depend on him. It's a Joint Chiefs of Staff planning conference for our Fiscal Year 86 missions."

"Total Force, don't you love it?" said Irene sarcastically.

"Well, I've led a pretty sheltered life as a weekender. But Jay is going to let me represent us at the conference. He says he's got other business while I'm doing the negotiating with the regulars."

"Oh," said Irene.

She meant it. There was information here she didn't need nor want. So she tried to change direction.

"Don't forget who works for who, Brian," said Irene.

"Sure, I won't forget. Weekenders work for the full-time air technicians, no matter what rank. Right?"

"Don't ever give in!" said Irene.

Brian had things pretty well figured out, and he worked comfortably within those bounds. He was good for Jay, knowledgeable yet not demanding. Jay and Brian made a good team; full-time sergeant and part-time officer.

"I don't get out on trips very often," said Brian. "So a flight all the way to San Francisco is quite a treat."

"On a Herk?" kidded Irene.

"Beats having to find a parking space at Burbank and waiting in line for an airline flight."

"True," noted Irene. "

"Would you believe I've been out-of-state only twice before on a C-130?"

"Join the Guard and see Southern California."

"That Panama trip with Jay was great, so I guess I do leave the shelter of Van Nuys once in awhile."

"It's really a small world," said Irene. "Even if you expand aviation to the entire Air Force, it's still tiny."

"True," said Brian. "The maintenance control officer we worked with at Howard during Volant Oak is at Travis now. One of the supply officers, too."

Irene fluttered inside. It wasn't the kind of flutter she enjoyed. In fact, she avoided it at all costs, but now it had happened. Jay had spoken of Shawna a few times, and she knew there was a relationship that was more than cordial.

"See, I told you it's a small world," said Irene.

* * * * * *

Shawna stepped into the kitchen to retrieve her cup of still-hot cocoa. She had left it on the counter a few minutes ago while answering the telephone. She should have let the phone ring; it was just another solicitor, a newspaper saleswoman this time.

As she reached for the cup, she reached too fast and too far. The cup, perched on the edge of the counter, fell directly to its doom, smashing onto the floor and spilling cocoa everywhere. It spattered against the dishwasher and under the refrigerator. Some mess.

And so her otherwise routine evening was interrupted by an unwanted phone call, a mess on the kitchen floor, and no more hot cocoa. To make matters worse, now she had to mop up the aftermath. It was best to be prompt before the gooey liquid spread any farther or started to dry.

When Shawna returned from the storage closet with the mop, she hesitated for a moment at the kitchen door. The floor was no longer wet. On the counter, the broken cup was reassembled into its original maroon order, and steam was still coming off the cocoa.

This wasn't a reason to question her sanity, nor was it a minor miracle. It was simply a momentary reversal of time. And Shawna knew it.

The Lady

She sits on her haunches,
Lifeless and quiet.
This lady is growing older,
And her wrinkles show.

Twenty-three years old and aging,
With cracks in her legs.
Ten thousand hours behind her,
But she has lots of life remaining.

She sports a new radome nose,
But most of her is old.
This is her second set of wings,
And her nineteenth engine.

The lady's man is the crew chief,
His name painted on her brow.
But there have been other men before,
And still more tomorrow.

An ugly beast to some,
There is a gentle grace in her stance,
To those who understand.
Over one hundred thousand pounds of beauty.

What noise she can make,
What sights she has seen.
She sits in the cold evening air,
Waiting for her man.

Our Year 1986: Distant Planet

1 Year Later

Space is not nothingness. Violent events cause space-time to vibrate.

Marcia Bartusiak (1999)

Chapter 25

Power

Where would the energy come from? Even if the signal connected properly, what would provide the power for the subsequent data transmission? The Minds had calculated it would take more energy than was currently available on this planet. But their job was to make the initial contact and establish the foundation for the data transfer. It wasn't their job to question the source of power. That was left to the Force. Reportedly, that work was being done in the astronomical realm. But there were still no hints of success.

In the meantime, a timeline had to be established. The Guides were pushing for the establishment of a schedule that was as immediate as possible. But that didn't take into consideration the progress of the Minds or the energy search by the Force. The Minds weren't even sure the current receptor was an intelligent being. And the Force lacked the necessary transmission power. The Minds weren't talking to the Force, and the Force was being paid little attention by the Guides.

But now, regardless of all the problems, they were all committed.

1986: Earth

There is no nature apart from transition, and there is no transition apart from temporal duration. This is why an instant of time, conceived as a primary simple fact, is nonsense.

Alfred North Whitehead (1938)

C-130E Hercules

Chapter 26

Fraternization

Senior Master Sergeant Ron Strickland sat on the squadron commander's brown naugahyde sofa, moving the toothpick from one side of his lips to other with his tongue. After all, the colonel had said to be at ease. It was more an act of defiance than anything else. He was a senior NCO on the fast track, with an amazing record of accomplishment.

The colonel sat behind his desk reading the report. It was only two pages, stapled at the corner. As he turned to the second page, he glanced at Sergeant Strickland, and then went back to his reading. When he was done with the report, the colonel flipped back to the first page and studied it briefly before he spoke.

"Ron, you really want this to go on record?" asked the colonel.

"Yes, sir."

Ron Strickland refused to say anything more until prompted.

"This is a serious charge," said the colonel.

"Yes, sir, it is."

"And it could get Captain Whitney into a lot of hot water," stated the colonel.

"I know that, sir."

"And she's your boss," said the colonel.

"No boss of mine," said the sergeant.

* * * * * *

Shawna had built her own empire in Transient Maintenance. Within the Field Maintenance Squadron, her section performed duties far removed from the rest of the other shops. The gas-and-go orientation of Transient Maintenance was a lot different from the typical FMS mechanics assigned to a shop where most of the work was on the bench. In a typical workday, most of the squadron's mechanics never left the shop. A flightline dispatch workorder was considered a nice change of pace.

Shawna's mechanics, on the other hand, were flightline APGs, airplane general mechanics. That specialty code was more of a non-specialty designator than anything else. This was the world of crew chiefs, quick-service teams, and follow-me trucks. Thus, Shawna's Transient Maintenance operation shared a strong similarity to the Organizational Maintenance Squadron, the caretakers of the wing-assigned aircraft. The on-going battle between OMS and FMS put her right in the middle.

She had done a commendable job. Her daily routine ranged from being on-the-carpet for delayed departures to getting the glory at the Chief of Maintenance's afternoon briefing. If all was going well on a particular day, it was best to enjoy it, for tomorrow could be a disaster.

This was the pace Shawna loved. She liked the "generalist" approach to aircraft maintenance and her direct involvement in the airlift mission. The job suited her well, and the squadron commander usually let her perform that job without serious intervention.

Now all had changed. In a moment, she had gone from the golden girl to the squadron's albatross. Her own number one man, Ron Strickland, had taken care of that.

Everyone knew about Shawna's transgression, and many sympathized with it. Fraternization within the regular Air Force was a quietly ignored policy. All were taught in their basic training, both in the enlisted and officer ranks, that the division of labor between workers and management was to be adhered to under all circumstances. The whole concept of military discipline revolved around that premise.

Even more important was the border involving love affairs. Men and women from enlisted and officer ranks weren't supposed to interact on a personal basis except in the most formal of military situations. It was totally unacceptable for the word "relationship" to enter that formula. By regulation.

But the reality of the situation was somewhat different. Fraternization occurred all the time, and it was generally considered harmless. Except of course when someone challenged the system. Or someone complained. Prudence was considered the byword for the interaction of men and women who crossed the boundary between the enlisted and officer ranks.

Senior Master Sergeant Ron Strickland had taken care of any prudence exercised by Jay and Shawna. And Jay's lack of seriousness toward the concept of fraternization and toward the regular Air Force's administrative policies had been their shortfall. The Air Guard put common sense first in such transgressions, whereas the real Air Force placed regulations at the top of the list. Shawna straddled that fine line, and paid the price.

* * * * *

"**Y**es, sir, I did," said Shawna.

The colonel looked like he didn't want to be in this position, but he had no choice. Shawna was sure it wasn't his desire to have her sit in this straight-back chair facing his desk, while he reclined in his cushy upholstered office chair. But she knew he had no choice in the matter. It was procedural.

"And did you meet with Chief Master Sergeant Rotella in civilian social situations, knowing the position of the United States Air Force regarding fraternization between officers and enlisted personnel?"

It sounded like the colonel had carefully rehearsed these words. There was undoubtedly an Air Force manual that specified the exact wording that must be used.

"Yes, sir, I did," said Shawna.

"Captain Whitney, I want to say something off the record."

The colonel looked frustrated.

"Yes, sir."

"This has nothing to do with the fine job you have done with Transient Maintenance. You know that, don't you?"

"Yes, sir," said Shawna. "And thank you."

The colonel wheeled his soft chair farther forward into his formal desk position.

"Captain Whitney, I need to ask you some personal questions regarding your relationship with Sergeant Rotella," said the squadron commander.

She felt uncomfortable, as she had since the colonel had closed the door to this room a few minutes ago. But she couldn't resist the temptation.

"Do you want to know if I fucked him?" asked Shawna with a perfectly serious expression.

The colonel raised his eyebrows in an unexpected gesture of light-heartedness. While frozen in that position, he began to smile.

"Well, Captain, the Air Force needs to know. I don't."

"Well, I'll tell you so we can get this over," said Shawna. "I did. Was that so wrong?"

The colonel paused and put both of his forearms solidly on the desk in front of him.

"In the eyes of the Air Force, yes," said the colonel.

There was nothing more to lose.

"Sir, what would have happened if this had been brought to your attention by an NCO other than Sergeant Strickland."

"It wouldn't have made any difference," said the colonel.

"But Sergeant Strickland has a lot of weight around here, doesn't he?"

"He's one of our most senior NCOs," replied the colonel.

She wouldn't let it die.

"But he worked for me," said Shawna. "Don't you think it was a bit out of line for him to bring it directly to your attention, bypassing me completely?"

"It was within his rights," said the colonel. "And this Air Force goes by the rules."

* * * * * *

When the administrative action was taken, Captain Shawna Whitney could have resigned her commission as an Air Force officer and exited the Air Force with a general discharge. She would have been "relieved of her command" and allowed to walk out into civilian life with barely a blemish on her otherwise fine record. Although such an exit would be a significant step down from a general discharge, it would be appreciably less crippling than a dishonorable discharge. Still, it certainly wouldn't help her find a job in civilian life.

The Article 31 action that she accepted instead was equivalent to a letter of reprimand in the file of a civilian employee. But administratively, a lot worse.

Shawna was to be reassigned, and it was no coincidence that her choices in the matter excluded installations within easy commute of Southern California. Dover Air Force Base in Delaware seemed a possible compromise, for both the Air Force and Captain Shawna Whitney. In her new assignment, the Article 31 would be removed from the eyes of her peers and those whom she supervised. To her superiors, it would be available as open knowledge.

As Shawna awaited the final decision on her base relocation, she was locally reassigned to the Aerospace Ground Equipment Branch. Generally, assignments to AGE were reserved for butter-bar second lieutenants. Shawna had skipped that step in her career. Now she would have a chance to see how the real Air Force handled the concept of documented fraternization.

* * * * * *

Jay Rotella sat on the yellow sofa in the Chief of Maintenance's office. Colonel Ted Main sat behind his desk in his high-back office chair, burnt-orange in color and a bit out of place in a military office.

"Jay, what in hell were you thinking?"

"I was thinking I liked her, sir," said Jay. The "sir" came out a little weak.

"You liked her, did you?" said Colonel Main. "Did you think about the trouble that could cause her because you're an NCO?"

"Briefly, sir," said Jay, a bit more sincere.

"Briefly? Shit, Jay, this is serious stuff for the real Air Force."

"We're the Air Force, too, sir." Said Jay.

"You're right about that," said the colonel. "I could have the book thrown at you."

"I know that." There was no "sir" this time.

"Jay, listen to me," said Colonel Main. "This has nothing to do with your professional competence, either hers or yours."

"Yes, sir, I know that," said Jay.

"But you've gotten this woman in trouble, primarily because you refused to recognize the regular Air Force has some rules you just can't monkey with."

"Yes, sir," said Jay. "I recognize that now. But I really like her."

"So you like her," said the colonel. "That's just great."

The colonel propped his right elbow on his desk and leaned his jaw on his knuckles. He paused before he spoke.

"I want you to use extreme care in this matter."

"What's that mean?" asked Jay.

"Damn, Jay. How about just pulling back from this, at least for now. The Air Force has got to do what they've got to do, and you could make it a lot worse, for her as well as for yourself."

"Yes, sir," said Jay. "I understand, but I bet you could do something to help."

"And what might that be?" asked the colonel. "You expect the regular Air Force to listen to the Guard in a case like this?"

"Well, maybe you could talk to the Chief of Maintenance at Travis," said Jay. "I bet he has a big influence on her reassignment. She really wants Dover."

Colonel Main pushed himself back from his desk. The meeting was clearly over.

"Okay, Jay, I'll do that. But no promises. In the meantime, just be glad there isn't any impact on your personnel file, at least so far."

"I'm grateful for that, sir."

Jay said it with obvious sincerity. The colonel nodded in understanding, and then motioned with a wave of his hand and the simple words: "Outta' here."

Jay got up from the yellow sofa. Instead of walking to the office door, he walked around the desk, extended his hand, and looked the colonel directly in the eye. He held out his hand, and the colonel grasped it firmly.

"I'm sorry I've caused this trouble for you," said Jay.

"No problem, Jay," said the colonel. "Just cool it for awhile, please."

"Of course, sir. I will."

* * * * * *

"That bastard!" said Melissa Henesie. "I'm glad you called, Shawna. "But I don't like what I'm hearing."

Shawna scrunched her neck to the left, cradling the telephone against her shoulder. Both hands were still on the telephone directory, aimlessly pondering the map of area codes. She hadn't talked to Melissa in months, but this required talking to someone. Not Jay. A woman's view was better now.

"I never really knew Strickland that well," said Shawna. "He was always a bit threatening, particularly when he smiled at me with that condescending look of his."

"Sounds like a real asshole," replied Melissa.

"By-the-book, sometimes too much so," said Shawna.

"And Jay?" asked Melissa.

"Oh, I haven't talked to him since my meeting with the colonel. I'm a bit wired right now, so I need to cool off."

"A bit wired?" Melissa's voice was up an octave now. "I'd be infuriated – outraged!"

"I guess I am."

"Well you should be. Can't you fight it?"

"Not worth the effort. And certainly not worth the attention it would get. I'd rather let it die, Mel."

Melissa gave the words a chance to settle. She cared about Shawna, and Shawna could feel it in the silence. It was finally Shawna who broke the stillness.

"It's not that bad, but I wanted to talk to you."

"Sure. I'm glad you called. It'll pass, just like all things do."

"Some things pass easier than others," said Shawna. "But I'm glad I found you. How's the new assignment?"

"Great!" said Melissa. "It's my first slot as a public relations officer. A dream come true."

"But Illinois is a long ways away. I miss you."

"I'm right here when you need me, Shawna. Come visit soon, or I'll come find you."

"I'm not sure where to tell you to look," replied Shawna. "But my guess is it will be a long way from California."

"And a long way from Jay," said Melissa.

"That's exactly the point."

"Some point," said Melissa. "That's what we need around here. More assholes like Strickland."

Chapter 27

F-19

In the dark, early-morning hours of July 11, 1986, Major Ross Mulhare, possessing only 54 hours in the Air Force's new stealth fighter, contacted Los Angeles Air Route Traffic Control Center and requested permission for his aircraft, radio call sign "Ariel 31," to descend to 17,000 feet. When the request was granted, Major Mulhare pushed the nose down an almost imperceptible amount, immediately changing the airplane's attitude just enough for a swift descent. As he passed through 18,000 feet, he cancelled his instrument flight plan.

The night sky over the Tehachapi Mountains was clear, with a thin crescent moon. But Major Mulhare's aircraft continued to descend rapidly, disappearing from both military and civilian radar at 1:45 am.

The aircraft impacted fourteen miles northeast of Bakersfield, California, in a hilly area adjacent to the Kern River, with a nose-down attitude of approximately 60 degrees. Major Mulhare was killed instantly upon impact, and the wreckage was thrown over a large radius, starting a forest fire that burned for sixteen hours.

Firefighters and other rescue workers arrived at the scene prior to Air Force representatives. Soon after arrival of the military personnel, the civilian rescue workers all signed papers provided to them by these officials, swearing them to secrecy in the cause of national defense.

The crash of USAF tail number 81-792 resulted in the immediate establishment of a National Security Area for a five-mile radius from the crash site, from the surface to 8500 feet.

The next issue of *Aviation Week* reported some sketchy details of the accident. This prestigious aviation publication declared that an F-19 stealth fighter had been involved in a crash. However, an Air Force spokesman was quoted as saying the accident didn't involve an F-19. That statement was technically correct.

Newsweek erroneously reported the Air Force already had seventy-two F-19 stealth fighters operational and hidden from the public. That media report was in error.

On August 11, 1986, one month after the accident in the Kern River Valley, the cordoned-off area surrounding the site was released from military control. Civilian visitors afterwards found evidence of a severe aircraft crash. Scattered small pieces of wreckage still remained, but most of the area had been swept clean.

Chapter 28

Absence

Alaska was about eight hours flying time via C-130, and Jay didn't make the trip very often. There were a few official flights, since the Alaska Air Guard was a sister wing of the 146th TAW at Van Nuys. But the flight north was a long weekend jaunt.

Shawna's new duty station at Elmendorf Air Force Base in Alaska was far removed from Jay in California. Maybe this would resolve the problems with their relationship without requiring a lot of decision-making on Shawna's part, or Jay's. Shawna wished she had more of a choice in the matter.

Jay's interest in Shawna didn't seem to dwindle, but the distance was a persistent problem. There were opportunities to make the trip, but the two of them built in their own obstacles. Absence makes the heart grow fonder. It also makes the heart seek new solutions.

Shawna talked to Jay for hours on the telephone, but the distance between them led to increasing frustrations. Most of her concerns were intensified by the knowledge that this was a four-year controlled tour, and it had just begun. For reasons even she didn't understand, she discouraged Jay from coming north, at least for now.

Captain Shawna Whitney, Aerospace Ground Equipment Officer, was beginning to think she might retire from the Air Force as a captain. But hopefully in command of something other than AGE.

After arriving at Elmendorf in October, the days were already short, and the sun was going to disappear for the winter very soon. The shortening of the days and the cold forecast magnified her attitude, an attitude that approached depression.

Jay tried to provide her with hope. He discussed leaving Channel Islands Air National Guard Base to join the Alaska Air Guard's C-130 operation at Elmendorf, but that would be difficult. The line chief for the Alaska Air Guard wouldn't retire for at least five years, and Jay would have to take a flight chief position until then, and even the flight chief jobs were currently full. The only alternative would be for Jay to return to the inspection docks, more than a few steps backward. And all of this was keyed to the availability of both a civil service and military position becoming available simultaneously. The lack of a civilian position was the tough part, to say nothing of having to abandon good ol' 826 in California. Besides, both Shawna and Jay realized, there were sergeants like Strickland everywhere.

It seemed hopeless, an ending for a relationship that never was built on stability. They had lived with impermanence for five years, bolstering their tenuous affair by drawing eagerly on the moments they had together. Now those moments were nonexistent.

Shawna began turning her telephone off when she was at home. There was nothing critical in her life these days that demanded reacting to the ring of the phone. Besides, when it did ring and it wasn't Jay, she found her day ending with a good cry. Many of her days began that way as well.

* * * * * *

You weren't supposed to know when they were coming. But you did. At least you had a good idea, and Shawna knew the Operational Readiness Inspection was right around the corner, probably this week. Her maintenance squadron was going to show the ORI team a thing or two, including the efficiency of the Aerospace Ground Equipment Branch. AGE wasn't exactly the garden spot of the modern Air Force, but it was getting a lot of scrutiny on recent ORIs at other air bases.

Shawna's contacts at other bases provided good clues about what the inspectors were looking for. For the moment, equipment accountability was the big thing. So Shawna's personnel had been fine-tuning their equipment responsibility procedures for months.

It was a simple process. Maintenance Control couldn't keep track of all of the ground equipment, so that job was delegated to Shawna's shop. In preparation for the ORI, a new equipment locator board had been developed, and Shawna looked forward to showing it to the inspectors. But Shawna knew the rule of thumb – never offer anything to the inspectors, unless it was stupid-simple and guaranteed not to raise additional questions.

* * * * * *

"How's your equipment control," asked the lieutenant.

We feel it is excellent," said Shawna.

Was there any other answer?

"Well let's take a look," said the inspector.

Shawna led the lieutenant from her office to the other side of the hangar, a short walk. Along the way, Shawna pointed out some of the equipment repairs being conducted on a variety of power carts. All the important repairs had been completed soon after the inspection aircraft arrived, and before the inspectors set foot in the shop. Another valuable axiom – complete major repairs before the inspectors are looking over your shoulder. The only activities in-work now were minor repairs that stood the least chance of being controversial in the eyes of the inspectors.

They stepped into the spic-and-span control room, with its new equipment locator board. Circles and squares of various colors were attached to the magnetic board, grease-pen markings designating the type and identification number of their assigned ground equipment.

A staff sergeant called the room to attention, but Shawna gave the two enlisted men in the room an immediate "Carry on" before either could get to their feet. The lieutenant looked around for a few seconds and then headed directly to the equipment locator board.

"So is this up to date?" asked the lieutenant.

No, stupid, we keep it out-of-date just for laughs.

"Of course," replied Shawna. "We like to think we have a good handle on equipment location."

"Okay, what's that one?" asked the inspector, pointing to magnetic square in aircraft parking spot number 14.

Shawna didn't reply immediately, allowing the staff sergeant at the locator board to show his knowledge.

"That's a pneumatic start cart, sir," replied the staff sergeant. "Unit number 43, standing ready for a pressurization check of a C-141."

The young inspector jotted some notes in his spiral notebook and asked similar questions regarding the location of other equipment. After a few more minutes of note-taking and small talk, the inspector announced he would be back. Shawna knew where he was going.

* * * * * *

Shawna was in the base theater, along with nearly everyone else in the airlift wing. This had to be the low point in her Air Force career. Her assignment to AGE hadn't been pleasant from the start. The dispatch section was a particular problem, since it tended to accumulate those who didn't fit in elsewhere in maintenance. One of those assigned dregs was a twice-busted airman by the name of Freehold who was looking for a quick exit from the Air Force. If he kept it up, he would earn his wish.

When Freehold was first assigned to AGE, Shawna had assigned one of her NCOs to watch him like a hawk. Freehold's record during his previous assignment at McGuire Air Force Base had culminated in the complete destruction of a power cart he had been assigned to repair. The McGuire shop chief had noticed Freehold banging on the power cart's fuel tank with a hammer, an obviously inappropriate method for removing fuel tank straps. After a thorough chewing out by the sergeant, Freehold apparently felt his method was well within safety limits. As he told the shop chief, the power cart had been completely defueled, allowing little risk of explosion. The supervisor attempted to explain the danger of fuel vapors in a defueled tank, but there wasn't a lot of listening going on.

As the boss walked away, shaking his head, Freehold got the sergeant's attention: "Hey, Sarge. See, I told you so!" As the sergeant turned to face Freehold again, he observed the airman ignite his cigarette lighter and proceed to lower it to the filler neck of the fuel tank. The explosion shook the building, destroyed the power cart, and placed Freehold in the hospital for a full week.

Upon return to AGE, Freehold was reassigned to the dispatch function and taught how to drive a towing tractor, considered a less risky assignment than equipment repair. The AGE shop somehow managed to keep Freehold alive for the remaining two months of his assignment at McGuire.

Freehold, now assigned to Elmendorf under Shawna's supervision, worked the night shift where he would cause the least damage. At least that was the theory until one night when he attempted to deliver a power cart to a transient C-5. The aircraft was parked within a restricted area, with a one-person guard shack providing the controlled entry point. The security guard was huddled within the telephone booth-like structure, fighting the cold Alaska night.

It was later revealed that the guard was suspected of dozing off, probably not an unusual situation on an isolated Alaskan ramp during a dull winter's night. In any case, the guard was brought to attention rather suddenly by Freehold's approach, gunning the engine of his tow tractor as he wheeled up to the entry point. The exit from the adjacent ramp access road required a ninety-degree turn, and Freehold was never one to waste time. Nor was he one to abide by the sacred rule of AGE tow tractor operators to engage the locking pin to firmly secure equipment to the tractor.

At approximately 2:30 am on this frigid winter's night, the power cart came loose from the rear of Freehold's tow tractor and headed directly for the telephone-booth structure that housed the unsuspecting guard. The power cart was severely damaged, the guard shack completely demolished, and the security guard was hospitalized. Freehold got two weeks off.

Upon return to his AGE assignment, Article 31 disciplinary action pending, Freehold was reassigned to the day shift, where he could be supervised more closely. There was another key rule for the towing of equipment. Although AGE tractors could accommodate multiple tow bars on three side-by-side towing connections, the center position was most often used by itself. Occasionally, side-by-side towing of equipment was authorized on the outer hooks. However, with two pieces of rolling stock in-tow, it required care when entering a congested area.

On cold winter days, the hangar bays were cracked open to their minimum acceptable extent, to keep as much heat inside as possible. Thus, when Freehold arrived at the hangar with two power units in side-by-side tow (at his accustomed speed of travel), there was little doubt what would happen next. As he sped through the partially-open hangar doors, the extended width of the equipment behind him didn't allow for clearance of the opening.

One power unit impacted the hangar door, and because Freehold again hadn't connected the locking pins, both power units were launched in separate directions. Shawna's night shift supervisor heard the crash from his nearby office, as one power cart nearly decapitated a mechanic working under a MD-3 unit, and the other sailed into the dispatch office wall. Miraculously, no one was hurt. But the repercussions were endless.

And so, as Shawna sat in the base theater awaiting the arrival of the ORI inspectors and their final report, she wasn't at the peak of her career. The inspectors had easily uncovered Freehold's notorious record, and it had set a bad tone. But by comparison, Freehold's reputation was minor, compared to what the ORI team discovered regarding AGE equipment control.

The first piece of equipment the ORI inspector attempted to locate on the ramp wasn't in parking spot 14, as advertised. So there would be hell to pay for that infraction. Not only was pneumatic start cart number 43 not located in that parking location, there was no pneumatic cart at all. After that chilling report by the inspector, Shawna launched an immediate search for start cart number 43. Meanwhile, the ORI inspector quietly watched.

For nearly a full week, during the entire visit of the ORI team, Shawna's personnel scoured the base for unit number 43. Unfortunately, the inspectors themselves found the start cart on the fifth day of the search. It was sitting in a remote tarmac location – on jacks, with all four wheels removed.

After the ORI team departed the base, Security Police finally solved the case – they discovered the stolen wheels mounted on a personal utility trailer parked at the home of an AGE employee. The airman was later convicted in military court, but that wouldn't help Shawna one bit in the theater today. Nor would it improve Shawna's goals for promotion.

As the ORI team marched into the auditorium, Shawna was shivering in her boots. Her squadron might pass this ORI, but her AGE Branch certainly was going to make the spotlight.

Using a snazzy two-projector system, the first slide was the logo of the ORI team from Scott Air Force Base, Illinois. The second slide was a photo of a pneumatic start cart on jacks, without wheels.

Shawna sunk into her theater seat just as far as she could go. The pain was more excruciating than anything she remembered in her brief Air Force career, even the fraternization disciplinary action. As she slumped in her seat, she muttered a silent obscenity regarding where this all began. Her thoughts reverted to toothpick-sucking Senior Master Sergeant Ron Strickland.

Sunset on the Flight Deck

Behind the graying clouds, the red orb dips,
And skims quietly in gentle illumination.
A glance at my watch reveals nothing coherent,
As biological clocks float in purgatory.

"MacDill Airways, MacDill Airways, MAC 21811."
No answer, except for the crackle of the HF.
Three hours out from the Azores, headed home.
The sun is quickly forgotten as floodlights click on.

Movements are slow and relaxed, even for the navigator.
He slides his plotter forward, and it effortlessly stops,
Almost exactly on the course line through nowhere.
The Doppler computer counts down to a nonexistent point.

"MacDill Airways, MAC 21811," harks the futile call.
The navigator punches the Omega keyboard with determination.
"McGuire at zero one thirteen. Only six hours more."
There is silence in the darkness.

Our Year 1988: Distant Planet

2 Years Later

Our present picture of physical reality, particularly in relation to the nature of time, is due for a grand shake-up – even greater, perhaps, than that which has already been provided by present-day relativity and quantum mechanics.

Roger Penrose (1989)

Chapter 29

Life Spans

The decision regarding a specific date and time had to be made well in advance. Without a precise schedule, the Force wouldn't be able to orchestrate the energy required for the task. It would take an entire orbit of this star to accumulate the required energy, and then the power would be expended quickly.

The Minds were entrusted to set the date, but the Force set the limitations. It couldn't be accomplished until after their planet completed its orbit around the star at least ten more circuits. On a lifetime scale, it meant that many of the Minds who had conceived this experiment wouldn't live to see the results. But it had always been considered an experiment for future generations.

How long would the receptor on the watery planet continue to live? The being's life span was entirely conjecture. There was only so much the Minds could do. And if the receptor died before the Force mastered the energy needs, no data could be transmitted. The entire experiment would have to begin again, probably under the administration of new Guides. It wasn't expected that the experiment would be repeated a second time.

So the Minds set a date. It wasn't distant enough for the Force. It wasn'tt early enough for the Guides. And it was awaited with anticipation by every being on this planet.

1988: Earth

The distinction between past, present, and future is only an illusion, however persistent.

Albert Einstein (1955)

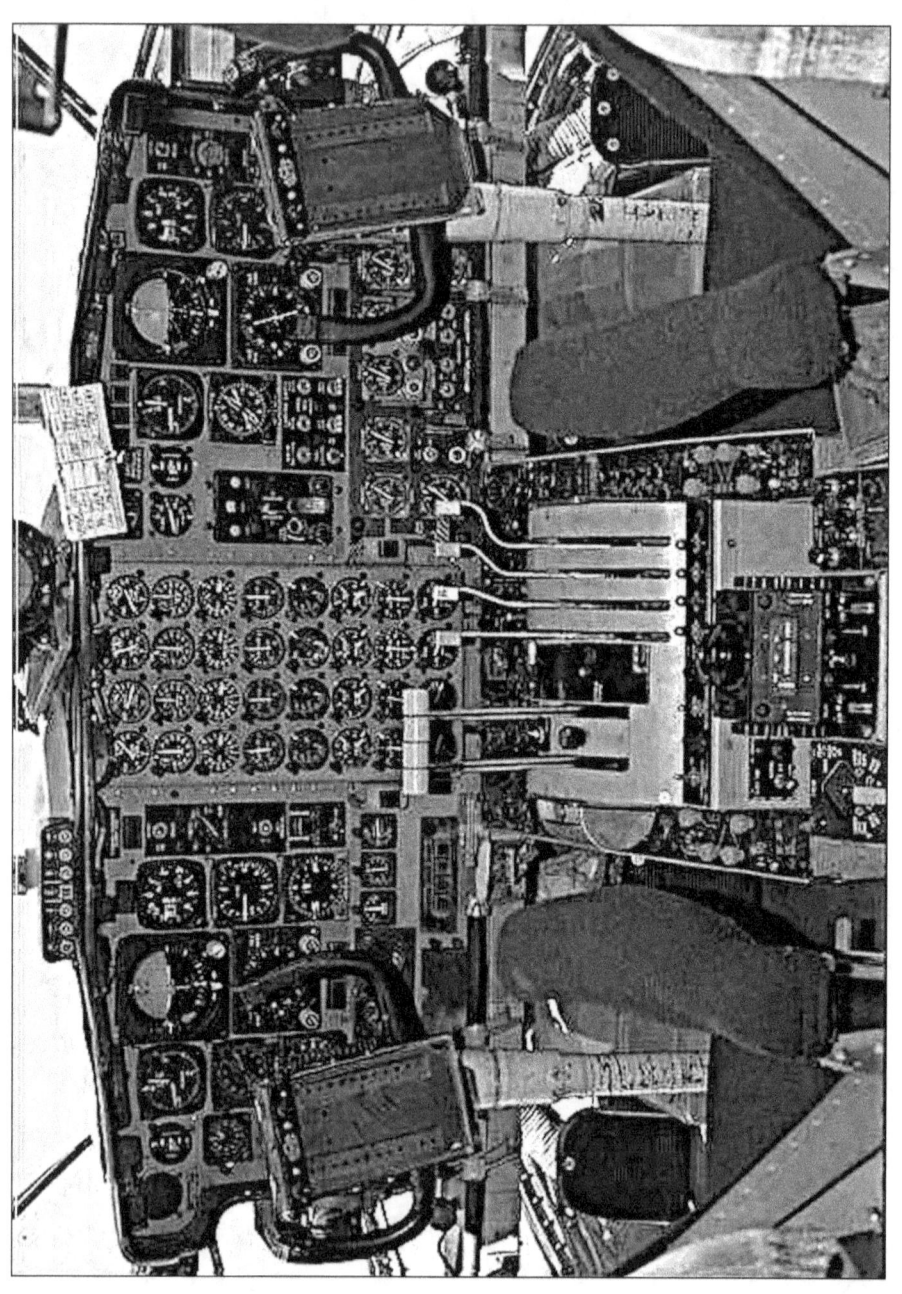

C-130 Cockpit

Chapter 30

Jackfrost

There was something wrong with this exercise. Everyone knew it, but the California Air National Guard was quick to accept orders from the Department of the Air Force. So did the cowboy aviators of Wyoming.

For two weeks, the C-130 sister wings at Channel Islands ANG Base and Cheyenne, Wyoming, would operate four aircraft each in a joint forces exercise at Elmendorf Air Force Base in Alaska. Exercise Jackfrost would be the military's attempt to determine the acclimation characteristics of C-130 aircraft and support personnel in a simulated war environment.

The results should have been obvious. It didn't take a lot of experimentation to realize aircraft and humans become acclimatized to their environments. Take an aircraft from California and watch the prop seals leak and internal parts scream in horror during the cold of winter. Similarly, take an aircraft flown primarily in cold climates, send it into the heat, and don't be surprised when it breaks.

An even more suspicious aspect of the Air Force's experiment was "Why Alaska?" There were far colder places in the United States than Alaska. The Minnesota Air Guard resided in one of these locations. But both the California and Wyoming units accepted the mission, as if they had a choice. January in Alaska was the plan.

Jay was quick to volunteer for the mission. His communication with Shawna had become increasingly rare in recent months. The moment the mission was announced, he was on the phone, but Shawna didn't sound at all excited. In fact, he perceived a sense of foreboding, as if his visit was doomed from the start. He told her: "Don't even think of telling me not to come." She didn't, but it sounded like she would have liked to.

* * * * * *

Elmendorf Air Force Base in January wasn't that cold. In fact, Jay ran into a tourist in downtown Anchorage who was "on holiday" from his blustery home in Edmonton, Canada. The Gulf of Alaska provides wet warmth (by comparison) to the Alaskan coast during the winter, while the interior of the state is chilled to some of the coldest temperatures on the continent. But if cold wasn't the enemy in January, darkness was.

Shawna had been reassigned from AGE to the Propulsion Branch. She was the low officer on a two-officer totem pole, working the graveyard shift, a remnant gift from her fraternization record. Jay thus volunteered for the Jackfrost night shift, leaving one of his flight chiefs to run the day operation. The Air Guard maintenance officer, a major, questioned this decision, particularly since Jay's expertise on the shift that typically launched aircraft would be missed. On the other hand, the major liked the idea of a chief master sergeant protecting the night shift.

So it was decided. Jay would work the same shift as Shawna, and be able to play with her during their time off. If, indeed, they played at all. When he arrived, Shawna failed to respond to his phone calls. He left repeated messages on her home answering machine, but she simply didn't reply.

The solution seemed simple, since Shawna had to answer her duty phone. But she refused to talk to him on that line, and firmly suggested he shouldn't come to her duty location. Jay certainly understood that request, since there were lots of other places to meet on the base.

To Jay, this seemed a significant change in her attitude. After the Article 31, Shawna accepted the reprimand as a temporary situation.

The administrative damage had already been done, and now it was over. Maybe she had found a new Sergeant Strickland to worry about. But that didn't explain her avoidance of Jay's phone calls.

Jay was both mystified and crushed. He entered the third day of Jackfrost determined not to violate the privacy Shawna was clearly requesting. But to toss away two full weeks together seemed unacceptable.

Besides his frustration regarding wasting precious time together, Jay faced his own personal challenges with January darkness near the Arctic Circle. He was depressed and professionally inefficient, two characteristics that were new to him. And far from pleasant.

* * * * * *

"**T**hanks for calling," said Jay.

"I know," said Shawna. "I'm sorry I've been this way. I didn't think you would understand my situation. I'm sorry."

"Try me," said Jay. "You might be surprised."

"Jay, my life is finally turning around. At least I hope it is. I've got a chance anyway."

"Good. I'm glad," said Jay. "I knew it would. You're a great maintenance officer, my favorite, and it'll all settle down."

"I hope so," said Shawna. "But your favorite maintenance officer still has some problems to solve."

"Well, I'm ready to see her, if she's ready," said Jay.

"I need to explain," said Shawna. "I can't see you at work, no matter what. It just has to be that way."

"I understand," said Jay.

He was feeling better already. If only they could get together and talk, everything would be fine again.

"How's Jackfrost?" she asked.

"Dark," replied Jay. "We're doing okay, but those Wyoming cowboys are making me mad. Before every flight, we have to hook our birds up to three or four ground heaters just to warm the props and keep the avionics black boxes under control. But our airplanes still puke every liquid they possess – hydraulic fluid, fuel, you name it. Our abort rate is atrocious."

"It doesn't look that bad," said Shawna. "I saw the week-to-date figures at our maintenance briefing today."

"But that's only because the Wyoming birds are flying fine," said Jay. "Those cowboys aggravate the hell out me. They don't even use heaters, and they mosey out to their aircraft and crank 'em up just like that."

"Not your fault," said Shawna.

"Still makes me mad."

"You haven't been calling on my shop for much of anything," said Shawna.

"Well, that isn't because we haven't had engine problems. You know the Guard. We're not going to cry uncle until the bailing wire runs out."

"I bet it's not as bad as you think," said Shawna.

"Right. It's worse. Of course, missing you hasn't helped."

"I'm sorry, Jay. I feel bad about not communicating with you lately. I was afraid you wouldn't understand, and I thought it might get better soon."

"The military's harassment of you might get easier? Don't count on it."

"No," said Shawna. "It's something else."

"What?"

"Well...," said Shawna.

She paused, and Jay gave her a chance to pick her words.

"I'm with this guy quite a bit these days."

"Oh," said Jay.

He was so surprised by this that he didn't know what to say. He wanted to make sure he said the right thing. Losing Shawna was like the end of the world. But he knew he could blow it right here.

"It's nothing serious," said Shawna. "But I'm grateful to him. He takes my mind off things."

"Things like me?" said Jay.

Those weren't the wrong words. They were worse.

"No, he doesn't take my mind off you. But there's a lot going on right now. Some of it isn't so good. I just have to concentrate on what's on my plate, and it's pretty full right now. I'd like to tell you more, but later."

"Okay," said Jay.

He did understand, sort of. She hadn't told him it was over. There was just this temporary tough period they both had to get through.

"Is it okay, Jay? I'm really sorry I didn't tell you before you came to Alaska."

"I bet you tried," said Jay. "Sometimes I just don't listen."

"And sometimes I just don't know what to say," said Shawna.

There was no rush now. Jay felt it was time to face things slowly and carefully. He was confident their relationship would persevere. At least he wanted Shawna to think he could be brave.

"Thanks for telling me," said Jay.

"Thanks for listening. I really didn't think you would understand. In fact, I don't understand myself."

"No problem," said Jay. "I'm going to work real hard at understanding. Give me a call when you can."

"Sure," said Shawna. "Keep 'em flying."

He tried to, but it wasn't easy.

Chapter 31

Total Force

The morning never really dawned. It just began. By the time the January sun finally rose above the horizon, it would be the middle of the day.

Jay was determined to improve his mood, so he was using his day-off to fly on an out-and-back to Fairbanks. The pre-dawn flight should get the adrenaline flowing. Flying in a C-130 never failed to rejuvenate his spirit.

As the aircraft climbed out of Anchorage and broke through the overcast, there was light after all. Once the clouds were below, the orange horizon glowed prominently to the southeast. In another few hours the sun itself would appear for its brief trot across the southern sky.

The flight was short, and soon they began the descent into Fairbanks. Mount McKinley thrust upward through the clouds off the left wingtip. The sky was sparkling clear, and getting even brighter as the still-unseen sun inched upward towards the horizon.

Jay had volunteered to serve as the only mechanic aboard, with the airplane's regular crew chief receiving an unexpected last-minute day off in the process. Jay was pleased to play mechanic today, although a chief master sergeant in the real Air Force would never be caught slinging chocks.

Fairbanks was crystal-clear, and extremely cold. But when they taxied in, Jay's view from the crew bunk on the flight deck revealed a civil service marshaller in a military olive drab parka that was completely unzipped. Underneath his parka was a gray sweatshirt, and Jay swore he saw the marshaller's naked belly button at the bottom of the shirt. Maybe it wasn't so cold after all. The man appeared to be a native Inuit, as did the two members of the loading crew who emerged from the flightline shack as the C-130 pulled into its parking spot.

Following orders from the aircraft commander, the loadmaster hadn't raised the cargo door nor lowered the rear ramp as they taxied in, although that was traditional for quick-turns. Losing their cargo compartment heat was to be delayed until the last minute. The flight deck was open to the airflow from the cargo bay, so a gaping hole back there would cool everyone.

Thus, the first door opened at this stop was the small crew entrance on the left forward side of the airplane, and it was Jay who undertook this simple task. He twisted the yellow locking lever, and the door immediately unlatched and swung down under its own weight to reveal a the civilian marshaller with his open parka, exposed belly button, and a broad smile. The cold that hit Jay was like nothing he had ever felt. It was bone-piercing, stunning cold.

"Aren't you cold, man?" asked Jay when he'd recovered his breath.

The unzipped civil service worker just smiled.

"We're having a warm spell today."

It may have been warm to him, but for Jay it was enough to snap his sinuses to attention. Warm spell, indeed.

* * * * * *

Total Force, 1980s style.

The Joint Chiefs of Staff were determined to fit a round peg in a square hole. Thus, the concept of "Total Force." The round peg was the U.S. Air Force. The square hole was the Army, Navy, Marines, and the Reserves of all the military services. Put them together and make them work for common goals. Sure!

Getting the Army to work with, rather than against, the Air Force was a lofty goal. Throwing the Reserves and Guard into the mix was just asking for trouble.

In later eras of international conflict, including Afghanistan and Iraq, the concept of Total Force finally came to fruition. Bodies actually worked together. But not in the 1980s.

Total Force. Total chaos.

The chaos began because the Army was late, and that was probably on purpose. The aircraft couldn't be loaded until the Army showed up, and maybe the Army was simply punishing the Air Force. The number of paratroops to be buckled into the red-strap cargo seats determined the amount of cargo-of-opportunity that could be carried. And the how many paratroops was still undetermined. Total Force. Total frustration.

Part of the frustration was because no one was talking to anybody else. The mission was scheduled to depart in twenty minutes. That left just enough time to get everybody loaded into the aircraft, with the cargo pallets still a big unknown. The baggage pallet sat on the ground near the rear of the aircraft with two four-by-fours underneath to allow a forklift to hoist it aboard. But that pallet couldn't load until the paratroops arrived. And it had to be the last pallet loaded.

The other equipment destined for King Salmon Airport included a Jeep and several pieces of rolling stock. None of this could go up the ramp until the number of troop seats was determined. Total Force. Total mess.

The mess didn't resolve itself. To make matters worse, it was still morning – cold and dark. In a matter of minutes, a thick layer of fog suddenly replaced the clear skies, and it wasn't the warm and friendly kind. Ice fog surrounded the C-130 to the extent that the light-all carts were creating near-zero visibility. Their powerful beams reflected off the tiny frozen water droplets to produce a complete whiteout.

From his position on the ramp behind the rear cargo door, Jay could barely see the Herk twenty feet away. This wasn't a good morning. The Army either didn't know what they were doing or they refused to share it with the Air Force. Total Force. Total headache.

The headache intensified when the brown Army bus finally appeared out of the fog. Only it's parking lights were illuminated, to prevent confusing reflections from getting worse. The paratroops began exiting the bus, a process that took way too long. This flight was going to be late. The Army captain at the bus door was yelling at his troops, and it didn't sound like yells of encouragement.

Aerial Port, the real Air Force's contribution to Jackfrost, was standing by to load the equipment, but they too had no idea what was going on. Regular Air Force, Army, Air National Guard. What a combination. Total Force. Total joke.

It was a cold joke, and Jay wished it was over. He'd been in this situation before, too many times. The Army wouldn't talk to the Air Force, and the Air Force wouldn't talk to the Air National Guard. And it was the Air National Guard that was supposed to be pulling this mission off. No one even knew how to load the airplane.

On this cold, dark morning, with ice fog, and Army troops, and forklifts, and whiteout, and yelling, Jay resolved to get this bird out of here. Be done with it, go back to bed, and wait for go-home day. Total Force. Total confusion.

When the C-130 finally pulled out of it's parking spot, Jay huddled on the cold aft ramp with the airplane's loadmaster. As the Herk rounded the corner, and pulled out onto the taxiway, Jay yelled over the noise: "I wonder if anybody has told the aircraft commander where he's going?"

"Total Force," said the loadmaster.

"Total disgust," replied Jay.

* * * * * *

Go-home day.

Jay had waited for this day more than on any previous military mission. Being so close to Shawna, but so far away, had proven nearly impossible. He hadn't called her after her only phone call to him. He kept waiting for her to call him again, but she didn't.

The four Wyoming C-130s were already gone. Now it was California's turn. As usual, Jay was on the last airplane out. This aircraft had most of his squadron's mechanics, a pickup truck, and the "war ready spares kit," a pallet of spare parts that was the life-blood of any deployment mission. More important, this aircraft carried the mission's supply of souvenir king crab. The crabs were freshly frozen and stored in rows of boxes on the aft ramp, the coolest spot in the cargo compartment. This C-130 had a special level of importance, since no one wanted to risk a delay in the delivery of crab to the families of the returning heroes.

If all sixteen engines would start, all four aircraft should be home in California soon after sunset. A refuel stop at McChord Air Force

Base near Seattle would be required, since C-130s typically didn't have the range for a nonstop flight to Southern California, unless the winds aloft were extremely favorable.

Cold. Dark. And more cold. This morning, it was snowing besides. But all sixteen engines responded, and the last plane out was finally "out."

Performing admirably in the cold dense air, the four C-130s climbed one behind the other, separated by only a few minutes. This would be an in-trail formation flight all the way to Seattle.

The Jackfrost mission had taken its toll on Jay. The night shift hours coupled with the nearly perpetual darkness of "daytime" and his remorse over Shawna had left him exhausted. As the last aircraft slipped out of the Elmendorf traffic pattern, Jay found himself nodding off. All of the other mechanics with him in the cargo compartment, twenty-four in all, seemed alert and excited. But for Jay, it was everything he could do to keep his eyes open. He didn't try very hard.

"Chief, wake up!" yelled someone. He had barely fallen asleep.

"What?" said Jay in a voice too low for anyone to hear.

"Chief, come take a look," yelled the hydraulic mechanic.

As Jay awakened, he could see several of his mechanics gathered on the opposite side of the cargo compartment, looking out the small oval windows. The deck angle was distinctly upward, so they were still climbing. He must have been asleep only a few minutes.

Through one of the cargo compartment windows, Jay saw the problem. Number one propeller was at attention, fully feathered.

As Jay regained his perspective, he peeked out the window closest to him and estimated they were at an altitude of about ten thousand feet, still climbing. Number one engine was shut down, and Jay knew the rules. So did everyone else. An engine failure during departure necessitated an immediate air abort, with a return to the nearest suitable airport, in this case Elmendorf. Jay had finally escaped the cold and dark only to be recaptured.

"They want to see you in the cockpit," said the hydraulic mechanic.

As the ranking maintenance man on board and the official troop commander, Jay climbed the steps to the flight deck and plugged his headset into the interphone system. The conversation he tuned into was calm and focused.

"Well, Bill, we're going to have to decide pretty soon," said the aircraft commander.

"Yes, sir," said the co-pilot. "You call it."

Jay looked around the cockpit. Everybody was busy except Terry, the aircraft commander, whose pilot seat was pushed back in its tracks, his feet up on the yellow foot rests.

"Okay, any inputs from anybody?" asked Terry.

"I wanna' go home!" cried the flight engineer.

"Withstanding that, any other thoughts?" asked the aircraft commander.

Silence. Jay surveyed the flight instruments. The co-pilot was hand-flying the airplane, with the flight director activated but the autopilot disengaged. The altimeter was winding upward through twenty-one thousand feet. He had probably been right; the engine shutdown had likely occurred at about ten thousand feet.

"Okay, we're going to need to decide real soon" said Terry. "Let's get ourselves level first."

They were leveling now at twenty-four thousand feet.

A voice crackled on the UHF radio.

"How you doing back there, slow poke?"

The transmission was from one of the aircraft in front of them. The remaining C-130s used that teasing radio call as their cue to harass the three-engine aircraft. Apparently, all of the other C-130s had already been advised of the situation.

"See you on the ground in Seattle, if we don't beat you home before you get out of Canada," said another taunting voice.

Jay looked out the co-pilot's front window and could see one of the C-130s, perhaps two miles ahead. Scanning farther, another C-130 was a tiny speck, barely visible on the horizon. It was already evident that their buddies were starting to pull ahead. The C-130 wasn't known as a particularly speedy aircraft, even slower with only three engines.

"Keep those crabs cold for us," chimed another voice on UHF.

The aircraft commander refused to acknowledge the teasing from the other aircraft. In this loose formation, he was wise enough to know it would end sooner if he just kept quiet.

Terry now spoke to everyone on the wounded airplane's interphone link: "Okay, let's buy this. The rules are clear. If an engine failure occurs during departure, including initial climb, we're required to divert to the first 'practical' military base with C-130 maintenance. If that's not feasible, we're supposed to go to the nearest civilian field that can handle a C-130."

No one corrected the aircraft commander. He continued.

"However, if the failure occurs in cruise, we can continue to our original destination. Now, the real question is whether we were in a climb or in cruise when the failure occurred," noted the aircraft commander.

"Looks like level flight to me," said the navigator.

"Me too," said the co-pilot.

"Hey pokey, how's it goin' back there," kidded someone on the UHF radio.

"Don't take any bird strikes from the rear," added another voice.

At that moment, probably everyone on interphone knew what the decision was going to be.

"Engineer?" asked the aircraft commander.

"Definitely cruise flight, sir."

"Troop commander?" said the aircraft commander.

"Sir," said Jay, "I've never seen a more beautiful demonstration of straight-and-level cruise flight."

* * * * * *

An hour after the engine shutdown, the flight engineer provided an unexpected report to the aircraft commander. After the shutdown, the engineer had been busy with the cross-feed of fuel to the remaining engines. If they were to continue their flight, he wanted to be sure to properly redistribute the fuel from the E-model's eight tanks to the remaining three engines. Due to the reduction of overall fuel flow with one engine out, he cheerfully reported their range had been extended just enough to make it all the way home – nonstop. Considering the lower power output, forecast winds aloft, and the required reserves, they should be able to make it all the way to Van Nuys. They would need to reevaluate their fuel consumption as they approached Seattle, but it looked like the McChord fuel stop could be eliminated. And that meant their engine repair could be delayed until they arrived home.

Four hours later, as the three-engine C-130 looked down on Mc-Chord Air Force Base from twenty-four thousand feet, three other C-130s could be seen huddled on the ramp far below. There's a constant truth about flying – no matter what the calculations indicate, a one-hour fuel stop always takes twice as long as expected.

"It's too bad, isn't it?" said the flight engineer to no one in particular. "Looks like we're going to beat those guys home."

The aircraft commander took his right thumb, placed it to his nose and waived a four-finger salute from flight level 240. Everyone else in the cockpit, in perfect military formation, immediately followed suit.

Chapter 32

Summer Roads

Summer in Alaska was a wonderful time of year. But for someone assigned to the graveyard shift and preferring to sleep in the dark, the long summer hours had drawbacks. Shawna went to work just before midnight, when the darkness of the night had barely begun. When she came off work at 8 am, the entire night had passed. That left her with about 15 hours to try to sleep, all of in it daylight.

But it did provide her with opportunities to crank up her trusty bicycle and tour the remote highways that adjoined her apartment complex. Not that remote, by Alaskan standards, but certainly scenic, relatively untraveled, and wonderfully flat. Usually she slept, often unsuccessfully, for the first few hours after she arrived home from work. She tried to stay in bed until at least 4 pm. Then she would take her bike for a workout before her late evening breakfast. Her world was a bit backwards, but it had its advantages.

* * * * * *

As Shawna made the broad turn, feet pumping at maximum speed in tenth gear, she was flying as fast as she dared. The generally flat road was banked slightly in this curve, and there was a gentle uphill slope as she came off the sharpest point of the turn. Her calves were working hard, and she raised herself off the seat to add a final burst of thrust.

She would be sweating hard for the next mile, but then it would be over. So she laid into the bike, shifting her weight forward over the handlebars.

It was actually beginning to get dark. The late evening overcast was speeding the twilight. Someone had swiped her bike's red rear plastic reflector, a fact she hadn't noticed until today. Riding without a headlight and no rear reflector was an unwise decision this time of night, but her apartment complex was now within easy reach. Her well-toned legs came down hard on the pedals, as she leaned forward just a bit farther for that final sprint.

In her helmet's miniature rearview mirror, she caught a glimpse of a pickup truck pulling a small travel trailer. It caught her a bit by surprise on this normally unoccupied highway. She didn't recognize the vehicle. Probably summer tourists, escapees from the Lower 48, taking advantage of the long Alaskan days. The truck's headlights were on, a good sign, indicating the driver was trying to keep his attention on safety in the twilight. Or maybe it was a Canadian truck that came equipped with running lights.

The image in Shawna's rearview mirror was growing fast. Maybe it was just her perception from this point in the uphill grade. No, this guy was moving fast, and she had better move over as far as possible. There was plenty of room to pass, as long as the truck moved across the yellow line just a little, and no one was approaching from the opposite direction.

Just in case, in an instant of routine decision-making, Shawna edged her handlebars ever so slightly to the right to straddle the shoulder of the road. There was a two-inch lip on this recently repaved stretch of highway, so Shawna was careful not to inch too far to the side. At this speed, she needed to be careful. Her tires were narrow.

The amount of handle bar movement needed to move a cruising bicycle three feet to the right at highway speed is exceptionally small, barely perceptible. The human brain and the body's cooperating nerves and muscles automatically make such judgments. But on this evening, Shawna judged wrong.

Just as the truck's roar behind her became an audible sound, the front tire of Shawna's bike moved closer to the lip of the highway than she intended. She caught the error immediately and tried to turn back to the left as the bike balanced on the edge of the pavement. For a moment, it seemed the correction might be enough. But it was too late.

The front wheel caught the road's edge at a glancing angle, fell off the pavement, and then wobbled uncontrollably. The bicycle started to tumble, and Shawna's forward weight sent her over the handlebars. She hit the pavement hard, felt the scraping pain across her left hip, and saw the roaring truck bearing down on her. That was the last she remembered.

* * * * * *

Shawna saw the medical technician's half-smiling face above her. She remembered immediately what had happened, and she was ecstatic. She wasn't dead. This uniformed fellow was a handsome blond-haired lad, and she was grateful to awaken to youth staring her in the face.

"Take it easy," he said.

His face was reassuring, with that hint of a smile.

"There's no hurry," he said. "Just lay here for a minute. You're fine. Don't move."

Shawna obeyed, but she wanted to speak. The wind was completely knocked out of her, and she couldn't manage a word. She tried very hard to relax her body, but she heard her heart thumping in her ears. She heard the voices around her and saw another uniformed man walk across her line of sight, behind the blond medical technician. Now she saw the flashing light reflecting off the bushes at the side of the road. It was almost dark.

"Stay right there on your back," said the blond voice. "Hardly a scratch. Don't know how you got away so easy. You're a lucky lady."

She was convinced.

"Wow." She could speak now.

"Keep still, please," he said. "We'll let you up in a few minutes, but first let's make sure you're as unhurt as your vital signs indicate. As far as I can tell, you didn't get a scratch. One of those miracles that happens all too seldom."

* * * * * *

A few minutes later, Shawna sat up, guided by the blond in uniform, but mostly unassisted. She felt fine. She saw the travel trailer and its truck parked on the right shoulder of the road in front of her. Something was hanging off the truck, low to the road near its front fender, maybe part of her bike. The rescue truck was right behind her, at the side of the road, flashing lights blazing away.

She sat quietly and surveyed the side of the road. About twenty feet in front of her, barely in her line of sight and apparently dragged off the road by the police, was her bicycle. It was lying on its side, bent into a sharply twisted shape. The spokes were poking outward at weird angles. Her bike was a total wreck, but this blond fellow seemed assured she was unscathed.

Something on her bike caught her eye. As the flashing light of the rescue vehicle throbbed out into the darkness, she focused intently. Each flash caught her bike in penetrating brilliance. Every time the strobe-like reflection hit her bicycle, a glint of light bounced back from her bike's red rear plastic reflector.

* * * * * *

On November 8, 1988, over two years after the Air Force accident near Bakersfield, the Pentagon released official photos of the top secret stealth fighter that had dominated speculation for nearly a decade. The stealth aircraft had been assumed to possess the designator of F-19, but Department of Defense officials announced that no such aircraft designator had ever existed. This aircraft was the F-117A stealth fighter.

Military officials also revealed that they hadn't told the firefighters who fought the blaze at the scene of the accident that the stealth material involved in the fire was highly carcinogenic. This classified decision, they said, was necessary in the interest of national security.

Last Leg Home

This takeoff has special meaning.
The flight crew feels alone.
Eight hours ahead, but it's all downhill,
On the last leg home.

Sixty-three thousand pounds of fuel.
That will get us there.
But watch the torque gauges during takeoff,
In the cold winter air.

Twenty-four thousand feet assigned.
The controller is exact.
Alaska's mountains sparkle in the clear air,
For this last aircraft.

No more HF or Doppler,
For the airways now are kind.
Warmth is straight ahead.
Frigid Elmendorf is behind.

On up to flight level two-four-zero.
To the rear is the common tone,
Of memories, some best forgotten.
It's the last leg home.

Our Year 1993: Distant Planet

5 Years Later

Relativity has taught us to be wary of time.

Wolfgang Rindler (1977)

Chapter 33

Mind Games

Finally the signal was registering success. Just as the Guides were on the verge of canceling the experiment and diverting the signal to a new location, the reflection of the powerful energy wave returned to the distant planet. It wasn't a true reflection, but it was the result of receipt and reemission of the original signal by an intelligent being.

The Minds hoped they hadn't been so successful that they had killed the host. Their own planet's beings could never withstand such an electromagnetic pulse. Hopefully, other intelligent forms of life could.

The projected data download arrival time and grid coordinates had been transmitted to the life form. Hopefully, the receptor understood their meaning. There wasn't enough power on this entire planet to carry out the final transmission more than once during its annular orbit.

The initial return pulse had included sufficient data to allow the use of numerical coordinates. The numbering system was simple and amazingly similar to the grid system of their own planet. The watery world's celestial coordinate system was probably planet-based, necessitating use of the world's axis of spin. Since that axis was precisely known, the first coordinate should be fairly obvious to the receptor, reducing the stellar location to only two possible positions. If the world's intelligence was smart enough, the rest should be simple to interpret.

A non-spin axis grid system was entirely a different matter. Then the coordinates would be a complete guess, with an arbitrary starting point that the Minds couldn't predict. But maybe the scientists of this wet world could find their planet with only one coordinate. That would take both innovation and luck. Intelligent beings were expected to have the former; and, hopefully, the latter.

1993: Earth

Where does this difference between the past and future come from? Why do we remember the past but not the future?

Steven Hawking (1988)

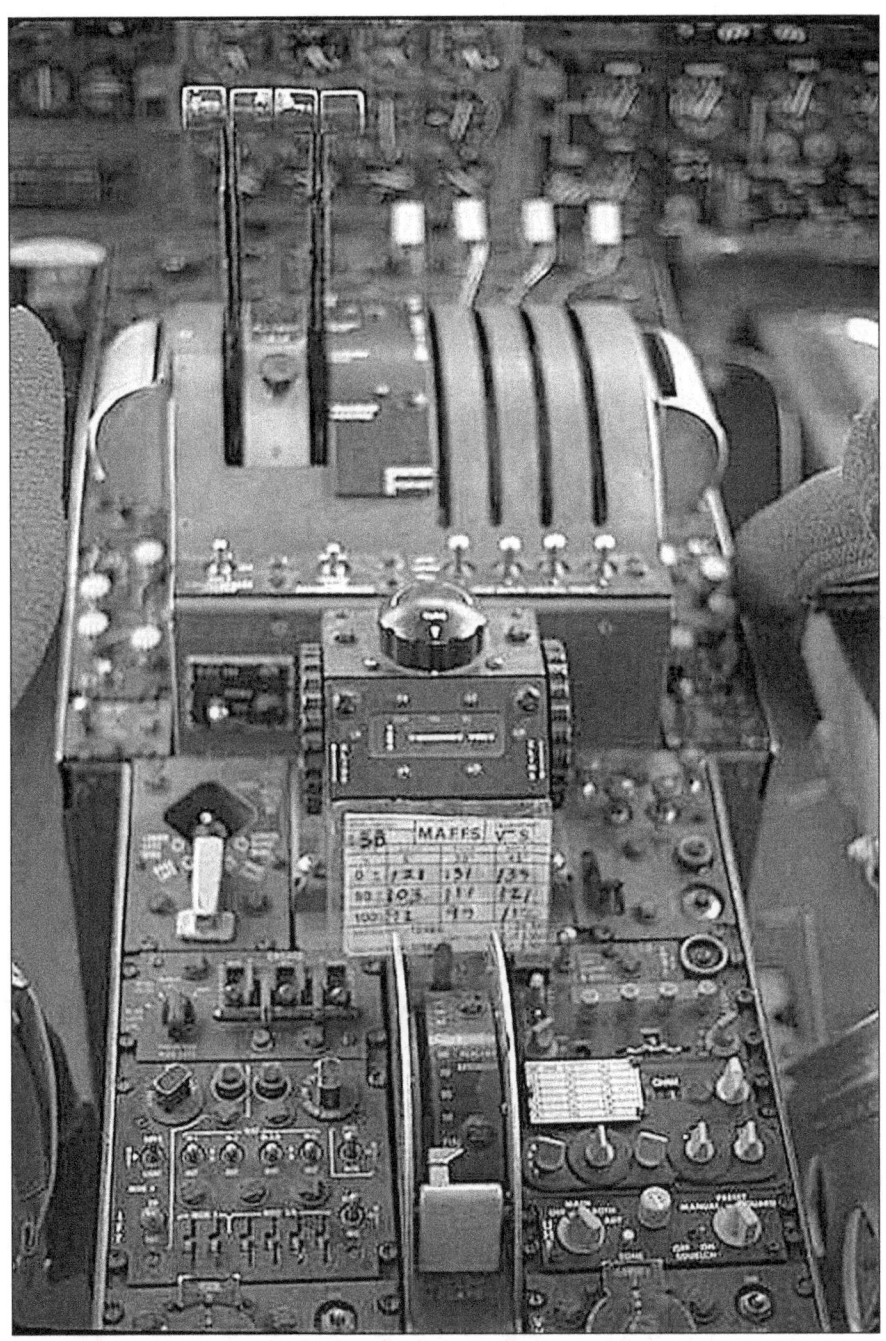

C-130 Throttle Quadrant

Chapter 34

Elmendorf

Colonel Kevin Leah stood before the KC-10 aerial tanker, contemplating the mission. It should be routine, if only the inertial navigation system would fix itself.

He didn't have a lot of confidence in these mechanics, but it should be just a matter of swapping black boxes. If you judged by the repeat discrepancy rate on INS squawks, their level of knowledge wasn't very adequate. He doubted these avionics specialists cared whether his airplane even flew today. There was a big gap between maintenance and operations. Some of it resulted in open animosity.

Kevin Leah wasn't prone to cooling his heels on the flightline. He was more comfortable behind his desk as Disaster Preparedness Officer. It was a position that didn't receive a lot of glory, but he found the job challenging and more interesting than flying these lumbering airborne gas stations. In his younger days, flying had a lot of appeal. Now it was simply a function that allowed him to continue to earn a high grade of pay.

When this maintenance delay began, he had called Shawna from Base Ops, hoping for a priority on the INS repairs, but she reminded him that her Aerospace Systems Branch had nothing to do with avionics. She almost laughed when he even suggested she intervene. Still, Shawna was concerned about the impact of the delay on Kevin, and promised to visit Maintenance Control and call him from there with an update on what she could learn about the avionics problem.

Mechanics were mechanics, and Kevin Leah figured nobody in maintenance really understood these black boxes. Colonel Leah just hoped he didn't have to depend on the inertial navigation system too much today. But in this part of the world, INS was the primary means to mate up with the receiver aircraft, usually young fighter pukes who were always in a hurry for gas. Over this territory, that was understandable. Those fighters were heavy on fire-power and light on range. The KC-10 was big on range and a boring beast to fly.

* * * * * *

Major Shawna Whitney was in her second tour in Alaska, seven years altogether, and there were times when she cherished the assignment. These long summer days were enough to make her temporarily forget about the depressing winters. As best as possible, she avoided reflecting on her days in California. Seasons were almost nonexistent in San Francisco, with the winter nearly indistinguishable from summer. Disturbing memories of California were still impossible to push aside. Her enthusiasm for the Air Force had been different then, much different than here in Alaska.

The job was part of the problem. When Shawna arrived in Alaska in 1986, she had been assigned to the Aerospace Ground Equipment Branch, a thankless position that became the horror assignment of her career. She had tried to make the best of it, and her reassignment to the Propulsion Branch was a big improvement. She worked in harmony with some strong NCOs in the propulsion area, and it was never her desire to move on to the Aerospace Systems Branch. But as a captive of the Field Maintenance Squadron, she had to go where the squadron commander assigned her in this frustrating game of musical chairs. Her new job as Aerospace Systems Branch Officer caused her to routinely exhibit her lack of knowledge in many of the areas she supervised, particularly hydraulics and electrical systems. That awkward display usually occurred at the morning staff meeting in the squadron commander's office.

Three squadron commanders had come and gone during Shawna's assignment to field maintenance. All were flight-rated lieutenant colonels, working their way through the maintenance squadron on their way to real jobs in operations or to an early retirement.

Shawna, now age 36, was feeling a lot older than she looked. She had grown into her 30s gracefully, and as she matured she kept her athletic look. Her nearly-black hair was short now but still tightly curled and long enough to maintain its constant windblown look. She avoided makeup, except on formal occasions, and those were becoming disgustingly more common these days.

Shawna certainly never envisioned being at this particular job for so long. She had a chance for reassignment several years ago, but by then her life with Kevin was tangled in everything. He was going to stay here; so would she.

Mrs. Shawna Whitney-Leah had been married for four years, and she had adjusted well. The biggest relief was her relative success in putting her relationship with Jay behind her. Ending that bond was the release of a torturing weight. For that reason alone, marriage to Kevin made sense.

Shawna and Kevin were the ideal couple. At least that's how those around them viewed their relationship. Kevin was a very successful full-colonel (called a "bird colonel" by his friends because of the eagle insignia on his shoulders). He was well on his way to becoming a brigadier general before he retired. Kevin was married to a younger, intelligent non-rated officer who outwardly appeared ripe for promotion to lieutenant colonel before she retired. As a couple, everyone saw the dollar signs – a prosperous retirement at a very young age, particularly young for Shawna.

Kevin knew everything about Shawna's past, or almost everything. He knew about a passing affair with an NCO from the California Air National Guard and the Article 31 on Shawna's record from Travis Air Force Base. He didn't know the real extent of her relationship with Jay, but Shawna would probably have told him, if he asked.

Kevin was very protective of Shawna's Article 31. Their friends didn't know a thing about it, and they had a lot of friends at Elmendorf Air Force Base. None of them knew Shawna had little chance of ever making "light-colonel." She considered her belated promotion to major to be the good fortune of being a woman in an Air Force that was trying to right decades of inequality.

One aspect of Shawna's life that Kevin didn't understand involved her memories of the future. Nor did he try very hard. Only Melissa and Jay had ever come close to grasping the significance of those memories. Melissa had missed the mark by a rather wide margin. Jay had accomplished a nearly direct hit.

Chapter 35

ORI

Chief Master Sergeant Jay Rotella felt stupid in his chemical warfare suit. This was his third time in the confining multi-layered outfit and gas mask in the past twenty-four hours. And this time he was stuck in Maintenance Control, with inspectors looking over everybody's shoulders. Jay had stepped into Maintenance Control to make a phone call when the siren went off.

This was one of those rare moments when Jay felt the half-century mark of his age creeping up on him. At 48, he kept in good shape by running almost every day. The only real mark of aging that he noticed was his vision. Getting used to glasses was difficult. He hated sweating in them when he jogged. Inside a chemical warfare suit, without his prescription goggles, he could hardly see well enough to function.

This was the second time he had suffered through an Operational Readiness Inspection in the past six months. The first time had been a war game heaped in overconfidence, accompanied by a Command Post that was an exercise in miscommunication. The ORI team's out-briefing was a blow to everyone, and a great lesson regarding the strength of the whole when weakened by a single important link.

So now they were doing it all over again. The embarrassment factor was huge in the Air National Guard, since every C-130 outfit knew the other units so well. News spread fast after the first ORI failure, and that made this retest all the more important. It had to be an *Excellent* or an *Outstanding*, not merely a *Satisfactory*. The good news is that no one ever failed an ORI twice in a row. The 146th TAW didn't plan to be the first.

The latest word in Total Force was mobilization. You were allowed to pick your destination, but you had to go somewhere that demonstrated your capability to get the job done in a remote location. You had to be able to work with the rest of the military, the Total Force concept. The Air National Guard couldn't be a stand-alone fighting component any longer.

"Mobility" wasn't the favorite word within the airlift wing, nor was it ever a pleasant process for tactical troops. Part of the unpleasantness involved the overkill in the area of equipment preparation. If any item (or person) had to be shipped as part of the mobility package, it required a stream of paperwork that no one person seemed to comprehend. In terms of speed, mobility slowed down the deployment process. But without mobility, an ORI was impossible. To put it in Jay's words: "Mobility sucks."

But that attitude was reserved for closed-door meetings at the squadron level and occasional outbursts on the flightline. No one disputed those words, but few at higher levels were free to echo them.

The 146th's choice for deployment was El Toro Marine Corps Air Station, a brave selection. Only 90 air-miles from Point Mugu, it seemed like a good choice. It also showed the unit's ability to work with a completely different branch of the service, the Marines. The 146th was about to learn what a different world they were dealing with.

* * * * * *

Through the faceplate of his gas mask, Jay could see the inspectors looking around the makeshift deployed version of Maintenance Control, trying to find anything astray. Since everyone in the room was a captive audience, the inspectors once again launched into their frustrating "be proactive" speech. Moving around in these suits only created sweat, and the inspectors knew that too. So they laid it on – easy to do in their unsuited condition as outside observers.

Jay was aware that ten feet overhead was an unauthorized stock of C-130 parts, those little extras that made a tough mission a lot easier. Sitting within the false-ceiling were tachometer generators, torque indicators, and hard-to-find components essential to success. If the inspectors discovered this illegal cache, the 146th would be more quickly dead than from this simulated chemical attack.

As Jay peered out of the faceplate of his gas mask, without his prescription goggles underneath, he could hardly see the symbols on the aircraft status boards. He wouldn't be in this mask for long. But it would be nice to be able to see.

There was little he could do. The success of the current phase of the ORI depended on completing this engine maintenance run before the control tower closed for the night. That was another loose end no one had considered. The neighboring community was extremely noise sensitive, and when the tower closed, all engine runs stopped. The maintenance crew working on the sick engine held all the marbles tonight, and Jay hoped they didn't drop them. The engine run couldn't occur until the engine was fixed, and that needed to be before the control tower closed. Without this aircraft, tomorrow's mission would go unscored and a definite failure. They were running out of chances.

Jay glanced around. The two production controllers, a supervisor and one female NCO, were sitting as still as possible. There was nothing they could do to control the situation now, and the more energy they exerted, the more sweat dripped within their chemical warfare suits. They were simply waiting for the radio call. And hoping.

In addition to these clumsily garbed figures, two inspectors were sitting in the luxury of their short-sleeve blues. It seemed like an unreal simulation, with the inspectors sitting around waiting to be gassed. The Maintenance Control supervisor sat at his computer keyboard, unable to do anything constructive with two layers of bulky gloves. His hood was on a bit crooked, but his mask seemed to have a secure fit, so the inspectors would probably ignore it. Chemical warfare was ranked right up there with mobility.

Mobility sucks. Chemical warfare sucks even worse. How could we ever win a battle, to say nothing of a war, in this klutzy garb?

The female controller, holding a three-ring red notebook in her lap, sat back in her chair. With her clumsy, thick gloves, she would probably be unable to turn to the correct page of the emergency action checklist if she had to.

Just as the clock was about to hit the fatal minute, when the engine run battle would be lost, the voice of the First Sergeant came over the radio.

Why is he involved in an engine run? First Sergeants are important fellows, but never involved directly with the maintenance of airplanes.

Then it became clear that the First Sergeant was located in the control tower, and it sounded like he had made a new friend. He announced to the engine run crew that they had an additional fifteen minutes before the tower closed for the night. Apparently he had found a case of Corona beer for the tower chief.

Jay laughed to himself, but the sound didn't make it through his multiple layers of shielding. The inspectors seemed to be mentally scratching their heads. First Sergeants in the real Air Force didn't do things like this.

In this room now, there was a feeling of pride. The female NCO sat up straight in her chair, clutching the red notebook even tighter. When you outwit the inspectors, you give yourself a special pat on the back.

What Jay didn't know was that some bad decisions were being made while they were struggling with the engine run. A few hundred feet away, the Command Post had fucked up again. They, as a whole, had already failed the ORI for the second time. And there was going to be hell to pay.

* * * * * *

On the same day as the ORI out-briefing at Point Mugu, Irene Bennett died in a hospital in nearby Ventura at the age of 52. There was no surprise in her death. Her body had given up its ability to adequately function years before, and the past three years had been little more than a period of extended life. When she died, her unpublished manuscript, entitled *Personal Finances for the Unafraid*, was on the verge of finding a publisher. Jay promised himself that he would see that it was printed. It was Irene's final request.

* * * * *

Page A3
Los Angeles Times

Panama Prepares for Transfer of Control of Canal

The Panama Canal Commission, previously directed by a U.S. administrator, is now under the leadership of a Panamanian official. This swap of duties of the Commission's administrator and deputy administrator occurred three years ago in 1990, and so far there seem to be few problems. Panama is preparing to accept complete control of the Panama Canal in 1999.

U.S. military forces contributed to stability in the region during the turbulent 1980s when two strong dictators kept tensions at a maximum. But now the country of Panama seems prepared to run the canal and to prosper from its economic benefits to the region.

(continues on page A9, "Panama Canal")

Chapter 36

Coordinates

Shawna fumbled for her flight cap. When the memory collided with her, she had tumbled to the floor near the hydraulic test stand. And now she was trying to recover in front of two frightened mechanics. She quickly regained her composure, grabbed her cap, and started to push herself back up to her feet.

"Turn that fucking thing off!"

She said it with as much lack of emotion as she could muster. Not very military, and certainly not the way a female officer should speak. Inside she was on fire.

"Are you okay, Major?"

The two-striper looked stark pale, gaping down at her. His NCO was more collected, as he reached over and flipped the switch off. Shawna wasn't sure if these mechanics were more intimidated by her fall or by her inappropriate language.

"No problem," said Shawna. "I just stumbled, that's all. But the screech of that test stand starting up is enough to make me puke."

"Sorry, we didn't mean to startle you like that," said the airman.

"Forget it," said Shawna. She was on her feet and under control now, cap back in place.

"Do you want us to fill out a ground safety report?" asked the NCO.

"No way," replied Shawna. "I'm fine. Sorry I yelled. It's not you. It's that damn test stand. Nobody's fault."

Major Shawna Whitney-Leah walked briskly out of the Hydraulic Shop. As she left, it took every ounce of strength to keep herself rigid. Inside she was trembling.

* * * * *

"**A**nd this happened before?" asked Kevin.

"I've told you about it," replied Shawna. "The stealth fighter incident."

"But that was one of those coincidences that might have been due to all the news you heard about a new stealthy airplane."

"Same thing," said Shawna. "And that memory had detail. So did this."

"You sound a bit like a psychic."

"Let me guess," said Shawna. "You think people like me are looking for the Jesus thing."

"The what?" asked Kevin.

"Never mind. Maybe I'm a bit psychic. I don't know. But this is a memory of the future. I'm sure of it, although I don't know exactly what I'm remembering in this case. It's very technical this time, with lots of complex numbers."

"And you're not a technical person," said Kevin. "You're a maintenance officer."

"And what does that mean?"

"Well, I'm just saying you aren't someone who would dream about technical details, particularly mathematical stuff."

"So I'm just plain nuts," said Shawna.

"I didn't say that, and you know it. But this is just a dream. You've talked yourself into it. Like you did before."

"Nothing like being open-minded," said Shawna. "I didn't say this was real. I'm not sure what it is."

"Well, if you keep thinking about it, this will become a big thing. We don't need that," said Kevin.

"No we don't," said Shawna. "And I don't need your advice on this. What little there is."

"I don't have any advice," said Kevin. "I think it's just a dream."

"When I'm not asleep," said Shawna.

"Well, I'm not sure what it is."

"Neither do I, Kevin. Let's forget it."

* * * * * *

For the past year, Jay had been thinking about a career change. It was tough to imagine leaving his C-130s. Most of them were the same tail numbers he had mothered for the past twenty years. 826 was still going strong, but Jay seldom traveled with her these days. The energetic young tech sergeant who now served as her crew chief had his own pride in the aircraft, and Jay managed to let go, at least a little.

Changing careers this close to retirement, at first glance, seemed ridiculous. He would be 55 in seven years, and that would put him at the civil service minimum limit. Then he could leave the Air Guard as a civilian air technician with a nice monthly pension. He would have logged 35 years of Air Force service as a weekender, leading to substantial financial double-dipping during his retirement.

But the FAA was now hiring maintenance inspectors all over the country. He could learn to love Boeing 737s. His civil service time would follow him to the FAA, and he could still stay with the Guard as a weekender, at least until he hit 30 years. Then they would probably try to push him out, if he was no longer a civilian air tech. All of his friends said this wasn't the best time to leave. Then again, maybe it was.

This recent ORI had prompted his thinking. This was a young man's game, and he wasn't so young anymore. A third ("repeat-repeat") ORI was next, and that wasn't going to be any fun at all.

* * * * * *

"I'm seeing numbers and exact dates this time," said Shawna into the telephone.

This was an embarrassing way to start a conversation after five years of nearly complete silence. But it was easier than starting on a personal note.

"Another memory?" asked Jay. "It's wonderful to hear from you."

"And great to hear your voice," said Shawna.

There! – the ice was broken. She had dreaded this moment. The only real communication with Jay in recent years was when she telephoned to tell him she had gotten married. It seemed only fair to call then, although it had taken every ounce of her fortitude. They had spoken only briefly on the phone since then, and it was awkward each time. Shawna knew Irene was seriously ill, and she knew it was taking its toll on Jay.

"How's Kevin?" asked Jay.

To Shawna, it sounded like he really wanted to know. Maybe he was hoping this was the "I'm divorced call."

"Doing fine. You don't mind that I called?"

"Mind?" said Jay. "You gotta' be kiddin'. I'm really glad to hear from you."

Jay paused but didn't say anything more for the moment. Shawna knew Jay well enough to know there was something he was thinking about, trying to word it right for her.

"How's Irene?" asked Shawna.

Jay's silence made Shawna fear what he was about to say.

"Irene died last month," said Jay. "I should have called, but..." His voice was soft, on the verge of trembling.

"Oh, dear," said Shawna. "I'm very sorry, Jay. I know she was awfully sick. Such a terrible loss."

Shawna wanted to say more, much more, but she didn't have any idea what words would work. Jay broke the silence.

"It was time for her. Not a pleasant last few years."

"I don't know what to say," said Shawna. "She was a wonderful woman, and I'm glad you were able to be with to the end."

"It was an unusual relationship," said Jay. "But an important one for both of us. She was still without a publisher for her books, so I'm trying to get that going. Know any good literary agents?"

"Although I never met Irene, she always sounded like someone very special."

"She was. I miss her a lot."

Shawna felt guilty. It wasn't the years of absence from Jay that bothered her. She was convinced their years apart were for the best. But hearing about Irene's death was unsettling, and the reason for her phone call seemed so inconsequential now.

Jay broke the awkward silence. He tried to get the conversation back on track, obviously grateful that Shawna had called. But he talked haltingly, like a kid who was frightened and wanted to change the subject. Their discussion drifted to their work – Jay's thoughts of retiring and Shawna's latest news from the real Air Force.

"What about you?" asked Jay. "Tell me about yourself."

"Well, I'm the Aerospace Systems Branch officer-in-charge, and I'm still over my head, but no one seems to notice."

"I bet you're doing a great job" said Jay. "You always have. You made major, I bet."

"Yes, it rather surprised me after all the hoop-la, but I made major."

"Light-colonel is next," said Jay definitively.

"Never, as I see it. That jerk, Strickland, took care of that for good."

"It doesn't have to be that way," said Jay. "You made major on target."

"Not true. They held me back long enough to give me the hint."

"What else?" asked Jay.

"Well... I'm pregnant. Due in late January."

"Wow, now that's news! January. That's wonderful."

"They'll let me work as long as I want before my maternity leave."

"You'll make a wonderful mom."

"We'll see about that. Jay, I want to talk to you about this memory episode sometime soon."

"Why not now?" said Jay. "This is the first since the stealth fighter incident?"

"Nothing since then, although there was a weird time warp episode when I wrecked my bicycle and should have been killed. And a busted cup of cocoa that somehow put itself back together."

"What!"

"Too strange to tell you about now. And they weren't premonitions. I'm more concerned about last week in the Hydraulic Shop. Since then, this strong memory has recurred three times. Each incident seems to be related to powerful electrical motors. I need to stay away from those pesky electrons."

"Tell me more," said Jay.

"Well, it's very specific this time, with an approximate date, sometime in 2016. And it's in the desert, maybe near Phoenix."

"What else?" asked Jay.

"There are numbers. I've written them down. I could see them clearly in my memory for a few minutes after each incident. They're like an afterimage when you look at a bright light."

"You have the exact numbers?" asked Jay.

"Not all of the digits, but I do have most of them. I've tried to jot down everything I see right after it happens."

"Good," said Jay. "I really think this is something important. Maybe not just for you."

"Give me your email address?" asked Shawna. "I'd like to send you the numbers I have so far. I'd say they're similar to geographic coordinates, but they don't make sense on a map. Yet they seem very precise."

Jay gave Shawna his email address, and Shawna told him more about pictorial graphics she saw in her recent memory episodes. Most of the images involved electronic equipment that seemed, to Shawna, like high-tech avionics gear.

"And I should mention something else," said Shawna.

"I'm listening," said Jay.

"Well, there have been some minor situations, increasingly frequent in recent years."

"What kind of situations?" asked Jay.

"Time reversals, I think," said Shawna. "Some may be just my imagination, but several are certainly real. Like when I added bubble bath to the tub last week."

"And no bubbles?" asked Jay.

"Oh, lots of bubbles," said Shawna. "But then they simply disappeared."

"I don't know much about bubble baths," said Jay.

"Well, I can assure you the bubbles don't go away just like that. These did."

"Like the bull in the china shop," said Jay.

"What?"

"The perfect example of the second law of thermodynamics," said Jay. "Can you imagine a bull going into a china shop and things being more organized after his visit?"

"No, I'd say you could expect a disaster."

"Right," said Jay. "And the second law of thermodynamics is as sacred as you can get. Things seek maximum chaos once headed in that direction. Everyday processes can't be reversed, at least according to that law."

"I've been breaking the law," said Shawna.

"Or time is breaking down," said Jay.

"I wish you would tell me it happens to everyone now and then," said Shawna.

"But you know that's not true," replied Jay.

"Yes, and that's what has me worried," said Shawna.

* * * * * *

Subject: Shawna's Weird Memories
Date: 9/04/93 9:04 am
From: shawnal@aol.com
To: 78265.3043@compuserve.com

I've attached the data I've been able to accumulate as an MS Word attachment. I've jotted it down in tabular form. There are further digits to the right, I think. I'll try to provide a more complete list of numbers as I remember them in future memory episodes (maybe there won't be any!). Please let me know what you think.

Hope all is well with you.

- Your Shawna

* * * * * *

Jay liked the signature element. It reminded him of all that he and Shawna had shared. They could probably never share that again, but their memories of being together couldn't be taken away. He certainly never planned to let go of them.

Jay opened the Word attachment and found two pages of data, most of it seemingly repetitious. One of the lines of numbers was duplicated three times. He doubted Shawna did that for emphasis. That must be how she remembered seeing it.

Like Shawna, Jay was drawn to the tabular data that appeared to be coordinates. The data was even aligned in numerical format with entries similar to geographic latitude and longitude, but there were no north-south or east-west indications. It was decimal in nature, base-10 rather than base-60, but it could still be coordinates. These days, satellite navigation receivers were starting to promote digitized base-10 figures for latitude and longitude. At first glance, these numbers certainly looked like geographic coordinates in degrees, with the minutes and seconds converted to decimals:

15.952361133
89.935666787

Jay went to the den and reached to the top of the bookcase. He grabbed the globe that hadn't been used in years, removed it from its wooden cradle, and brought it to the living room. He placed the globe on the floor and sat down beside it with the printed copy of Shawna's email attachment. The first numbers should be latitude, although there was no north-south indication, so he found the 16-degree North line. Getting it any closer than a few degrees was ridiculous on this small-scale globe. He tried matching it with the other digits by assuming it was a westerly longitude. The numbers, 16 degrees North, 89 degrees West, put him along Guatemala's border with Belize, near the Gulf of Honduras. He tried another match, assuming the first number was southerly latitude. Using westerly longitude again, he located the position, in the Pacific Ocean, nearly 1000 miles west of Peru and an equal distance south of the Galapagos Islands.

Jay spent the evening playing with the numbers, checking the longitude both east and west of the prime meridian and completely reversing the latitude and longitude sequences. The digits of the remaining permutations put him in the Bay of Bengal east of India and then further south in the middle of the Indian Ocean. The 89.9-degree line, treated as latitude, resulted in a location within 50 miles of the north or south pole. Jay remembered Shawna's mention of Phoenix, and none of these locations was a sandy desert.

Chapter 37

Declination

Subject: RE: Shawna's Weird Memories
Date: 9/04/93 11:14 pm
From: 78265.3043@compuserve.com
To: shawnal@aol.com

Have you ever been to Guatemala? Do you dream of vacationing on a cruise ship in the Indian Ocean or trekking across a polar icecap? I'll meet you there!

Those numbers certainly look like coordinates, but they don't lead me to any immediate conclusions. Let me play with the data a bit more. Do you still like to play?

Your RSP

* * * * * *

Jay was being bold with his reply, but not nearly as bold as he used to be with Shawna. He thought she would take it lightly. But he hoped she wouldn't.

He also had another idea, and it involved another set of coordinates, celestial right ascension and declination. Jay used an old copy of a children's star atlas for assistance. This was one of his favorite astronomy books, since it simplified the overview of the constellations while still portraying the primary Messier objects and the brightest NGC nebulae. More importantly, the entire sky was displayed over only eight pages.

Jay sat down at the kitchen table and opened the book in front of him. The map's celestial grid was overlaid on the charts as thin labeled lines. First he considered the right ascension coordinates relative to the numbers in Shawna's data. There was no obvious correlation. Right ascension, labeled in hours and minutes, didn't seem to equate to anything in her listing. Dismissing right ascension as a dead end, Jay considered the declination coordinates on the sky chart. There were no pluses and minuses in Shawna's figures, so he started with a northerly coordinate line first. He began at plus-16 degrees in northern Orion and worked his way west. Using a ruler and a red pen, he drew a line on the chart that spanned the two-page centerfold. There were a few bright stars right along the red line, including a nondescript star named Markab in Pegasus; also Sualocin in Delphinus. The bright star Aldebaran in the constellation of Taurus was slightly off the red line at a declination angle of about +16.5. No Messier objects or NGC nebulae were reasonably near the line. Of course, the child's astronomy charts, marked with his ruler and pen, might not have the accuracy that would be available on a more detailed map. And on a larger-scale chart, many more dim stars would lie near the line.

Now Jay duplicated this procedure, using the two pages of the book that displayed the southerly declinations. Once again, a few bright stars were near or on the 16-degree south line, including Tau Ceti in Cetus and Skat in Aquarius. The brightest star in the sky, Sirius, in the constellation of Canis Major, was reasonably close to his 16-degree south line at a declination of -16.7 degrees. No nebulae were near this southern declination.

Finally, Jay tried the other permutations involving the swap of right ascension and declination. That put the location nearly on top of Polaris, the North Star, or near the starless south celestial pole. The coincidence regarding Polaris drew Jay's attention. This star was the benchmark for the artificial rotation point of the universe as seen from earth.

Jay's list of things to do tomorrow included a more in-depth investigation using his *Norton's Star Atlas*, but that would take some time. The large scale of that chart would cause the 16-degree declination line to span many pages. This had become an absorbing challenge. He would give the project a high priority. Besides, here was a great excuse to call Shawna.

* * * * * *

Jay walked into Plans and Scheduling, finding Christine huddled over her computer.

"When's our next Anchorage trip?" asked Jay.

Christine looked up from the keyboard, and raised her eyebrows at him.

"Business or pleasure?" she asked.

Everyone remembered Jay's maneuvering years ago to divert C-130s to Travis at every opportunity. Jay had been pretty open about the maintenance officer who had moved to Alaska. If anyone in the airlift wing knew about an interesting relationship, soon everyone else knew.

"Business, of course," said Jay. "Anything this month?"

"As a matter of fact, there's an AME flight next Friday."

She turned to the magnetic strip board behind her and pointed to the light green strip labeled *Elmendorf*.

"The next closest is a two-day McChord run this Saturday. Of course, you wouldn't try to divert it to Alaska, would you?"

"Never," answered Jay. "But I'll keep it in mind."

* * * * * *

Subject: Coordinates
Date: 9/07/93 7:24 pm
From: 78265.3043@compuserve.com
To: shawnal@aol.com

Interesting numbers. I'm working on them, but this might require mouth-to-mouth attention. The values may be celestial coordinates, so I'm researching it further.

We have a mission to Elmendorf in 3 weeks, an overnight turnaround. I'd like to show you the details of what I'm working on. Meet me at Base Ops on Friday, September 17 at 2330Z?

Your Jay

* * * * * *

Subject: RE: Coordinates
Date: 9/09/93 6:16 pm
From: shawnal@aol.com
To: 78265.3043@compuserve.com

Jay,

You're a definite problem. I'll meet you at Base Ops, per schedule. I suppose it will be 826, and you'll both expect cookies.

- Your Shawna

* * * * * *

At the Elmendorf Base Ops cafeteria, Jay sat across from Shawna. He was dressed in his battle dress uniform, barely wrinkled after an eight-hour flight. BDUs had replaced the fatigues of previous years, but the only real change was in the name and the wonder of permanent-press. Shawna wore a still-zipped maroon ski jacket, extra large but unable to conceal hints of her pregnancy. Her thick blue jeans and half-calf after-ski boots made her look typically athletic, even in her pregnant condition. A loud overhead heater behind their cafeteria table blew noisy, warm air over them.

"What's the chance of getting away for Gallant Eagle?" asked Jay.

Just like the old days, he liked to keep Shawna off guard, and this was a good way to do it. What a way to start a face-to-face conversation after all of these years.

"Gallant Eagle," replied Shawna. "Pope Air Force Base in November. Now that sounds perfectly terrible."

"So your unit is going?" asked Jay.

"We're committed to a bunch of exercises like that," said Shawna, "But my squadron's part is minimal. The wing has to produce one maintenance officer, and no one is volunteering."

"Wonder why?" said Jay. "Good ol' Poop Air Force Base has a bit of a reputation. But I'd love to see you there."

"I figured that was why you were asking," said Shawna. "You've never spoken fondly of that place."

"To say the least. But if you were there, my attitude might be completely different."

Shawna thought briefly about it, but had a difficult time concentrating on the image. What a reversal; she had been in this position before, worrying about Irene. Now she was worrying about Kevin. The strangest part was that she considered the trip for even a moment.

"You can't be serious," said Shawna.

"Perfectly."

"And you're not just talking about a get-together after work at the officers' club," said Shawna.

"As a matter of fact, no," said Jay. "But that would be fun too, if only I was welcome in the officers' club. We've never really worked on a mission together since Panama."

"It's crazy," said Shawna. "I'll be like a balloon in November."

This is the old Jay. Way too bold for the new Shawna. After all, I'm pregnant.

"Yes, it is crazy," said Jay.

He waited, giving Shawna time to react further.

"Well, forget it. I'm married, quite happily, thank you. I thought you came here to talk about this memory."

"That was the pretext," said Jay. "But do think about it. I won't volunteer unless you do."

"I have thought about it, Jay. Can we change the subject?"

Shawna shifted her weight in the chair, trying to get comfortable. Jay grinned at her, reached into his briefcase, removed a book, and opened it on the table. He placed a copy of her email attachment next to the book.

"Take a look at this chart," said Jay, referring to the children's astronomy book. "The red line represents the northerly declination angle that might be represented in your figures."

He pointed to the printout of her email attachment and then continued: "There are two possible lines," he said. "That's based on the assumption this is really celestial declination. The two lines represent north and south in celestial coordinates."

Jay flipped two pages ahead and showed her the other red line.

"That's southerly declination," he said.

Jay gave Shawna a chance to absorb the pages. She flipped back and forth between the pages that portrayed the northern and southern hemispheres.

"What about the longitude coordinate?" asked Shawna.

"Not at all clear," said Jay. "That's called right ascension, and I can't match it up with anything. Your number 90 is simply too large. If it is right ascension, it's a number that makes no sense to me."

"Does anything interesting lie along this line?"

Shawna was running her finger along the red line on the southern hemispheric chart.

"Several stars, and that's about it. But now let me show you this."

Jay reached into his briefcase and withdrew a large woven cloth book with a light blue warped cover. Shawna hadn't seen many of these thick hard-cloth covers, and she wondered whether they were still being manufactured.

Jay opened the book to a page that had a paper clip as a marker at the top. The pages of the book, like the cover, were warped from time, moisture, or both. Another narrow red line crossed this page, cutting directly across a star in the constellation of Cetus.

"Tau Ceti," said Jay. It's only twelve light years away. Almost next door, by astronomical standards. Its composition and size are rather similar to our sun. But there's also another star that has caught my eye."

"Which is...?" prompted Shawna.

"Polaris" said Jay, with maximum dramatic emphasis. "If this second coordinate is declination, then it points nearly directly at Polaris, and that's a much more popular location than Tau Ceti."

"The North Star," said Shawna.

"Right. But the coordinates are a bit off for Polaris, by about three minutes of declination. That's still very close."

"Any other hits or near misses?" asked Shawna.

"Nothing very interesting," replied Jay. "Tau Ceti fits the data most closely, even closer than Polaris, but it isn't exactly on the line. Real close though."

Shawna looked down at the children's astronomy book, still open to the page showing the region that included Tau Ceti.

"It looks like it's dead-center on Tau Ceti," said Shawna.

"But it isn't. This red line is within one second of declination of the star's actual position. That displacement doesn't show up on the scale of either of these charts, but it definitely isn't Tau Ceti's exact location."

"So how far off is it, in miles, light years, inches?" asked Shawna.

"Way off on a real-miles scale," replied Jay. "At a distance of twelve light years, that displaces Tau Ceti from your memory coordinates about 912 billion miles. That's only a fraction of a light year, but it's about ten thousand times the distance between the sun and the earth."

"So my coordinates are probably not Tau Ceti, after all," said Shawna.

She felt something here, but now it was fading. She didn't want to lose it.

"Well, there's still something exceptionally strange about this," said Jay. "The numbers in your memory are extremely accurate, more accurate than astronomical measurements of stellar locations. And this southerly declination is very close to Tau Ceti. Yet not exact."

"I've tried to record the details of the coordinates accurately," said Shawna. "Part of my critical nature, I guess."

"I know," said Jay. "And that's why such a small error is so interesting."

"So the error in itself is food for thought," said Shawna.

"Exactly," replied Jay. "How could you, by chance, come up with extremely accurate figures pointed almost precisely to a specific star but still missing it by just a tad?"

"But there's nothing there. At the exact coordinates, that is," said Shawna.

"But it's only an arc second, a tiny fraction of a degree out of alignment," said Jay. "That's extremely close, and plenty accurate enough to convince me that only Tau Ceti fits the data. Why the numbers aren't more exact is hard to figure."

"Maybe they don't want us to know the exact location," said Shawna.

She spoke as matter-of-factly as if they were discussing an aircraft system they were troubleshooting.

"They?" asked Jay with a smile.

"Well, 'me' then," replied Shawna. "I'm the one who has been having the memories. But I can't help but wonder if someone else is sending this information."

* * * * * *

Total Force. Total joke. The moment the advance party C-130 arrived, it was evident nothing had changed. The Base Housing Office didn't even know they were coming.

How could that be? The planning conference in October had made their lodging requirements clear. No off-base quarters, please, had been the request. It would be the worst of all situations to spread their mechanics all over Fayetteville, taking hours to get them to the flightline. That didn't mix well with twelve-hour shifts. But the Housing Office didn't know they were coming.

Yet the flight crews had on-base quarters reserved. The pilots would have probably preferred staying in town, but they were kept near their aircraft and away from the frustration called Fayetteville. The city tried to cater to the military at Fort Bragg and adjacent Pope Air Force Base. A welcoming sign on the city's theater-like marquee said "Welcome *International* Guard." Spend your money in our wasteland.

To some this was a region of gorgeous terrain, forests and rivers. To others in the military, it was a true wasteland.

* * * * *

Gallant Eagle was a milk run for Colonel Dana Munson. Maybe it would have been more demanding if he wasn't so used to this exercise. This was an annual affair at Pope Air Force Base and just a short hop from the North Carolina Air Guard Base in Charlotte. Dana never expected to be flying with the North Carolina unit, but his transfer from Minneapolis to the east coast had been fortunate. He was at the whim of his civilian employer, and software developers moved around a lot. The North Carolina Air Guard was glad to get a pilot with Dana's background, although they gave him a lot of flak about his roots in Minnesota. His personal military call sign was now "Viking."

Dana's squadron wasn't directly involved in Gallant Eagle this year. Today was just a local flight diverted to help out the Air Guard forces who needed an engine fuel control assembly as quickly as possible. This wasn't the way it was supposed to work, since the Air Force supply system needed to be tested as part of Gallant Eagle. But lateral support was a lot quicker. The California Air Guard was struggling in Fayetteville without a replacement fuel control, and his folks had one. C-130 units were competitive with each other. They were also brothers.

Colonel Dana Munson sat in the left seat of the C-130, droning along at eight thousand feet over his beautiful adopted home of North Carolina. So green, even at this time of year, and so wet with wandering streams. As aircraft commander, he had relinquished control of the aircraft to his co-pilot, just as aircraft commanders before him had let him fly. It was a huge gift, because he loved the feel of this aircraft in his hands, but similar privileges had contributed crucially to his own career.

Colonel Munson was flying with a co-pilot who was like Dana in his early years. Much taller than Dana, of course. Who wasn't? But this pilot still needed Dana's help, although he was well past the mentoring stage. Thus, he let the lieutenant in the right seat get the thrill of handling this wonderful aircraft one more time. The younger officer was well seasoned, due to his prior stint as a C-130 mechanic. He'd worked hard to make it through flight school.

Fayetteville was straight ahead and the skies were cloudless and smooth. The co-pilot was now as seasoned in C-130s as other young flight officers, but he was still visibly pleased to accept this gift. His call sign might be "Hillbilly," but he would go a long way in this powerful Air Force.

"You can have the landing," said Dana.

He turned his head to watch the reaction from the right seat. It was as expected – the red-headed lieutenant beamed a broad smile back at him.

"Brave man," said Lieutenant David Ricardi. "I'll make you proud."

* * * * *

The bus situation was a disaster. Jay was briefed on the Blue Line and the Red Line, but it obviously wasn't going to work. Mechanics simply didn't finish work or even begin it on a logical schedule. By the second day, the only practical alternative was being exercised. Vehicles dedicated to the flightline were pulled away to make pickup and delivery runs at the four spread-out hotels that housed the 146 TAW mechanics. Four hotels spread over ten miles. Meanwhile, if a truck was needed on the flightline, sore feet in combat boots would replace the poorly scheduled buses.

Jay was supposed to have a pickup truck for his assigned use. Of course, that was the plan rather than the reality. The reality was that there was no vehicle, nor was there one for his squadron's maintenance officer. They could take the Blue Line. Thank goodness for Avis.

Gallant Eagle – a Joint Chiefs of Staff Exercise conceived in hell. The Army was already there. They simply rode shuttle buses to Pope Air Force Base from their barracks at adjacent Fort Bragg. The Air National Guard and Reserves had arrived to the tune of confusion. It was the second day of two weeks of flying, and everyone was already primed to go home. The flying schedule was a mess, with an operations team from Charleston Air Force Base trying to call the shots. The regular Air Force was trying to tell the Reserves, Air Guard, and Army what to do. It didn't work.

The Air Force C-141s hadn't arrived yet, nor the C-5s. Yet the second night's missions included them. They were expected to just plop down after long flights from Travis, McChord, and Elmendorf, and begin paradrops that evening. It wouldn't work.

Total Force. Total disgust. But none of that mattered. Jay thought about Shawna, winging her way towards Gallant Eagle, probably descending into Pope by now. Coming to be with him.

The C-141s appeared, one after another. This might be the nightmare of Total Force, but it was also what made the Air Force mission so exciting. Giant Starlifters winging in from across North America, concentrated on a dreary patch of runways in a dismal place called Fayetteville, North Carolina.

Jay seldom visited the Airlift Control Element, since it was the command operation for the flight crew side of the house. He avoided the ALCE as much as possible. But today he was sitting in their air-conditioned temporary shack, awaiting the inbound call from Shawna's C-141. The moment he heard it, he felt himself explode with excitement. It was a dream that seemed too good to be true.

Jay was waiting at the parking spot when the sleek C-141 shut down its engines. A cascade of unburned jet fuel dumped from the overboard masts on all four engines simultaneously, the final cleansing of the engines. Mechanics slowly started to pile out of the Starlifter, hauling bags and toolboxes. But the fifth person off this aircraft was a female in battle dress uniform, and Jay thought she looked quite pregnant. She also looked wonderful.

As Shawna stepped down the air stairs at the front of the C-141, she appeared to be peering down at the steps, careful not to trip. Then, as she stepped to the tarmac, her large bag in her left hand, she looked up and caught Jay's eyes. He locked onto her gaze, and regardless of protocol, she provided him a quick and intimate wave. This was the Shawna he knew. The Shawna he still loved.

* * * * *

Shawna steadied her step as she exited the C-141. These crew entrance doors weren't exactly airline jetways. She hesitated as she put her foot onto the top anti-skid step. It wasn't only the stairs that bothered her. It was what she expected to see in her first look outside. She expected to see Jay.

Although her short stature didn't require it, Shawna stooped slightly to clear the door. Kevin, not Jay, was on her mind at this moment. He was a good husband. Not an exciting husband, but a good one. Good for her at this time in life. Jay had been only a passing memory in recent years. Until the last few months, that is, when she'd been forced to think about him again.

This mission would be challenging. For one thing, she would be stuck behind a desk, her pregnant status limiting her flightline activity. It would also limit her interaction with Jay. She was here to support the Elmendorf C-141s, and that would be her focus. She was here by assignment rather than her desire to be with Jay. She had drawn the short straw at the low end of the wing's maintenance officer totem pole, and that's what brought her to Gallant Eagle. Through a strange mix of coincidence on her part and active planning by Jay, they found themselves on the same ramp in North Carolina.

Glancing down, as if afraid these steps would cause her to lose her grip on life, she felt her heart pound. She had to look up sometime, she couldn't put it off a second longer.

Jay's eyes locked onto hers immediately, and she couldn't resist a quick wave. Shawna suddenly knew that all was soft and easy again. Or rough and complicated. There was a fine line in between.

The Game

It's a big game.
We sit patiently in Maintenance Control.
Waiting for something to happen; anything.
But the radios and telephones are silent.

All is ready.
Fifteen C-130s sit poised for launch.
There is tension in this room; nothing to do,
And so we wait.

No one dares speak.
We want to pass this test.
All is too perfect; it's only a game.
Everyone acts nonchalant.

So much can go wrong.
Sixty starters must rotate, each like a light bulb.
One day it works; next day it doesn't.
Now it is time.

Fifteen Herks make a lot of noise,
When their starters simultaneously engage.
Will all of the boost pumps work? The anti-skid?
And what about the fuel correction lights?

Trucks are parked on the outer ramp,
With mechanics perched on the hoods.
Everyone acts confident; in charge.
It's only an act.

The first bird breaks ground.
It only a test, but the landing gear sucks up for real.
More noise on the runway; more airplanes, more props.
It's only a game.

Our Year 2016: Distant Planet

23 Years Later

If the motion of every particle of matter in the universe were precisely reversed at any instant, the course of nature would be simply reversed forever after.

Lord Kelvin (1863)

Chapter 38

Last Chance

The Minds knew this was their only chance during this orbit around their sun. The amount of energy to be used was more than any other scientific experiment in history, and there had been many energy-hungry tests on this planet.

If a new receptor had to be sought, it would require starting all over again, locating an intelligent being and hoping something would be different the next time. There was no reason to think it would be.

When the powerful pulse went out into space-time, everyone perceived the sense of last chance. This was an experiment that wouldn't be approved again unless it succeeded the first time.

The results would be nearly immediate. There wouldn't be the normal delays caused by the speed of light. The Minds and the rest of their world would know right away whether the signal was received. Interpretation of the signal by the receiving intelligence was an entirely separate problem, and was the part of the equation beyond the control of the Minds.

No one doubted that the intelligent beings of the watery planet would try to intercept the signal. The receptor had been a good choice in that regard. This member of their species was easy to read and appropriately skeptical of the signal – ideal characteristics. The Minds might never know whether their choice of receptor was a typical intelligent being of this world or a miraculous trick of chance, a kink in the curvature of space and time.

Making this contact was only the beginning of the experiment. But all else hinged on this moment.

2016: Earth

But Easter Day is Christmas time,
And far away is near,
And two and two is more than four
And over there is here.

W. Williams (1924)

C-130 Flight Engineer's Overhead Panel

Chapter 39

Reawakening

For the first time in over twenty years, Shawna's memory of the future awoke her. She wanted to call Jay immediately. But she couldn't.

She rolled over and looked at Kevin, sleeping peacefully on his stomach. He was looking old now, although 64 wasn't ancient. Shawna was 58, and she felt at least as old as Kevin. Both were retired now, doing quite well on their Air Force pensions. Kevin had never made brigadier general, and separated from the Air Force only months after Shawna. He exited the military with twenty-five years of service.

Shawna was promoted to lieutenant colonel as part of her retirement. She never got to pin on the silver leaves, but she would get the pay. This loophole in the Air Force regulations had opened and closed several times in recent decades, and it would probably be gone again soon. But for Shawna, it spelled financial benefit, so she took it. But it didn't help her self-esteem. The Air Force wouldn't let her stay beyond the minimum of twenty years necessary for retirement.

After military retirement, they found themselves adjusting to civilian life with some difficulty. Kevin was better at it than she was. He seldom talked about his flying and never discussed his military positions. He found a new aerospace job behind a desk that suited him, and he moved on. The Air Force didn't hold a lot of pleasant memories for Kevin Leah. He had new interests now, and even Shawna was of reduced importance in his life. Or at least he was more independent of her. But that wasn't due to lack of love for Shawna. It was simply due to a sense of peace within his own world, an adjustment to civilian life that had been kind to Kevin.

Shawna, on the other hand, openly admitted missing the Air Force. Not all of it had been perfect, but lots of it had been pure excitement. She missed her friends, she missed the airplanes, and she missed the mission. But she loved Kevin. She also knew they had increasingly separate interests, and they were both comfortable with that concept.

She brushed back her tightly curled hair – longer than ever, just touching her back, and barely streaked with gray. Shawna quietly slid out of bed, pulled on her robe, and shuffled into her slippers. She skipped the normal wake-up brushing of her teeth and walked to the adjacent room. Nikolas lay sound asleep, his bedroom window wide-open with the curtains waving in the morning breeze. She went to the window and slid it closed. Nikolas didn't stir.

Shawna walked to the balcony door and looked down on the brushy ravine below the house. She pondered her isolation. There were few friends here. Flagstaff was a far cry from the bigger cities she had enjoyed throughout most of her Air Force career. Phoenix was within driving range, but it was a long trip. Flagstaff had some of the things she liked in society, but many of the things she liked weren't here.

* * * * * *

Jay Rotella, age 69 and looking ten years younger, power-walked or kayaked on a small lake near his house nearly every day. He could hardly wait to see Shawna. She would arrive in Burbank later that day, and he was feeling fidgety. Jay sat in the living room, trying to concentrate on the latest layman's astrophysics book by Tom Rogus. It wasn't beneath Jay's level at all, particularly when Rogus went into detail regarding the latest cosmology theories. Jay respected someone who could describe complicated concepts in layman's terms.

He scanned the obvious preparations in the living room. Every-thing looked tidy and organized, just the way he wanted Shawna to find it. This house was only blocks from his old townhome, but it was a lot roomier. He wasn't sure it was worth maintaining a yard and doing the normal homeowner chores, but it gave him an area of concentration, something he had never needed when he worked for the Air Guard.

Retired from the Guard for over ten years, Jay was employed for another seven years after that, full-time as an FAA maintenance inspector at LAX. The daily drive in the freeway traffic had been horrendous. And the job was too much like punching a clock. He left the Air Guard knowing it could never be replaced. He was right.

But the FAA job was cushy, embarrassingly so. And the big airliners were fun to work with. There just wasn't that sense of mission he loved so much. The money was great, but there was something missing, and it wasn't just the C-130s.

Now he had all the time in the world to enjoy in his second retirement. There was the great outdoors, some freelance consulting for an aviation company, and the nighttime sky above.

Jay looked at his watch. Only six more hours before his Shawna would be with him again.

* * * * * *

"You cleaned things up for me," said Shawna as soon as she walked through the door.

"Now what makes you think that?" asked Jay. "I'm always this organized."

"Right," laughed Shawna.

This house was a reminder of what drove Jay. He didn't live in the past, but C-130 photos formed a big part of his home's decorative theme. The walls harbored Herk photos, and a carved wooden C-130 model rested on the coffee table. How could an airplane so ugly be so beautiful?

On the hearth, proudly displayed, was the hardcover edition of *Personal Finances for the Unafraid* by Irene Bennett. It was a book that hadn't been a best seller, but it had been well received. The content was timeless, although the book's numerical examples had to be extrapolated for the wild financial inflation of the past few years.

Shawna was pleased to see Irene's book displayed in this home. She loved this house for all of the right reasons. She loved this city. She loved Jay. She looked for the words to start things in the right direction. They seldom faced a problem with words these days.

"How's Nikolas?" asked Jay.

"Big day," said Shawna. "He's invited his dad to the new 'Aquanauts' movie. It's real 3-D and there's a full-size portable aquarium at the theater. You can even splash around in the water with the fish afterwards."

"What about fathers?" asked Jay.

"They get to watch. It would be quite a site to see a theater full of seniors in bathing suits."

They talked comfortably about Kevin and Nikolas, as well as Shawna's oldest son, now in his senior year at the University of Arizona. Shawna tried to explain about Kevin's increased desire for privacy. It wasn't lack of love. Their relationship had never been deeply sensual, and now Kevin was developing other interests. There was no misunderstanding. Finally Shawna broke the trend of the conversation.

"Mind if tell you about the latest?" asked Shawna.

"That's why you're here," said Jay. "But first let me get dinner going."

* * * * * *

After dinner, Jay cleared the table while Shawna read the bookmarked chapter of a book he had placed in front of her. The chapter was entitled "Space-Time," and it was part of a large-print book with a beautiful photo of the M51 Whirlpool Galaxy on the cover. It looked like a coffee-table book for amateur astronomers.

As Shawna read her assigned chapter, Jay placed the dishes in the sink, added some hot water to let them soak, and returned to the table. He sat quietly in his pushed-back chair. Shawna knew he was trying very hard not to fidget and disturb her reading. And she knew that was difficult for Jay.

Shawna understood most of what she read, but she turned the pages of the book back several times to reread some paragraphs, to assure she wasn't missing anything important. When she finished the chapter, she closed the book, placed it in front of her on the table, and pushed her own chair back.

"Well written," she said.

"I thought so, too. Does it make sense?"

"Mostly," said Shawna. "Of course, I'm not quite the expert that you are, but I followed most of it."

"What did you think about the concept of curved space-time?" asked Jay.

"Well, I don't pretend to understand it, but I get the general idea. Even on our earth-like scale, curvature of our planet disappears."

"Yes," said Jay. "That's the whole point."

"Are the Lorentz transformations important? I really didn't understand them."

"Nothing to worry about," said Jay. "Leave it to us physicists. What about imaginary time?"

"Well, I read it," said Shawna. "But it didn't build a fire in me."

"The theory is pretty mathematical," said Jay. "But the basic concept isn't very difficult to grasp. Imaginary numbers are fairly easy to understand. Yet they give negative values when multiplied by themselves."

"So maybe time is similar?" said Shawna.

"Mathematically, yes," said Jay. "But the arrow of time always goes forward, as far as we know."

"Do you think a reversal could occur in an isolated instance like myself?" asked Shawna.

"I'll admit to being perplexed by that," said Jay. "The biggest mystery is why it would happen so infrequently to you. I think I could accept time reversal, but it would be a lot easier if there was some consistency."

"Back to the future again," said Shawna with a grin.

"Or forward to the past," said Jay. "Space-time is so encompassing that cause and effect can get intertwined. The Butterfly Effect is my favorite example."

"I've heard about it," said Shawna. "But how does it relate to this?"

"It's just an example of the complexity of cause and effect. Meteorologists like to use the example of the butterfly flapping its wings in Africa."

Shawna was staring at Jay now, wondering where this was going. She knew Jay well enough to know he needed to use examples to explain things, and she liked it. But she didn't always follow the details.

"So the butterfly flaps its wings, and..." said Shawna.

"Well, there's an effect on the atmosphere. Not much of an effect, of course, but it disturbs the air surrounding the butterfly. And that influences, on a very tiny scale, the atmosphere in Africa, and that influences the world's weather in an unexpected way."

"And so on and so on," said Shawna. "But the effect isn't unexpected."

"No, but the flapping of the wings was unexpected, so the meteorologist's otherwise accurate forecast is thrown for a loop. The point is – it's impossible to be entirely deterministic in predictions. Anything is possible."

"That bails the weatherman out," said Shawna. "Don't blame him, blame the butterfly."

They both laughed, but Shawna got the point.

They discussed the concepts of space-time a bit more, but Jay wasn't intent on having Shawna become an expert. He was more interested in the details of her most recent memory.

"It's the desert again?" asked Jay.

"Yes, but definitely not Flagstaff. That's high desert or chaparral."

"So low desert, maybe Phoenix?"

"Could be," said Shawna. "Does the electronic gear I described make any more sense?"

"Well, it sounds like a sensitive receiver with a very high signal-to-noise ratio. Nothing we don't already have on the astronomical shelf."

"Where?" asked Shawna.

"At almost any modern radio astronomy observatory," said Jay. "The details from your recent dreams are pretty specific, even the manufacturers' names sound somewhat familiar. I plan to look into that."

"Good. So do we still have that appointment?" asked Shawna. "I need to leave by one o'clock tomorrow to catch my flight."

"No problem," said Jay. "In the morning, we'll take that little field trip to Jeremy's office. He's quite a guy."

Chapter 40

Signature

Jeremy was a huge fellow. He weighed well over 250 pounds and stood 6-foot-3. His blond hair might have been bleached. He even looked like a California surfer, probably no older than twenty-five.

UCLA's medical labs extended throughout the campus. Jeremy's abode was on the fourth floor of a tall modern brick building that still smelled new. As Jay and Shawna entered the room, they were greeted by loud rap music they hadn't heard in years.

"I'll turn it down!" yelled Jeremy. He clicked the stereo remote control, and the music dropped so low they could barely hear it. He clicked again, and the soft sound of classical music filled the room.

"Beethoven," said Jeremy.

"Man of many interests," replied Jay.

"Music drives my experiments. You gotta' listen to the world's background. It can tell you a lot."

Jay and Shawna didn't know what to say, so they ignored the concept. Jay had warned her this guy was different.

"Jeremy, this is Shawna. She's the astrologer I was telling you about."

Jay winked at Shawna, and she shook her head in mock disdain.

"I'm a Virgo," said Jeremy. "You never know. Could be something in that stuff. Have a seat on the table, Shawna."

The table was a typical doctor's office examining slab, complete with a hand-cranked paper cover.

Jeremy rolled a computer worktable toward her.

"We won't shave you, although it's the best way to get accurate readings. That's my standard disclaimer."

Jeremy began hooking up electrodes. Then Shawna laid down on the table and tried to relax.

The electroencephalogram took only a few minutes. Jeremy started reviewing the results immediately, as Shawna sat up and brushed her hair back into shape. Jeremy seemed to detect something unusual right away.

"See here," he said, pushing the EEG cart closer to Shawna. "This tracing is the one that we're most interested in. It shows a lot of activity, and it's usually latent. Look here, Jay."

Jay leaned over to inspect the tracings, but they meant nothing to him.

"Normal brain activity shows up as rather irregular bursts, like you see here," said Jeremy. He used a pen to point out the uneven pulses.

Then Jeremy shifted his pen to the right and circled an area of steep peaks on the EEG.

"But this is what I'm interested in, because these pulses are more rhythmic."

The blond giant continued to survey the tracings, saying nothing more. Finally, after several more minutes of investigation, he spoke again.

"I'm not prone to jumping to conclusions. But based on what Jay has told me, I'm rather surprised to see such a clear peak right here."

He pointed at a double-spike on the tracings.

"What's it indicate?" asked Jay.

"Well, I've never seen an EEG quite like this. And I've seen a lot of them. But it sure looks like what I prefer to call the 'fortune teller' signature."

* * * * * *

Shawna and Jay sat in Burbank's small airline terminal, trying to ignore the television newscast blasting from the far wall.

"Enough probing for one day," said Shawna.

"Admit it. You love it when I probe," said Jay.

"Most of the time," said Shawna. "I'm not sure about this."

"Let's give Jeremy some time to help us figure this out. He's a good guy."

"I do like him," said Shawna. "But I'm not sure I want him sharing this with the rest of the world."

"He won't," said Jay. "Jeremy's discrete, and he'll only discuss it with the medical experts we approve. Some of them have already been helpful. They compare this to an almost-forgotten case written up in *Science Journal* a few years ago. Supposedly, there was a somewhat similar instance at Purdue University at least two decades ago. It was ignored by nearly everyone until the case analysis was finally published as part of a recent investigation into epileptic seizures from victims who claim they have seen UFO's."

"Now there's a category I'm pleased to be a part of," said Shawna.

"Well, it just shows there may be a relationship between episodes similar to what you've experienced and some possible attempts at alien communication."

"With nut cases," said Shawna.

"Who's to say?" said Jay.

* * * * * *

As they awaited the departure of Shawna's flight, Jay tried to tune out the sound of the television. He wanted to explain this in a way Shawna would clearly understand.

"So here's the close-up of Tau Ceti," said Jay, showing her a letter-size sheet with a spiked starlike object in the center. "The exact coordinates from your 1993 memory are overlaid on it. Notice that the star is just a bit removed from that declination coordinate, assumed to be southerly."

He pointed at the appropriate spot slightly below Tau Ceti on the chart, and then he continued.

"Remember, we only have declination to go by, so we're running with only half the necessary data."

"What happened to Polaris?" asked Shawna.

"Well, it's still a candidate, but Polaris' location is further from your coordinate lines than Tau Ceti, and there have been some developments that convince me this is our candidate."

"Candidate," repeated Shawna. "Sounds like you've got something specific in mind."

"As a matter of fact, yes. The real breakthrough came when Tom Henkins, a UCLA astronomer, got involved. When I told him 2016 was the projected year for whatever was going to happen, he immediately recognized the problem."

"Which is?" Shawna knew Jay had promised some answers today, and this was already sounding promising.

"Which is – stars move. So Tau Ceti wasn't there in 1993 nor was it there when my old star atlas was published several years earlier."

"You're saying the coordinates mark the spot where Tau Ceti was sometime in the past?" said Shawna.

"Almost," replied Jay. "It's where Tau Ceti would be in 2016."

Shawna's face lit up. She saw the association and it made sense

"Let me show you," said Jay.

He penciled in an arrow with its base on Tau Ceti. The arrow pointed towards the bottom of the page, the head of the arrow resting on the spot provided by Shawna's memory coordinate.

"Imagine this arrow as a vector," said Jay. "It's got both direction and magnitude. Now, this isn't as precise as it looks, because we don't have an exact tangential velocity for Tau Ceti, and we're only working with one coordinate. Stars simply move too slowly for us to notice any motion in our lifetimes, except on a very precise astronomical scale. But it's generally a good fit with the data."

Shawna was bobbing up and down now, with a big smile on her face.

"So we almost missed it," she said. "If my memory episode had provided fewer decimal places, we would never have noticed the difference in location, would we?"

"In fact," said Jay, "that's one of the things that has convinced Tom Henkins this is a valid future prediction. The accuracy of your memory, unless you're an astrophysics whiz, puts Tau Ceti right where it will be this year, at least in declination."

"So he thinks this is an accurate prediction of the future?" asked Shawna.

"Yup."

"Well...," she said, "Maybe I can make a living as an astrologer after all."

Chapter 41

Temporal Familiarity

Shawna parked her pickup truck at the entrance to the gated house. Nikolas sat in the passenger seat, after a reluctant shopping trip to the mall. He got the hiking boots he wanted, but it cost him an hour of mom-son bonding in the sporting goods store.

"Do you want to go in with me?" asked Shawna. "I'll only be a few minutes."

"I'll stay here," replied Nikolas.

She hit the switches that rolled down both front windows. Then she stretched to grab the notebook from behind her on the rear seat and left Nikolas to himself with his electronic game-pad. A teen-age son could certainly entertain himself, but Shawna refused to leave him home on a Saturday when she needed to conduct real estate business. He was always good company, and the bribe of hiking boots worked well.

As she walked towards the gate, Shawna wiggled the "For Sale" sign, making sure it was still secure. There was no reason to think it wouldn't be. Her trademark realtor's uniform was a throwback to another decade – conservative bright green blouse with the company logo and an obviously tight mid-length skirt. Considering her age, it still got the customer's attention.

Shawna opened the gate with her hand-held remote, and started up the sidewalk toward the front door. Reaching into her skirt pocket, she felt the micro-size front door lock transmitter and hit the button without removing it from her pocket. A jolt of terror made her jump, and the memory poured into view.

It was a full-screen movie on a display too small to contain it. Data scrolled before her eyes, all a repeat of her recent memories. The dish of a huge radio telescope rotated before her, swinging down towards the horizon and stopping at a constellation she had finally memorized without having to connect the dots. It was definitely Cetus riding low near the southern horizon. She immediately focused on Tau Ceti, which she now knew quite well, although it wasn't a particularly bright star. Shawna had learned the exact position and could pick it out from the typically confusing background of nondescript points of light.

Complex electronic equipment was clearly visible off to her left. She was in this movie, and she had time to look around. The equipment was all clearly emblazoned with manufacturers' logos. Today, for the first time, the equipment had alphanumeric labels as well. Part numbers.

* * * * * *

Shawna finally stopped trembling. She stabilized herself on the walkway, did an abrupt about-face, and headed back out the gate towards the parked truck. Nikolas was still playing the same level of electronic *Rocketplane* when she climbed into her truck and quickly engaged the ignition. She ignored the seat belt chimes and started to drive away, buckling as she steered. She needed a telephone real fast, and her cell phone was at home. Wait a minute. There was a phone in that house. Too late, her vehicle was already halfway down the block. There was a telephone in her nearby real estate office. She couldn't get there fast enough.

* * * * * *

"I've reserved a room for you at the University Inn" said Shawna into the phone.

Jay was arriving on Monday, and from there they were flying to Socorro, New Mexico. Nikolas would stay with her real estate partner.

"Isn't that a bit of overkill?" said Jay.

"Probably. But this town is smaller than you think. Everybody loves to talk."

"And if they talk?" taunted Jay.

"Like I said, it's probably overkill, but it makes me feel better."

"A buffer for Nikolas, I suppose," replied Jay, his voice lower now, more understanding.

"And for me, too. Besides, I'll be leaving Nikolas alone for two days, so we could use the time together before I go. I bet that sounds like overkill, too."

"Well, he's old enough now to take care of himself. Or is he?"

"He'd be insulted if I hired a babysitter. But it's tempting for a teenager to get into trouble when his mom is out of town. It's something I should probably get used to."

"He's growing up fast."

"Too fast."

Their conversation turned to the upcoming schedule at Socorro. It was still a week away, but it occupied their attention every day, every hour.

"The part numbers helped a lot," said Jay. "I'll call Dennis at Socorro tonight and see if he has checked them out yet.

"Is there enough time?" asked Shawna. "My memory is focused on Thursday."

"I know," said Jay. "But the part numbers are only an additional detail. If this team really knows what they're doing, they'll find those part numbers match up to what we've already assembled. All of your past details have provided everything we need."

They talked about the timing of Jay's visit. He was planning to fly an older Piper Arrow he now owned, but this was too important to rely upon a single mode of transportation. If there were significant weather problems, Jay would meet her in Phoenix, and they would leave from there via airline. It was faster than connecting with the commuter carrier out of Flagstaff.

"The news media is in the dark, for now," said Jay. "There haven't been any leaks as far as I can tell. And if this doesn't turn out to be what we think it is, the National Radio Astronomy Observatory won't have a lot of egg on it's face."

The radio telescopes of the Very Large Array in New Mexico had been committed to this project after a scientist named Troy Doheney had taken a special interest in Shawna's memories of the future. Troy was originally associated with UCLA's search for a link between brain activity and the 'fortune teller' signature that was noted during Shawna's medical examination. Troy had led the charge on a concept many considered a waste of telescope time. But now all twenty-seven radio telescopes of the VLA were to serve as radio antennas linked simultaneously to this important moment in space-time. It was a far-out possibility, but it was worth the shot in the dark. Little routine research time would be lost on such a brief undertaking, and there was that one tiny but intense hope.

Chapter 42

Socorro

The weather was perfect. Fall in Flagstaff, just before the real snows came, was always a treat. The airport sat more than a mile high, and Jay was grateful for the low temperature. He had planned his arrival with a partial fuel load, keeping the gross weight down for the takeoff the following day in the thin air, just in case.

As Jay tied the airplane down for the night, Shawna entered the ramp through the passenger gate, which someone had unlocked for her. When she approached, Jay was reminded of her stark athletic beauty. No doubt she had dressed for him, and he liked it. She wore a heavy tan skirt, hemline well below her knees. Her wide-lapel matching jacket was open to reveal a soft knit white blouse. She was a picture of comfort. And he loved what he couldn't see.

"My RSP," Shawna said when she was within voice-range.

They used this term a lot lately, in defiance of their situation. There was a lot less sex these days, and a lot more understanding. Maybe it was a natural tradeoff.

"Careful," said Jay. "This is Flagstaff, you know."

"Sometimes I just don't care," replied Shawna with a grin.

"Nor do I," said Jay. "Tell me we're flying away together."

"We're flying away together."

"That's what I wanted to hear," said Jay. "Let's make one last call to Socorro to make sure everything is ready to go."

"Time's short," said Shawna. "For some of us it's so short that it's backwards."

* * * * *

Descending out of eleven thousand feet, Jay contacted Albuquerque Air Route Traffic Control Center and canceled his instrument flight plan.

"Remain on your present squawk code, and expect VFR traffic advisories en route to Socorro," said the controller.

"Roger, thanks," replied Jay.

It was still over a hundred miles to Socorro, but the Very Large Array of telescopes was lined up right along Victor 264, and Jay wanted a closer view. Saint Johns was a few miles behind them now. They had been confined to this small cockpit for almost two hours. The air was clear and smooth, so dropping lower seemed reasonable and a lot more scenic.

In a few minutes, Jay easily identified Interstate 60 and headed directly towards the bend at Quemado. From there it was a fairly straight shot to Socorro. The National Radio Astronomy Observatory, the Very Large Array of radio telescopes, was halfway down Route 60 between Quemado and Socorro, right along their path. Plenty of high peaks remained, so Jay stopped the descent at 9500 feet. The Albuquerque ATC frequency was silent, except for occasional chatter with an airliner up in the flight levels.

"There's a road coming in from the right," said Jay. "Just beyond that junction are the radio telescopes of the VLA. See it?"

Shawna peered through the windshield but didn't see the observatory antennas. Then she saw the pattern of the railroad tracks that held the telescopes.

"Y-shaped? It's huge!" said Shawna.

"That's it," replied Jay. "Imagine the resolution when all twenty-seven of those antennas are coupled together."

"Just for us."

"For everybody," said Jay. "But if this doesn't work out, I'm sure they'll remind us that it was only for us."

* * * * *

The small city of Socorro sat fifty miles from the VLA. The town certainly didn't feel like a scientific Mecca. Inside the Holiday Inn, Shawna and Jay joined UCLA astronomer Tom Henkins in his room. Tom had no background in radio astronomy, but his important role in resolving this astronomical mystery had tempted him to join the other scientists at this site. He wouldn't miss such an exciting event – a life's dream. Of all the astronomers and electronic technicians involved in the long hours leading up to this half-day event, Tom had been the constant cheerleader. Without his enthusiasm, it was doubtful the necessary money would have been allocated to the project. There were even some private investment funds Tom had successfully appropriated. Without that private money, the whole project would probably have been forced to go public with a news release that might become the laughing stock of the decade.

No one wanted to lose the opportunity, but few of the scientists considered the chance of receiving a signal better than 10 percent. Most considered the possibility quite a bit less. Still, in the realm of the search for extraterrestrial intelligence, this was relatively high odds. But it was a whole lot less than a sure thing.

Chapter 43

VLA

The end of November is a beautiful time on the Plains of San Agustin. The temperature is usually moderate during the daytime, comfortably cool. Evenings are downright cold, and the stars burn bright on clear nights. However, the weather conditions for this project weren't critical. Under overcast skies, day or night, these electronic telescopes can see just as well as under clear skies.

The Tau Ceti Project was scheduled to begin 30 minutes before midnight Universal Time on the date stamped into Shawna's memory, November 21. That equated to 4:30 pm local time, about an hour before Tau Ceti rose above the eastern horizon at 5:32 pm. Just in case of problems with the well-tested equipment, an advance start of an hour should provide enough time to recover from any start-up glitches. The radio antennas would be aligned nearly horizontally when initial signal from the star arrived.

The antennas would simultaneously track the star for nearly eleven hours until Tau Ceti dropped below the western horizon at 4:06 am. The project would officially end when the signal was cut off by the star's descent below the distant hills.

During the observing cycle, Tau Ceti would reach its highest elevation of approximately 40 degrees when positioned true south. The angle of the telescopes would hardly change throughout the prime portion of the observation period. Most of the movement would be horizontal.

This operation wasn't dependent upon the weather or the time of day, although lightning storms could temporarily interrupt the observations. There were no thunderstorms in the New Mexico forecast.

Final equipment calibration was complete by two o'clock in the afternoon, and there was nothing further for anyone to do. Among the visitors in the control room were Tom Henkins, Shawna, Jay, and Troy Doheney, serving as a physicist from the nearby Santa Fe Institute. Troy had most recently been working with social scientists regarding how to deal with a first-contact situation involving extraterrestrial intelligence. He had helped bring Shawna's memories of the future to the attention of scientists at the observatory. His national notoriety from his think-tank work in Santa Fe had been important in tipping the balance. Everyone listened to Troy Doheney.

But there were several points of controversy, even to those who believed this was a worthy effort. The greatest debate involved where to listen for the signal. The obvious target, Tau Ceti, was at a different physical location now than its optical place in the sky. In fact, it had already moved twelve years farther in its intergalactic journey since tonight's light was received on earth. So where it now appeared in the sky wasn't its true location. And if this incoming message were faster than the speed of light, targeting the optical location of the star would put the antennas too far afield. Thus, the biggest question among the believers was where to look.

The final decision had been to assume instantaneous communication, though such transmissions were only theoretical, and thus target a blank spot in the sky where Tau Ceti should be beaming its communication energy tonight. It was a location in the sky that was nearly on top of today's visual location for the star. But it was far enough away to miss a tightly beamed transmission from another world, if the signal was at tonight's optical location. There might be only one chance.

A separate and more threatening issue was the nature of the communication source. If it was a faster-than-light transmission, such a source implied the use of particles equivalent to elusive Tachyons, a purely theoretical atomic particle not yet verified here on earth. If the emitted beam were based on Tachyons or other undiscovered elementary particles, how would they intercept it? Unless, of course, the transmitting being had figured that out and encoded a special download signal for primitive earthlings. That implied a lot of faith in the transmitting intelligence. But there was no other choice.

Shawna and Jay played no part in the observational program, and they were wise enough to leave the VLA scientists and technicians to themselves as much as possible. With them in the glassed-in observation area were scientists Tom Henkins and Troy Doheney, and the latest arrival, Melissa Henesie. Melissa's late arrival had been a special thrill for Shawna. She had flown in from the Pentagon, where she now worked as a civil service public relations officer, to be with Shawna this day. It had taken a last minute flight to Albuquerque and then a drive by rental car to Socorro, but she had made it just as things were winding up that afternoon at the VLA. The security personnel hardly questioned her when she flashed her Pentagon ID card.

She had come almost directly from a meeting in Washington. And that too meant a lot to Shawna. In the observation area, there were some tearful moments between them. But now it was all high-pitched talk and anticipation. Just before the VLA receivers kicked on, Shawna wrapped her arms around Melissa in a full-body hug.

When 4:30 pm arrived, nothing special happened, except for a brief PA announcement by the duty controller who noted: "Tau Ceti Project is active." At that moment, all but one of the twenty-seven telescopes swung in their respective mounts to focus on the horizon to the east. The telescopes stopped their movement when they hit the projected spot for Tau Ceti's emergence from the horizon a little south of due east, and their tracking clutches were placed in idle. One telescope was out of commission for preventive maintenance, and that maintenance cycle was too important to be interrupted by any project. It wouldn't reduce the reception strength in any noticeable way.

Electronic monitors in the control room displayed self-test routines from all twenty-six telescopes. Linked together, these radio telescopes would provide detailed interrogation of the target. Tonight they would be listening on a specific frequency from Shawna's memory, and they were doing it with more sensitivity than normally reserved for a mere star.

The equipment was designed to intercept powerful electromagnetic signals transmitted from a specific spot in the sky. If all went well, the real heroes would be the chain of computers ganged together to accept the influx of data at an unheard-of rate. The biggest obstacle that could lead to failure of this tonight's attempt was the potential overload of these computers from the sudden influx of data from the magnified signal. An even worse scenario was what was expected by most of the personnel involved in this project – no incoming signal at all. They were used to such failures, taking them in stride.

* * * * * *

No one was surprised when the flat signal with occasional atmospheric noise spikes appeared on the master monitor at 5:34 pm. It was Tau Ceti's normal electromagnetic signature, overflow from the star's nearby optical position. Over the next few minutes, the signal showed less static and increased intensity as Tau Ceti edged upward from the horizon, out of the thickest swath of the earth's atmosphere. By the time the telescopes reached an elevation angle of only a few degrees, at 5:40 pm, the signal distinctly changed. This was all perfectly expected from a star rising in the east, escaping from New Mexico's horizon interference. One of the monitors now showed a star as it might look in an optical telescope, with a false-color image. But that monitor was for the novice visitors. The scientists attended to the electronic displays that indicated signal strength at a variety of frequencies. The displays were nominal for a 3.5 magnitude star that was slightly off target at the expected location of the communication signal.

Shawna knew Jay had brought his small telescope as a diversion from the boredom of an all-night wait. But she wasn't sure she would be able to leave this control room until the entire project cycle was over. The expected time for receipt of the signal was 10:49 pm, equating to the maximum elevation angle of Tau Ceti. That marked the moment when the earth's atmosphere would least interfere with reception from Tau Ceti's area of the sky.

By 7:00 pm, everything was boringly routine, and Shawna desired more than a coffee break. After over three hours of waiting in this room, she was ready for a change of pace.

"I'm ready for that telescopic view," she said.

"Let's do it," replied Jay.

They invited Melissa, Tom, and Troy to go outside with them. Tom was absorbed in a science journal and declined. Troy and Melissa said they'd join them after Jay's small telescope was set up. They knew how cold the New Mexico desert could be on a November night.

* * * * * *

The Meade ETX-125 was still a state-of-the-art telescope, though now over twenty years old. What made it most revolutionary was cost. In the past two decades, go-to commands were built into amateur telescopes in a manner that made them truly user-friendly at an affordable price. The world's professional telescopes had enjoyed this technology for a half-century, but now amateur astronomers could punch in a Messier nebulae catalog designator, and the telescope would swing promptly to its target. Even the rapidly shifting planets were included in the most basic database. The first telescope to really bring this capability to the low-budget amateur was the Meade ETX.

But it didn't just happen. First the telescope had to be aligned accurately, especially an older model like this one. If the movable tripod mount was off even a fraction of an inch, you could be looking at black sky, and you'd find yourself stumbling your way around just like the bad old days. Jay finished the alignment procedure in minimum time tonight. It was quite dark now, a full hour after sunset, and it was already desert-numbing cold.

Shawna stood quietly next to Jay, rubbing her wool mittens together as he finished the alignment.

"It's only appropriate," announced Jay, "for our first observation tonight to be the universe-famous star called Tau Ceti."

Shawna looked back over her shoulder at Cetus to the southeast. It wasn't an easy constellation for an amateur, riding low near the horizon. To see it as the ancients did – a whale swimming in the sky – took a lot of imagination. The five-point tail was quite evident, but most observers thought it looked more like a head. Shawna had already focused on this nondescript "head" the moment they had exited the building. She had seen Cetus in her memory episodes more times than she cared to count, not recognizing it for what it was for many years. It's configuration looked much the same in the cold New Mexico sky.

Jay dialed in "Tau Ceti" on the remote control's menu of stars, and punched the Go-To button. The small scope's tracking motor drove the black tube slowly to the southeast and promptly stopped about fifteen degrees above the horizon. The gears made a faint humming noise as the telescope continued to slew unhurriedly towards the star. Then the sound stopped, there was a quick beep, and the telescope was on-target. Jay approached the right-angle eyepiece and focused the star.

"It's yours," said Jay.

Jay pulled back to give Shawna plenty of room, and she approached the tripod. Shawna was immediately thrilled at the crispness of the image. It seemed in perfect focus for her eye. Maybe it was the telescope, maybe it was the clarity of the New Mexico night, and maybe it was her excitement this evening. Tau Ceti hovered in the eyepiece, strikingly three-dimensional.

"Wonderful," said Shawna.

"Just your routine yellow sun-like star," said Jay.

"Not at all. This one is very special."

Shawna backed away from the eyepiece and gazed at the constellation of Cetus, connecting the dots that formed the whale. Jay walked behind her and moved close. They barely touched, Jay's chest against Shawna's shoulders. A shiver went down her back, along with a flash-image of that night on the parade field at Howard Air Force Base. Shawna's thoughts dwelled on Panama, where history had demonstrated that a volatile political situation could settle into a semblance of order, against what seemed like insurmountable odds. Wherever you looked closely, good and bad were intertwined. And there was hope and exciting revelations waiting everywhere. She finally spoke.

"Beautiful night, don't you think?"

Jay didn't respond to that comment, but he did inch even closer, pushing his chest firmly against her back. Shawna spoke again.

"Really beautiful. Especially Tau Ceti."

* * * * * *

The signal they were waiting for was received at 0452 UT or precisely 9:52:21 Mountain Standard Time at the National Radio Astronomy Observatory on the Plains of San Agustin in New Mexico. It was an intense electromagnetic burst focused entirely in the radio spectrum, and it continued for three full minutes. Tau Ceti was almost precisely at its highest elevation at that time, but still relatively low in the southern sky. The electromagnetic burst was focused so precisely that no other observatory in the world reported anything unusual that night. Unless a radio telescope was focused precisely on the celestial coordinates, nothing would have been detected.

Two of the linked computers in the download array crashed immediately after detecting the intense signal. The remaining computers performed admirably, taking up the slack from the overloaded machines. The data streamed in for three minutes and then ceased for the rest of the night.

Initial analysis revealed extensive numerically-formatted material. Some of it formed spatial patterns of columns and rows that were obviously of intelligent origin. There were no graphic files. It was all numeric, and it would take months, maybe years or decades, to determine what had been received.

Dark Sky

Worlds spin, unseen in the dark
By even the largest telescopes on earth.
But they are there, as few would dispute.
Imagination provides the details.

There is a presence that can be felt
But seldom admitted by the night observer.
To admit the presence would be to dispute the data.
No earth-like world has been detected – yet.

Absence of data doesn't dispute the obvious.
Life in abundance could be just beyond observation,
Past the threshold of present technologies.
But it could be there just as surely as not.

And so does life look back at us?
Wondering as we do of the possibility of life.
Perplexed by the lack of contact
In a universe so vast.

Could life be everywhere?
Simply below the limits of communication
Over the distances and times required for success.
Technology may not be a universal obsession.

The earth-bound astronomer looks up
Into a dark sky.
Dark in appearance but bright in life.
Life may be everywhere, or nowhere.

Thus, the puzzle.
Is it best to search?
Or simply wait?
And how passionately do we desire the answer?

2017: Earth

1 Year Later

Have we reached some unity of knowledge, or is science broken into various parts based on contradictory premises? Such questions will lead us to a deeper understanding of the role of time.

Ilya Prigogine (1980)

A face only a mother could love

Chapter 44

Secrets of Science

Shawna awoke, and for a moment lost her orientation. This wasn't Flagstaff. But her mind was at ease. There had been no more nightmares. Or daytime bolts of memory.

She rolled over, and wondered why the other side of the bed was empty, with the covers pulled back. Dawn wasn't yet streaming into the room.

Even through the closed windows, she smelled the smoke. There hadn't been a fire like this in ten years. Malibu was only a few miles over the hill. When she had turned off the television the night before, the fire was already making its way up the ridge towards them, and nothing significant could be done until the air tankers got back on the job at daybreak.

* * * * *

The National Radio Astronomy Observatory had released the news the morning after the signal was downloaded, even before the data received anything more than a cursory look. The accumulated information was voluminous, and most of it not at all comprehensible.

The world's reaction was one of shock. For decades, the international Search for Extraterrestrial Intelligence had been examining the sky methodically for indications of life elsewhere in the universe. The communication event precipitated by Shawna's memories had come out of the blue, unheralded except by those few around her who were preparing for that November evening. Suddenly, and totally unexpectedly, her story was on the front page everywhere.

The National Radio Astronomy Observatory turned the data over to the National Science Foundation, keeping a copy of all the signal recordings for their own analysis. The Radio Observatory would come up with many of the initial discoveries on it's own. They had only a few hours head start, but their orientation was already in the right direction.

One of the first discoveries within the data was confirmation of the source of the signal. The second planet in orbit around Tau Ceti was quickly identified as the source of the signal. According to the download, the world orbited at a distance slightly farther from its star than earth orbited the sun. This newly discovered solar system, still invisible in the optical spectrum, was primarily composed of rocky worlds, with no gas giant planets, an apparent rarity in the universe. The world was the second of six planets in order of distance from Tau Ceti. Two of these planets had intelligent life, but the second one was by far the most advanced in terms of technology, and it had been the source of the signal. On the second planet of Tau Ceti, as on earth, this momentous event would be cause for great celebration.

The numeric data files contained limited descriptive information, but the format was well thought-out. Within the data stream was the code for the data itself. Already there were answers to many of the most recent concerns on earth, including the harnessing of nuclear fusion and medical miracles that would have otherwise waited another century. But it became clear early in the translation of the data that not all of the secrets of science were being provided. Critical issues involving technology were freely described, but the real mysteries of the universe remained just that. There was little doubt to anyone on earth that this planet of Tau Ceti had solved many of those mysteries long ago, but they were going to let the people of earth have the same opportunity on their own.

Much of the data involved the next step – the transfer of life from the Tau Ceti world to earth. Machines still needed to be built, and necessary break-troughs in science were still pending in both solar systems. But the strategy was in place, and few scientists believed there would be substantial delays now that the mold was set.

No earthling was removed from the debates. These were introspective times for humans. The greatest good from this unexpected alien contact was a world-wide reevaluation of priorities. It was precipitated by the new contact, but had lain dormant in humans for centuries.

On a practical scale, the improvements to society were immediate and immense. Even seemingly-unrelated aspects of culture broke through to new heights. The stock market soared on pure confidence in the future of humanity. The 20,000-barrier of the Dow Jones Industrial Average, flirted with for several years, was finally cleanly broken. A bull market pushed solidly into new territory, with no signs of stumbling. And so, even the financial foundation of society was affected by the discovery of life elsewhere in the universe.

The world was changed. Societies were changed. And most of all, throughout the planet, individuals were changed. It was the greatest gift of modern times.

* * * * *

Shawna walked downstairs, and the smell of smoke became more distinct. The patio door was wide open, and Jay was sitting at the picnic table in the backyard, the remote satellite television centered on the table. The TV displayed scenes of firefighters battling blazes that were consuming luxury homes right at the ocean shore. And then the scene switched to the aerial tankers. Shawna approached the picnic table, and Jay looked up and smiled in the edging light of dawn.

"Under control," he said. "They just got airborne – using the MAFFS birds from Mugu. I'll miss all of the action."

"You've had your share," said Shawna.

She gave him a start-the-day kiss on the top of his head, still crested by a graying crew cut. As she started to turn away, he took her hand and drew her back. Jay pulled Shawna's T-shirt covered stomach to his lips as he sat at the picnic table, and held her there for several seconds. Then he let her go, their hands slipping slowly apart.

"Is Nikolas up yet?" asked Jay.

"Not a peep," said Shawna. "No natural disaster will ever bother that kid. He probably smells the smoke and thinks it's burnt toast."

Jay looked toward the south. There was a wall of smoke rising from the other side of the ridge. He picked up the binoculars that were resting on the picnic table and pointed them towards the rolling clouds of white. Even to the naked eye, a few licks of flame could be seen jumping the ridge. The rest was dense white smoke.

"Look here," he said returning to the TV images. "There's a close-up of two of the C-130s in MAFFS paint."

The telephoto lens was following two Herks in trailing formation, dressed in florescent orange tail-paint, coming nearly straight at the camera. The lead aircraft was a J-model, the reincarnated version of the C-130s Jay had known so well. The second aircraft, only discernible to a perceptive eye like Jay's, was an older C-130. It was either an H-model or an even older "E," impossible to tell from the video.

As the J-model passed over the news media's position on the ground, the camera followed it overhead. Panning to the rear of the airplane, a high-tech fire-fighting nozzle could be seen protruding from the side, ready to disperse the water and Phos-Chek fire retardant.

"Not like the old days," said Jay. "We cranked the cargo door and ramp wide open and dropped right out of the back. It's a wonder we never lost a loadmaster."

Then the television scene panned to a blazing home in a hollow near the camera's position.

"There's one!" said Shawna. She pointed to the west, as Jay abandoned the TV image to watch a C-130 headed directly toward them. The aircraft, with its fluorescent-orange tail, was now descending as it flew along the Ventura Freeway, probably about to bank towards the ridge and Malibu.

"Beautiful birds," said Jay.

"Damn beautiful," echoed Shawna.

Jay picked up the binoculars again and turned them towards the approaching Herk. After studying the magnified scene for a few seconds, he spoke with pride and a cracking voice.

"826, I just knew it was you."

Night Drop

The desert is black at night.
Ahead is a checkpoint,
If you look quickly.
Behind is the weaving Colorado River.
Navigation backups mean little at this altitude.
The darkness absorbs us.

We descend through three thousand.
Ten minute warning,
And the pace quickens.
Back in the cargo compartment the scene has changed.
Loadmasters in gray helmets stand at assigned positions.
Checklists are taken seriously.

The moment approaches.
The cargo door cycles upward,
And the ramp goes down.
Behind is the gaping hole of darkness.
A few points of light twinkle in the void,
Swaying from side to side.

Our sister ship swings into view behind us,
And then disappears.
The hole is empty again.
A cool breeze permeates the cargo compartment.
A gentle wind flaps against a piece of loose insulation,
And time stands still.

Down low in the turbulence,
Our ship struggles for survival.
The gate is cut,
And a small pallet rolls off the ramp.
It disappears into the consuming darkness,
Towards a dim rotating beacon.

Our aircraft climbs sharply,
In a right bank.
From the cockpit, two sister ships appear to the left,
Formation lights casting an eerie glow.
For what reason would man be here,
Hovering in the darkness?

Our Year 2017: Distant Planet

Nothing is something. And nothing has energy.

Rocky Kolb (1999)

Chapter 45

Airborne

The Minds were beasts of the ground. They were confined to the study of science, by their own choice. Their rewards for contributing to this latest achievement included the knowledge that they had been the chosen few to lead their society forward in science. The results of contact with intelligent life outside their own solar system could only be estimated, but there was little doubt it would go down in history as the greatest scientific achievement of all time. There was little doubt that the benefits would be even more profound for the intelligence on the watery planet. Processed information, the lifeblood of intelligence.

The indirect benefits to those who initiated the search would also be great. They would learn from those of less intelligence, one of those universal truths. More important, they would achieve one of intelligence's greatest accomplishments – the privilege to assist another being, another culture, another world. What value could be higher in life?

In celebration, the Minds sat near the edge of the cliff. Their species was still primarily an airborne culture. But the wings of the Minds had atrophied from lack of use. They worshiped those who flew. And most of their world still could.

This day, the Minds sat on the bluff, watching their brothers and sisters playing in the updrafts along the cliff – soaring on the currents from the azure sea, dipping and climbing in celebration of the news from the future.

Other Science Fiction by Wayne J. Lutz

Order at:
www.PowellRiverBooks.com